Toby's Folly

**Penny Spring and Sir Toby Glendower mysteries
available from Foul Play Press**

The Cape Cod Caper
Death of a Voodoo Doll
Death on the Dragon's Tongue
Exit Actors, Dying
Lament for a Lady Laird
The Menehune Murders
Toby's Folly
Zadock's Treasure

MARGOT ARNOLD

Toby's Folly

A Penny Spring and Sir Toby Glendower Mystery

A Foul Play Press Book

The Countryman Press, Inc.
Woodstock, Vermont

To Betty and David Earle
with much love

Toby's Folly

WHO'S WHO

GLENDOWER, TOBIAS MERLIN, archaeologist, F.B.A., F.S.A., K.B.E.; b. Swansea, Wales, Dec. 27, 1926; s. Thomas Owen and Myfanwy (Williams) G.; ed. Winchester Coll.; Magdalen Coll., Oxford, B.A., M.A., Ph.D.; fellow Magdalen Coll., 1949-; prof. Near Eastern and European Prehistoric Archaeology Oxford U., 1964-; created Knight, 1977. Participated in more than 30 major archaeological expeditions. Author publications, including: What Not to Do in Archaeology, 1960; What to Do in Archaeology, 1970; Troezen Excavations —the final report, 1988; also numerous excavation and field reports. Clubs: Old Wykehamists, Athenaeum, Wine-tasters, University.

SPRING, PENELOPE ATHENE, anthropologist; b. Cambridge, Mass., May 16, 1928; d. Marcus and Muriel (Snow) Thayer; B.A., M.A., Radcliffe Coll.; Ph.D., Columbia U.; m. Arthur Upton Spring, June 24, 1953 (dec.); 1 son, Alexander Marcus. Lectr. anthropology Oxford U., 1958-68; Mathieson Reader in anthropology Oxford U., 1969-; fellow St. Anne's Coll., Oxford, 1969-. Field work in the Marquesas, East and South Africa, Uzbekistan, India, and among the Pueblo, Apache, Crow and Fox Indians. Author: Sex in the South Pacific, 1957; The Position of Women in Pastoral Societies, 1962; And Must They Die?—A Study of the American Indian, 1965; Caste and Change, 1968; Moslem Women, 1970; Crafts and Culture, 1972; The American Indian in the Twentieth Century, 1974; Hunter vs. Farmer, 1976; Feminism in the Twentieth-Century Muslim World, 1978; Voodoo and its Impact on Negro-American Society, 1980; The Changing Face of Polynesia, 1982; Pacific Studies: a Symposium, 1985; Trends in African Nationalism, 1987; Modern Micronesian Chiefdoms, 1989; The Marquesas: Today and Yesterday, 1990.

Chapter 1

Penny Spring was barricaded in her office, phone off the hook, door locked and in a mild frenzy of activity, as she tried to clear her desk of outstanding business against the start of her long overdue sabbatical, and, more importantly, against the imminent arrival of Dr. Alexander Spring, slated to arrive at Heathrow at crack of dawn on the morrow for an equally long overdue vacation and visit to his mother. To her impatient spirit the pile in her out basket was growing at a snail-like pace and there still remained a sizable mound of papers in her in basket. For the past minute there had been a persistent knocking on her door, which she had determined to ignore; the knocking, however, continued, growing in agitation and volume, so that finally she threw down her pen in despair and stumped over to the door in a fine fury. "Who is it?" she barked. "And whatever it is you want, go away!"

"Oh, Dr. Spring, it's me — Ada. Please open up, it's an emergency," the voice quavered.

With a growl of anger, Penny unlocked the door and flung it open. "This had better be good, Ada! I warned you not to disturb me for anything less than this place burning down or murder."

Ada Phipps reeled back, her bright strawberry hand-knit sweater stretched tight over her large bosom heaving with emotion, as she gazed at her favorite employer with panic-stricken eyes. "Oh, yes, I know and I'm ever so sorry, Dr. Spring, but it think it is."

"Is what?" Penny snapped.

"Murder," Ada gulped. "The Oxford police want Sir Tobias."

"Well tell them they can't have him — murder or not. He's up at the Folly and can't be reached — indefinitely. Not a suspect is he?"

"Oh no! Nothing like that!" Ada was horrified: even though her relationship with Toby had all the earmarks of a cold war, she was too loyal to her irascible employer to even contain such a thought. "It's the Brighton murder. They have the murderer in custody and have to talk to Sir Tobias."

"What Brighton murder? Anyway Toby hasn't been near Brighton in two years," Penny exclaimed.

"Oh, you must have heard it on the news, and it's been in all the papers," Ada said eagerly. "The murder of that Russian in the Royal Pavilion two days ago? Manager of the Leningrad Ballet company that's been playing in London? Done in by one of the ballerinas. They caught her at Oxford station this morning."

"I've been busy," Penny snapped, but she was puzzled. "If they've got the murderer, why do they want Sir Tobias?"

"They won't say," Ada wailed. "They just keep calling and calling and say they must talk to him. Oh, please, won't you talk to them? I keep telling them, but they won't believe me. They may listen to you."

"Oh, very well," Penny gritted and stamped down the

echoing stone stairs of the Pitt Rivers Museum to the office after the agitated secretary, thinking dark thoughts about her absent partner. After their return from Hawaii Toby suffered one of the most violent downswings in mood that she had witnessed in years. At these times he retreated completely within himself, and until such times were past literally retreated from the world.

His particular refuge was as unique as he was, an Upper Paleolithic cave-shelter that he have been excavating at such times on and off for the past twenty-five years. It was typical of him that to ensure this sanctuary he had not only bought the cave but the whole mountainside in which it was situated, the nearest habitation a small farmhouse — also his — a mile down the mountain, in which resided an elderly sheep farmer and his wife, who guarded his privacy with all the zeal of well-trained Dobermans. The farmhouse had no phone, and the only way contact could be made was a message to the local shop in the village, yet another two miles away, which eventually would find its way up the mountain with the weekly groceries. Penny had the shop's number but had never used it, and had no intention of doing so now. The last thing she wanted at the moment was to have to deal with the melancholy Toby.

"It's an Inspector Corbett who has been calling," Ada explained, as they reached her own cluttered sanctuary. "Shall I call him for you?"

"Do that," Penny said grimly, and waited while the crestfallen Ada dialed and after a minute's spirited argument got put through to the inspector. With visible relief Ada handed the phone to Penny. "Inspector Corbett? Yes, this is Dr. Penelope Spring. I just called to confirm what our secretary has already told you. Sir Tobias is not here and cannot be reached. There is no way to contact him. In his absence I am empowered to act and speak for him, and I have his power of attorney. So what do you want?"

The inspector's voice, despite its attractive Oxfordshire burr, sounded as exasperated as she was feeling. "Do you mean Sir Tobias is out of the country?"

"No, but he cannot be reached," she repeated firmly.

"That's absurd, if he's in England he obviously can be reached. It is vital that we talk to him. I must insist you tell me where he is."

"I'm sorry; not possible. Can't you tell me what this is about? My secretary tells me it's something to do with a murder in Brighton. Sir Tobias has not been near Brighton for two years," she retaliated.

"It is a very personal matter. I can only communicate with Sir Tobias," he insisted.

"Well, that's too bad. Then I'm afraid I can't help you," she snapped and went to hang up.

"Wait!" Corbett's voice was urgent. "Please listen, Dr. Spring. I know who you are and your affiliation with Sir Tobias, and I assure you that this is *extremely* important. It concerns the murder of Vassilev Litvov, so the case has international implications."

"All very interesting I'm sure, but what has that to do with Sir Tobias?" she demanded.

An exasperated sigh came over the phone. "Does the name Sonya Danarova mean anything to you? Has Sir Tobias ever mentioned that name to you?"

"Not a thing and no," she said promptly.

"Well we arrested her this morning at the request of the Sussex police, as a suspect in the murder of Litvov. She was seen at the crime scene and promptly fled before she could be questioned. She won't make a statement. In fact she won't say a word other than to demand to see Sir Tobias, and says she will not talk to anyone but him."

"But why him of all people?" Penny asked.

There was a long silence at the other end, then Corbett said, "She claims he is her father."

Penny was so thunderstruck that she could not get a word out, until the inspector called anxiously, "Hello, hello, are you still there?"

"Yes, I'm here," she managed to get out, "But I've never heard anything quite so absurd in all my life. The woman must be mad, completely mad! Have you had the police psychiatrist look at her?"

There was another pregnant pause before Corbett said, "To be frank, Dr. Spring, we are walking on eggs on this one and we do not want to do anything to upset the Russians. This tour is part of a cultural exchange under Gorbachev's 'glasnost' kick. We have a matching company of Sadler's Wells on tour in Russia at the moment, and we do not want to do anything that might bring down Russian ire on *them*. So it has to be kid gloves all the way, and so, no, we have not taken this obvious step, since the Russians might construe it as a 'brainwashing' device to get a confession out of the wretched girl."

Penny had been doing some rapid thinking. "There may be a quicker way of disproving her ridiculous claim. I have known Sir Tobias the best part of thirty years, and I know for a fact that he has never been to Russia during that time, nor, so far as I know, has he had any Russian connections elsewhere. And he certainly has never been married. Did the woman have her passport on her, and if so what does it say about her place and date of birth?"

"Yes, she did, and, though I'm no hand at reading

Russian, as far as I can make out she was born in Moscow on June 21st, 1960."

"So that would mean the conception was around September of 1959," Penny mused, rummaging in her memory banks. Where had Toby been that year? It was the year she had arrived, newly widowed, in Oxford with the four-year-old Alexander, to take up her lectureship for the Michaelmas term that had started in October. She had been there in September, but it had been such a hectic and stressful time, finding a place to live and finding someone to look after Alex while she worked, that she had not been very aware of anything else. But she was fairly sure that Toby had not been there; he'd been off digging somewhere, though where was beyond her recall. "Um, it's not as much help as I had hoped," she said into the phone. "I'm afraid I can't remember where he was at that time. He wasn't here I know. I tell you what, why don't I come down and take a look at this Sonya Danarova? She might open up to me as I am not connected with the police, and I've quite a knack with unwilling informants."

"It would be far simpler if you just gave us Sir Tobias' whereabouts," the inspector growled. "I'm sure you can appreciate the fact that if any of this leaks out — whether it's false or not — he'll be in for some most unfortunate publicity."

"Then it's up to you to see that it *doesn't*," she retaliated. "For I warn you that at the very mention of publicity Sir Tobias is likely to vanish without a trace. No, I'll come down and look things over. After that I'll decide whether there is any reason to try and contact him. Take it or leave it. I'm extremely busy." The inspector took it.

Feeling very hardly done by, and having instructed

Ada to hold the fort and say nothing to anyone, Penny sought her car in the parking lot and drove off down South Parks Road into the Broad and then into the Cornmarket, through the cacophany of Carfax and into St. Aldate's. Mindful of the congestion that normally existed in the narrow streets around the police station, she parked the car in a secluded spot near Pembroke College and walked the rest of the way. The desk sergeant indicated Inspector Corbett's office and she went in to confront a man whose mild appearance matched his pleasant voice. He was round in face and body, fresh-complected and rosy-cheeked, with sandy hair and a pair of twinkling blue eyes that currently were squinting with frustration. "I've just heard that Chief Detective-Inspector Grey is on his way up here from Scotland Yard," he said brusquely. "The authorities feel that this case is such dynamite that they are taking it out of the hands of both the Sussex police and ourselves. When he does arrive I warn you that he is not likely to be as pleasant about your continuing refusal to disclose Sir Tobias' whereabouts as I have been."

Penny raised an eyebrow at him. "Really, Inspector, just because we are dealing with a case involving Soviet nationals, it hardly seems appropriate for all of you to start acting as if *England* were a police state! I'm surprised at you. I came here in order to help. If you don't want it, then say so and I'll be on my way. You can send a dragnet out for Sir Tobias — or whatever it is you do — but I warn you he will not be easily found. Since neither of *us* is wanted for any crime, I consider all this a bit high-handed and unnecessary."

Corbett had the good sense to look abashed. "Yes, well, I'm sorry," he muttered. "I'm afraid we're all on the jump over this. From what little I learned from the

7

Sussex police, the main thing against this Sonya Danarova is that she ran away. We've got to find out why. Shall we get on with it then?"

"By all means," Penny said grandly, drawing herself up to her full five-foot-one. "Is there any way I can get a peek at her before actually going in? Oh, and does she speak any English?"

"Yes, we've put her in a regular cell by herself; you can see into it from the corridor. I'll give instructions to the policewoman on duty to let you in and out at will. And yes, she appears to speak English remarkably well. Then you'll check back with me?"

She nodded and he ushered her out and down to the holding cells. It gave her a queasy feeling as the steel gate clanged and locked behind her, and she followed the young policewoman down the grim corridor until the latter stopped and whispered, "She's in the one at the end. I think she's asleep."

Penny peered cautiously in to see a tall, slim form with very long and beautifully muscled dancer's legs lying totally relaxed on the cell bunk, her eyes closed. The face was purely Slavic, with high, broad cheekbones, a finely chiselled nose and clean lines to the jaw and sharply defined chin; her hair was almost blue-black and shiny, tightly swept back from the face into a bun at the back of the small and very round head. The shape of the head gave Penny a momentary qualm. She nodded at the policewoman who opened the cell door and let her in: the figure on the bunk did not so much as stir.

Penny stood for a moment looking down at the still form, then said softly, "Sonya Danarova, my name is Penelope Spring. I am a colleague and close friend of Sir Tobias Glendower, who is not in Oxford and is not available. In your present unfortunate situation it may be of help if you talk to me. I should like to know why you came here seeking his help and why you have told such a fantastic tale to the police."

The eyes opened and a terrible doubt shot through Penny: the eyes did not go with the rest of the face, for they were very round, very blue and very familiar. The girl with a single graceful motion swung her long legs off the bunk and sat up, the blue eyes narrowing. "I have heard of you," she announced in English that held only the slightest trace of an accent. "You are close to him for a long time, yes? About my father I know everything, you see, and to him I come for help. I am in great trouble. So only to him do I speak." The fine lips clamped in a determined line. "This you tell the police."

"Oh, come now!" Penny said with far less certainty than she had felt a minute before. "Why keep up this ridiculous story? If you have heard about his success in murder investigations and want to seek his help and advice, that's one thing. But to make up something like this is too absurd. I know you were born in Moscow and that Sir Tobias has never been near the place in his life! So tell me the truth and maybe I can help you."

The blue eyes blazed at her. "What I say *is* the truth! I am the daughter of Natasha Danarova and Toby Glendower. Ask him — and see if he denies it! Ask him about Dubrovnik and the summer of 1959."

"And what was this Russian Natasha Danarova doing in Yugoslavia, may I ask? And why, *if* this is true, has he never in the past thirty years even mentioned either her or you?"

"My mother was dancing there, as prima ballerina of the Kiev Ballet company on tour. And why would he mention her, when she ran off and left him? He did not know about me at all — either then or later," the girl said angrily. "My mother wished it so. Myself I did not know all this until five years ago."

Penny's thoughts were chaotic. Was this some crazy scheme of the Russians to bring discredit on Toby? That would make no sense whatsoever. There was no possible motive. "You speak English remarkably well," she temporized. "Is that part of this scheme, whatever it is?"

"I speak also French, German, Spanish, Italian and Polish equally well," Sonya fired back. "I have a natural gift for languages. I hear and I can speak. It is simple."

Penny's heart sank still further. Not that a cultural trait could be passed on, but the gift for languages just like the gift of music did tend to run in families. Not that the girl approached Toby's fluency in a dozen and a working knowledge of a dozen more, but still. . . . She decided to change direction. "Well, I'm afraid you came here for nothing then, because he is not here and will not be for the foreseeable future. So why don't you tell me what your trouble is and then maybe we can straighten it out with the police together? I know how frightening it is to be in trouble in a foreign country."

A glint of amusement appeared in the blue eyes. "Not half as frightening as it is to be in trouble with them in Russia," Sonya said dryly. "But I did not do this murder, however much I hated that filthy police spy. We all hated him — Mala and Peter and Mikail and Olga — all of us, but I do not think any of us killed him. Filthy KGB pig!" She literally spat.

Penny felt a mounting excitement. "I thought he was the manager of your group. You are telling me he was a KGB man? And why name those particular people — are they involved?"

Sonya looked at her, the animation dying out of her expressive face. "Already I say too much. I say no more.

Only to my father will I speak. He must be fetched. No, not if they pull out my fingernails will I say more. Goodbye!" And swinging her legs back on the bunk, once more she closed her eyes in dismissal. Penny looked down at her in frustration—of all the obstinate, pig-headed. . . . It was another familiar trait that brought her little comfort. "Well, be it on your own head," she said, and called for the policewoman.

Corbett was waiting to pounce beyond the steel gate. "Well?" he demanded eagerly.

"Very little, I'm afraid," she hedged. "I don't know if you are already aware of this, but she claims Litvov was more than a manager; he was a KGB man."

A faint groan burst from him. "Oh, no! That really tears it. Did she admit anything?"

"She denies killing him, but she did name some names that might be helpful because they must be just a few of the whole company—she named Mala, Peter, Mikail and Olga—and said they did not do it either. Does that help?'

He was studying the folder he had with him. "Ah—here it is!—Mala Oupenskaya is the prima ballerina, Peter Gregorivich is the lead male dancer, and the other two are the Kupinskis, a married couple. But that's the entire company who were in Brighton—it was just a small special show, you see. The main company stayed in London. So, no, it doesn't help us much. But will she give us a statement now?"

"No, I'm afraid not," Penny sighed. "She still insists on seeing her—on seeing Sir Tobias."

"Well then?" he challenged.

She was silent for a moment, then made up her mind. "All right, I'll do my best to contact him, but I warn you he may not answer my summons, and in any case it will take some time. He really *is* out of touch."

"You can use the phone in my office," Corbett said eagerly.

She shook her head, "No, I haven't the number with me. I'll do it from Pitt-Rivers as soon as I get back. You'll have to trust me on this, Inspector. I've agreed to help you and I will, but it may take some time."

"But Grey is expected any minute," he protested. "What can I tell him?"

"Set him on Litvov's possible KGB involvement and say you've got things in motion," she said severely. "Surely that's enough for him to chew on!" And took a hurried leave.

As Penny retraced her steps, her spirits sank even lower at the thought of dragging Toby back in his present state, and for something that might well be a complete wild goose chase. He would be furious, more than furious, but—well now she just had to know.

Reaching the Gothic fantasy of Pitt-Rivers, she parked the car and hurried back to her office. There she cradled the humming phone and searched frantically through her Rolodex for the vital number. Taking a deep breath she dialed. "Hello, is this Pen y Nai general store? This is Dr. Penelope Spring from Oxford University. I have a very urgent message for Sir Tobias Glendower who is excavating the cave of Pwhelli. Would you please see that this message gets to Pwhelli farmhouse as soon as possible and that the farmer—Mr. Williams, isn't it?—takes it *immediately* to Sir Tobias."

A lilting Welsh voice agreed cautiously that this could be done, and what would this message be?

Penny took another deep breath. "Tell him Penny Spring needs him back in Oxford immediately. Tell him it's a matter of life and death and that I cannot keep the police at bay without him. Tell him not to phone but just come. I need him *now*."

Chapter 2

"Good Heavens! Is it that time already? I had no idea!" Penny looked at her watch and ran a frantic hand through the new hairdo she had so patiently endured against her son's arrival, thereby ensuring its total destruction.

"A fine greeting for a long-lost son and heir I must say!" Alex Spring grinned as he crossed the office and bent down to kiss and hug her. "I went barreling out to Littlemore to find no one home at the cottage, no signs of a fatted calf, nothing. So I took a chance and drove back here, only to find you slaving away as usual."

Penny waved a despairing hand at her desk. "Oh, I'm so terribly sorry, darling, all this was supposed to be finished yesterday, but what with one crisis after another I didn't get finished last night. Can you amuse yourself until, say, lunchtime? Then I swear I'll be over and done with it for as long as you're here. That is if the police don't get after me again."

"The police!" Alex cocked a handsome blond eyebrow at his mother. "Don't tell me you're at it again!"

"Oh, not me—it's Toby they're after," Penny said gloomily. "Sit down, dear, I'd better tell you about it, because it really is rather worrying. By the way, you're looking marvelous." She eyed his handsome features hungrily, and thanked a merciful Providence that her one and only had turned after the tall and urbanely handsome Arthur Spring and not after her. The only thing she could lay any claim to were his eyes, which were the same mild greenish-hazel as her own.

Alex cleared a pile of books off a chair and seated himself with nonchalant grace. "Fire away, mother dear. What's the old boy been up to now?"

"Well, it's like this . . ." Penny began, and poured out the events of the previous day, ending with, "Of course he's going to be just livid if it all turns out to be false. But, as I said, there are some disturbing things about the girl, and well, I think there may be something in it."

"There'd be a simple way of finding out," her son said with mild authority. "Toby's medical records here by any chance?"

Penny looked startled. "Why, yes, down in his office. We always keep ours handy, because we've been dashing around the world at such a rate these past few years. But what good would they do?"

"If the police would let me take a blood sample from the girl, I could match it with his blood work-up. It will show right away if he is *not* her father, though it won't definitely prove that he *is*, even if there is a general match."

"I don't think they'd dare allow it, but . . ." Penny thought hard. "It is just possible she might let you. We could try it. But . . ." she went into an unaccustomed dither. "Perhaps we ought to wait until Toby arrives."

Alex's amused expression had faded into concern. "This thing has really got you rattled, hasn't it? Calm down, ma! I mean it certainly doesn't sound much like Toby, does it? A Russian ballerina?"

"Well, no—and yes," Penny said slowly. "Remember we are talking about thirty years ago." Relations between her son and Toby throughout that period had always been on the strained and combative side. Alex had always been resentful and a little jealous of her closeness to Toby, and Toby, for his part, had equally resented what he termed her determined "spoiling" of her son. What Alex had never understood—what no one had really ever understood—about their intense intellectual and emotional compatibility, was that it had never lapped over into the physical. Their personal relationships had always been a thing apart, a closed area that neither were in the least interested in investigating. She only had a vague idea about that side of Toby's life. She knew that he was definitely not homosexual—disliked homosexuality in either sex, in fact. And she knew well that, on the whole, he was deeply distrustful of women. However, he had shown on more than one occasion a marked soft spot for women who were unusual—like the remarkable Vashti Vadik. No, on those grounds alone, she certainly could not rule out a Russian ballerina.

"What is she like?" Alex broke in on her reflections.

She roused herself. "Oh, very attractive in an offbeat sort of way. Tall, slim, very Slavic in coloring, except for the eyes. . . . Not exactly a run-of-the-mill type. Her English is quite fluent and, according to her, is but one of six she can speak equally well."

"Does she indeed!" Alex was visibly impressed. "Sounds interesting. Any chance of just getting a look at her?"

Penny gave him a hard look. Like his father before him. Alex had a lively interest in, and an equally lively success with, women: a fact that had given her much cause to worry over the years, although he had early demonstrated considerable skill in extricating himself from tight corners and was still a happy, carefree bachelor. "She's not a peepshow," his mother said severely. "Whoever she is, the poor girl is in a mess of trouble."

"I was just thinking that I might be of some help," her son said mildly. "If she is just a disturbed delusional woman, I think I would probably spot it. If she talked to you once, she may again — and I still think a blood test might be handy for the police. Clear the air and so forth. . . ."

Penny cast a last despairing look at her desk. "Oh, very well then! I don't suppose the world will end if I don't finish this stuff today. Anyway I ought to touch base with Corbett to let him know I have carried out my promise about Toby. Will you drive or shall I?"

"Allow me," Alex said, springing up with alacrity, and they bent their steps towards the main police station.

Penny was mildly relieved to hear that the Scotland Yard man had been and gone, and was now *en route* to Brighton to question the other members of the company. Corbett was not immediately available, and while Penny fumed and fidgeted, a policewoman, under the spell of Alex's handsome presence, provided them with cups of tea, and, having established he was a medical doctor, proceeded to woo him with details of her sister's "interesting operation."

Corbett eventually arrived, looking flustered, and got even more so as Penny explained why they were there. "Well I don't know," he said, eyeing Alex dubiously. "We don't want to give the Russians anything to complain about. Of course, it would be useful to know if she is crazy. Maybe if I went in with you. . . ."

"If you do, she probably won't say a word," Penny fussed. "Can't you just lurk in the corridor or something, and just give us the heave-ho if you think things are going too far? What's to lose? Even if Sir Tobias decides to answer my summons, it will still be hours before he gets here."

Corbett reluctantly agreed and they all went down to the cells, where he gave a nod to the guard on duty and hung back in the corridor. This time Sonya was up and very much about. She was using the cross-bar of the cell door to limber up, her long legs flashing in graceful sweeps, as she rose and sank, apparently oblivious to her interested spectators.

"Sonya!" Penny called. "I'm back and would like to talk to you."

Sonya paused mid-plié and peered through the bars. "You have sent for my father?" she demanded eagerly. "And who is that with you?"

"A message has been sent to Sir Tobias," Penny countered. "And this is my son, Dr. Spring, newly arrived from America. We'd both like to talk to you."

Sonya backed away from the bars and they crowded into the small cell. She looked up at Alex appraisingly, then down at his mother. "You do not look alike—no, not at all." She peered at him closer. "Except maybe for the eyes—yes, there I see a likeness, just a little. You are a very fine looking man, yes? What kind of a doctor are you?"

"Oh, just the run of the mill medical kind," Alex was doing his own appraising. "Pills and potions for all contingencies. Service with a smile."

Neither he nor Penny were prepared for Sonya's reaction to this. The blue eyes dilated and she shrank away from them until her back was tightly pressed against the rear wall of the cell. "So that's it," she said in a scarcely

17

audible whisper, "Now they show their true colors. They send you to drug me, to kill me perhaps — well, go ahead then! Pump all the truth serum you want into my veins and I will still say the same thing — Tobias Glendower is my father and I did not kill Litvov. Yes, I will say it till I die."

Penny was searching frantically for something soothing to say to the frightened girl, when Alex surprised her. "Don't be such a melodramatic little idiot!" he said sharply. "You know damn well that in this country such stupid things aren't done. We come here to help — whether you believe it or not. So why don't you be sensible and sit down here with us and tell us all about yourself and how you got into this mess? However, while we're on the subject, it would help your claim if you'd consent to give me a blood sample that I could match against your father's — but that's entirely up to you, of course."

To Penny's surprise Sonya relaxed and flashed him a brilliant smile. "There is not need to be so cross with me," she cooed. "I am just a stupid ballerina, yes? How do I know about such things?" She thrust out her arms to him, on which the fragile blue veins stood out beneath the transparent ivory skin. "You want my blood? — take it! Take it all, if it will prove what I say is true."

Alex gave a snort of laughter. "You're so damned dramatic. And if you're stupid, well then I'm Queen Elizabeth!" He spread out his own long, large hands. "As you can see, I did not come equipped with my instruments of torture. I'll have to come back and I don't know if the police will let me do it, even with your consent. So let's just relax and talk a while." He sat down on the cot and patted the place beside him invitingly. Sonya detached herself from the wall and curled up into it cozily, gazing confidingly up into his face. His eyes widened slightly. Feeling more than a little *de trop*, Penny settled on the other side of him and held her peace—he seemed to be doing just fine.

Sonya, however, appeared in no hurry to talk about herself. She nestled a little closer and murmured. "You come from America? Where in America?" Her voice lingered wistfully, separating all four syllables of the word.

"I've just finished my specialist's training in internal medicine and gone into practice with two other doctors in Manhattan. That's in New York," he murmured back.

"Ah! Then you must have seen Mikail Barishnikov!" she exclaimed. "Micha is such a great dancer—if a little short." Alex admitted gravely that he had.

"That is always my problem, you see," she went on. "I am a good dancer, but never, *never* will I be a prima ballerina because I am too tall, much too tall! So for me it will always be the character parts, the special solos, because the men are always too short to handle me. Even Peter, who is my height, is not really tall enough. It is a great curse." She sighed heavily.

"It must be," he sympathized. "When you love your work."

She looked at him in wide-eyed surprise. "Oh, but I don't. I don't like it at all!"

"Then why do you do it?" He was equally surprised.

"No choice, none at all. My mother was great prima ballerina, so me, I have to be ballerina too—from five years old that was settled. *She* was right height, you see, just a little taller than she is." Sonya jerked her chin at the silent Penny. "But me, I grow and grow and there was nothing to be done, nothing at all."

"Where is your mother now?" Penny broke her silence.

"Oh, dead—for four years now. A plane crash in Siberia when they were touring. A little company—she was past it really, but did not want to stop," Sonya said flatly.

"I am very sorry to hear that. Then you are all alone now?" Alex took back the conversational ball with determination.

Sonya shot him an unfathomable look. "I have my friends." There was a touch of defiance in her tone. "And I did not get on well with my mother. We were not alike—no, not at all."

He changed direction. "So what would you really like to do?"

Sonya's eyes narrowed as she reflected. "I think I would like to be translator of books—children's books. At that I would be very good," she murmured. "Or maybe a cosmonaut. That would be nice, I think, to rise into the blackness and look back at the Earth spinning like a shining ball? Yes, very nice—it would make everything else seem so . . . unimportant." Her voice died away.

They were interrupted by a slight cough from outside and looked up to see Inspector Corbett peering in at them. Sonya tensed, but he said with mild authority, "I'd like to have a word with you, Dr. Spring, before you go, so I am afraid I must cut this visit short."

They got up, but Alex leaned down and whispered to Sonya, "We'll be back." They smiled at each other.

"Well, what do you think?" Corbett asked, when they were out of earshot.

"She's as sane as I am," Alex said definitely. "Probably saner. I'd say she is very stable."

"Humph!" The statement evidently did nothing to cheer Corbett. "Did she say anything to you about the murder?"

"We hadn't got around to that when you arrived," Penny said. "Though earlier she did repeat that she had not killed him. While we're here, could you give us a little more on the background of all this? Sir Tobias should be here shortly . . ." she hoped! ". . . and will want to know."

"Well, all right, come into my office and I'll give you what little I have," Corbett growled. "But you've got to understand I've only got the bare bones of it. It's the Sussex police and Scotland Yard who have all the info. Our sole responsibility is to hand her over to them once this business about Sir Tobias is straightened out."

They followed him back to his office, and after flipping through the slim file, he leaned back in his chair. "The sequence of events appears to be this: the whole company had been in Brighton for a single gala performance at the big conference center on the Front on Saturday. A small group of the dancers remained behind to give a special performance at the Pavilion on Sunday; some charity thing in which the Duke of Norfolk was involved and attended with a lot of the local nobs and bobs. Originally, this was to be held at Arundel Castle, the Duke's seat, but then it was changed at the last minute to the Stables Theatre of the Pavilion. This seems to have caused a certain amount of confusion. Anyway, the performance was held and after it there was a small reception for the dancers in the Pavilion itself in the re-done Music Room—the one that was burned up by some nut a few years back and has been restored? Sometime during that—between nine-thirty and ten-thirty—Litvov disappeared from view. He was subsequently found dead by a night guard in the great kitchen of the Pavilion. He had been beaten to death with repeated blows to the head. The weapon was one of the large copper frying

21

pans that hung along the walls. It was put back on its hook after the murder."

"So why did the Brighton police fasten on Sonya?" Penny demanded.

"Well, as I said, primarily because she fled the scene and the others stayed put — we have no idea where she was between the time of the murder and when she turned up here. And then . . ." Corbett paused, ". . . her fingerprints were found on the murder weapon."

"Oh!" Penny said blankly. She collected herself from this blow as well as she could. "Who else besides the dancers and Litvov were there from the company? Any other Russians?"

Corbett consulted his notes again and shook his head. "No, the only other person involved with the arrangements was a Selwyn Long, who has been acting as a liaison officer for the government on this ballet tour. He was there with another Foreign Office type who apparently has a place near Brighton — a Herbert Spence. But that's the lot." He looked expectantly at Penny.

"Have you got anything else on Litvov's KGB status?" she asked, feeling a little desperate.

"Nothing so far."

"Why not give Sonya a lie detector test? I'm sure she'd cooperate," Alex put in to his mother's dismay. "She has even offered to submit to a blood test to clear up this paternity business."

"I wouldn't touch either with a barge pole," Corbett said bluntly. "All I want is to get her off my hands."

"Just one more thing," Penny said, with a darkling look at her son. "What was the company's itinerary? Where had they been? Where were they going? Maybe there is more to this tour than meets the eye."

Corbett snorted his disbelief but went back to his

notes. "They've been touring for the past three months — mainly capital cities. Let's see, they came here from Paris, and after this London stint, which ends in two weeks, were slated to go on to Madrid."

"And where are all the dancers involved now?"

"Their statements were taken and they were allowed to join the main company back in London. The assistant manager, one Igor Borotov, has taken over, I believe. Of course, they have been warned to stay put until our investigation is finished, and we're keeping a close eye on them." Corbett closed the file and stood up in dismissal. "And that is literally everything I can tell you, Dr. Spring."

Penny thanked him absently and Alex followed her out. "What now?" he demanded as they got back to the car.

"Lunch — I need reinforcement." she said firmly. "And a little prayer that Toby is on his way. That girl is worse off than I thought."

They lunched lengthily at The Mitre in the High and talked of other things besides what was uppermost in both of their minds. "Now where?" Alex said at its conclusion.

"Back to Pitt-Rivers — I'll pick up my odds and ends and take the stuff back to Littlemore. I can do them at home a bit at a time. And I'll clue Ada in to alert us when — and if — Toby arrives." She sighed at the thought.

"Well, does a seasoned old detective pro like you see any leads?" he asked, trying to lighten her mood.

"There is one thing that strikes me as odd," she said. "Do you remember the layout of the Pavilion at all?" Alex shook his head. "Well, if the reception was being held in the Music Room, what was Litvov doing at the opposite end of the Pavilion? The kitchen is about as far away as you can get from the Music Room — and it's not a working kitchen, it's purely for show as it appeared in the time of the Prince Regent."

"Maybe he had lured the fair Sonya away from the crowd for reasons amorous and she beaned him when he went too far," Alex said brightly. "A clear case of self-defense."

"Oh really, Alex!" his mother said in exasperation. "Though she obviously had to be there at some point. But it looks to me as if he was meeting someone and wanted no interruptions."

Alex drew up with a flourish in the gravel drive of the University Museum and they made their way through its echoing mustiness and looming dinosaurs to the big double doors that led into Pitt Rivers. As Penny made for the stairway to the left, Ada appeared out of the museum office and beckoned frantically. "He's here," she whispered.

"Toby! — where?" Penny was galvanized.

"In his office."

"How is he?"

Ada rolled her large cowlike eyes heavenwards. "Terrible!" she moaned. "I've never seen him in such a rage. When I told him you weren't even here I thought he was going to murder me."

"Did you tell him anything?" Penny said in alarm.

Again Ada rolled her eyes. "Not me! I wouldn't have dared. Oh, Dr. Spring, I wouldn't be in your shoes for a fortune, that I wouldn't!"

Penny cast a despairing glance at her son. "Well, here goes!" she groaned. "Welcome to Merry England, darling. This looks like one hell of a vacation."

Chapter   3

Toby Glendower stood looking out of his office window, the pall of gloom encompassing him almost palpable in its essence and augmented by the cloud of blue tobacco smoke that encircled his knoblike head like an outer aura. As Penny rushed into the room, followed at a more sedate pace by the tall figure of her son, Toby wheeled about, his round eyes as hard and steely as ball bearings. "So there you are," he growled in his deepest basso. His eyes fixed malignantly on Alex. "And now I see who's here, I understand your panic. What's this young idiot got himself into now? And why the hell do you have to drag me in? It's nothing to do with me."

"It's nothing to do with Alex, either," Penny said, giving him a hard eye in return. "In fact, he was just on his way out to Littlemore." She wheeled on her son. "See you later at the cottage, dear, as soon as I've dealt with this."

"You're sure?" Alex said, gazing with equal hostility at Toby.

"Quite sure," she said, pushing him back out the door. "This won't take long, but don't wait." She turned back to Toby. "And for God's sake, Toby, sit down! I can't think with you looming there like an avenging angel, and this is very important."

Toby stalked over to the chair behind the piled-high desk and slumped into it without a word. Penny settled herself in his "visitor's" chair, but before she could get started he held up a minatory hand. "Before you begin, I want to make one thing very clear. While I've been up at the cave I've been doing a lot of thinking. I am *very* tired of being dragged all over the world and into things which basically are no concern of ours — mainly at your behest, I might add. I consider I have been wasting valuable time and neglecting my own work, which *I* consider very important even if you don't. So, if this is another of your bleeding-heart involvements, count me out! Since you are evidently in one piece, the alarmist message you sent was obviously just to get me here. Well, I am here because I felt I owed you that much, but I have no intention of staying — if you've got yourself mixed up in something then I suggest you enlist your son to help you." He stopped and puffed angry little smoke rings from his pipe.

"You quite finished?" Penny said with dangerous calm. "May I speak now?" He squirmed uneasily and nodded. "This matter does not concern *me* at all," she went on with quiet vehemence. "And I only sent for you under considerable pressure from the Oxford police to do so. They have in custody a Russian woman — a dancer — who is a suspect in the murder of another Russian, one Vassilev Litvov, in the Brighton Pavilion four days ago. The Russian will make no statement to the police until she has seen you. They are therefore anxious for you to confront her and get this settled before they proceed with the case. So far, out of consideration for your reputation, they have kept this out of the media. I have seen the girl myself and feel that you should do this as soon as possible."

"Out of consideration for my reputation! What the devil do you mean? What the hell has a Russian woman got to do with me?"

Penny dropped her bombshell. "She claims you are her father."

Toby looked at her in thunderstruck silence, then removed his pipe from between his clenched teeth and muttered, "Preposterous! What absolute rubbish!" He surged to his feet. "Obviously this creature is insane. I'll see to it right away."

Penny was watching him keenly. "Her name is Sonya Danarova, and she asked me to remind you of the summer of '59, Dubrovnik and Natasha Danarova, a prima ballerina touring with the Kiev Ballet company."

Toby staggered as if he had been hit and slumped back into his chair. "Danarova—did you say Danarova?" he whispered. "But that's impossible I tell you! Impossible!"

"Well I see the name does mean something to you," she said dryly. "I think you'd be well-advised to get down there right away and see for yourself. Ask for Inspector Corbett—he is more than anxious to see *you*."

He got up very slowly, the anger in him entirely evaporated, his eyes suddenly stricken and haunted, he looked at her. "Will you come?"

She shook her head. "No—not now—this must be between you and the girl. For what it is worth, Alex has seen her too, and feels she is quite sane. If you need me later, you know where to find me. I'll be at Littlemore with Alex. I hoped, for your sake, this would be all moonshine, but. . . ." She did not finish her thought, but got up and went to the door. He was still standing frozen, his eyes blind with inward pain. "Get it over with," she advised softly. "Get it over with quickly, my dear." And she left.

Back at the cottage, she made a determined effort to banish all thoughts of what was transpiring downtown out of her mind. "So what do you want to do while you're here? I'm entirely at your disposal," she demanded of Alex, who was busily browsing through the memorabilia of yesteryear in his room. He looked up at her with a sly grin. "Well, what about a couple of days in Brighton to start with, to look over the scene of the crime, and then on to London to take in some shows— like the Russian ballet—and see what develops after that?"

"Oh, Alex, this is your vacation and you've worked so hard for it, I don't want anything to interfere with that!" his mother protested feebly. "Besides, it may not be as we think. . . ."

"Oh, come off it, ma! I know what *you* think, and I must say I agree with you. And you'd be as miserable as sin if you weren't in on it. Besides, for me it would be fun—I've never been involved in any of your investigations. And, whoever she is, I like Sonya. So why not?"

"Well, we'd better wait and see what develops," Penny temporized. "It's no use going off half-cocked before we hear from Toby."

"No harm in making a few arrangements though," Alex got up and smiled down at her. "Where do you usually stay in Brighton?"

"Oh, the Royal Albion—Toby likes that," she said absently. "It's old-fashioned."

"And London?"

"London is so expensive these days," she fussed. "I try not to stay over."

"Not to worry—me heap rich American doctor, remember?" Alex comforted. "It's on me."

"Well, there is this one place—not too expensive either—the Clarendon on the Bayswater Road to the north of Hyde Park," she said. "I've stayed there sometimes and it's quite handy for getting around."

"Right! I'll make reservations then. Day after tomorrow for Brighton? We can always cancel you know, if it doesn't pan out." And with evident enthusiasm he went downstairs and applied himself to the phone.

Penny occupied herself for a while and in a halfhearted fashion to the remainder of her outstanding business, which now seemed totally trivial and irrelevant. "All set!" Alex called in to her. "How about a drink?"

"Fine!" she said with relief. "I could certainly use one," and shoveled her unfinished work into an overflowing drawer of her desk.

They had just settled to their drinks in her tiny lounge when Alex cocked an attentive ear. "I hear a car. Maybe that's Toby." They jumped up in unison and peered out of the latticed windows of the ancient cottage in time to see Toby's Rolls pulling into the small driveway. The Daimler he had driven for over twenty years had recently died of old age, and he had replaced it, typically, with an almost equally ancient Phantom Rolls-Royce. Toby crawled out of it and proceeded at a snaillike pace, his scholar's stoop accentuated, towards the front door: he walked like a somnambulist. Penny hurried to open it.

He stood on the threshold, his cherubic face chalk-white, his eyes glazed. "May I speak with you?" he asked, his eyes travelling beyond her to Alex. "Alone?"

Penny began to bristle. "Now look! This is Alex's

home and he knows all about this. So if you want to speak to me. . . ." Alex's hand pressed her shoulder warningly. "It's all right, ma. I think I'll go down and chat up old Thornton—see if he has any of that good homemade hard cider on hand for me." As he leaned down to kiss her cheek, he murmured in her ear. "And get some strong hot coffee into him as soon as you can—put a dollop of brandy in it if you like. And put the electric fire on for a bit. He's in a state of shock." He shouldered past the frozen Toby and strode off down the path.

"Come in then, come in and sit down," Penny said impatiently. "I'll get us some coffee." And she more or less pushed Toby into the living room and down into a chair before bustling out to the kitchen to make the coffee.

When she returned with a tray he was still sitting as she had left him, his long fine hands dangling limply, gazing straight ahead with blank eyes. She poured the coffee, laced it with a hefty slug of brandy and thrust it into his hands. "Drink it!" she commanded, bending down to switch on the electric fire kept in the open fireplace to ward off the chills of English summertime.

He drank it down like an obedient child, then placed the empty cup on the floor beside him, held out his hands to the glowing bars, shivered suddenly, and said in a wondering voice, "She's mine. She's my daughter. All these empty, wasted years when I thought . . . and all along. . . . You don't know how I have envied you having someone, having Alex. . . . This changes everything, everything. . . ." His voice grew stronger and for the first time he looked at her.

"You are sure?" she said quietly.

"Positive." And he began to talk, the years dropping away from him as he relived all the pain and pleasure of the past. She listened mutely, wondering how she, whose business it was to know people, could have remained so unaware, so obtuse about the man who had been closer to her than any other. He talked of the cold, rejecting mother whom he had loved; of the demanding, passionate father whom he could not love; of how he had early closed a steel shutter upon his emotions and retreated behind the barricade of his intellect. "I thought myself incapable of love," he murmured. "Until that summer, until Natasha. . . . It was like every cliché that has ever been written on the subject: love at first sight, moonlight and roses and passion. We were madly, insanely in love — despite all the obstacles that stood between us, we had it all planned; to run away across the border into Italy, to marry, to live in this bliss forever and ever, and then she . . . vanished, went. Not a sign, not a word. Then or later. After all my barriers had been destroyed the rejection was more than I could bear. I think I did go mad for a time. I certainly tried to blot out everything with drink. . . . Why I just didn't end it all right then, I'll never know, because I have never really recovered from it."

Out of the corner of her eye Penny spotted Alex peering in at the window, looking inquiringly at her. She shook her head slightly and made a little shooing gesture with her hand, whereupon he shrugged resignedly, made a "bottoms up" gesture and sloped off. She saw by the clock that The Dog and Dragon should be open by now and hoped he would find some solace in his favorite watering spot. What a homecoming, poor lamb! she thought gloomily, and tuned back in on Toby's stream of consciousness.

"And then," he was saying, "you were here and suddenly the world righted itself and I could think again. I'm sorry I've been so difficult all these years, sorry I've put you through so much, sorry I haven't been more understanding about Alex. Dammit, I'm sorry about everything!" He looked imploringly at her.

"Oh, Toby—don't be absurd! There's no need for this sudden breast beating, especially with me, and you know it," she said briskly. "The past is the past. It's what we have to do now that's important. How do you think we ought to go about this? It's a precarious situation, to say the least of it."

"It's a whole new life!" he exclaimed, jumping up and beginning to pace energetically up and down. "Yes, first I have to regularize our relationship—I'll get old Pontifex on to that right away. He'll know whether I have to adopt her or just recognize her relationship to me or whatever. . . . And then I'll have to make a new will, probably a trust will be the best thing, I imagine, and then. . . ."

Penny looked at him in utter amazement. "Toby!" she cried. "For God's sake, stop! I know all this has been a great shock, but for Heaven's sake *think!* Sonya is *Russian*; worse, she's accused of *murdering* a Russian. She says she is innocent, and I'm inclined to believe her, but you must have talked to Corbett and seen what a lot of evidence there is against her! She certainly has a lot of explaining to do. What did she tell you about the *murder?*"

Toby stopped pacing and peered down at her. "Oh, that! We did not talk about that, there was so much else to talk about. And of course she's innocent. No daughter of mine would commit murder!" He positively bristled.

She looked at him in exasperation. "Granted it's not every day one meets a twenty-eight-year-old daughter for the first time, but you don't know the first thing about her! What she's like, what she's been through, what has happened along the way: what, in short, this is

all about. If we are going to help her, we've got to
know. If you didn't talk to her about the murder, what
on earth did you say to Corbett?"

"I told him that I'd let his superior know as soon as I
had consulted with you and my solicitor and made arrangements for her release," Toby said in a hurt voice.

She gasped and felt a strong twinge of sympathy for
the much-tried Inspector Corbett. "Oh great! And I
thought I was the one who always managed to get on
the wrong side of the police. You'll be damned lucky if
he doesn't unleash the media on you. He must have
heard what passed between you in the cell."

"I very much doubt it," Toby said loftily, "Since we
spoke exclusively in Russian."

I might have known! Penny thought resignedly.
"Anyway he probably told you how impossible it would
be to get her out," she persisted.

"Certainly not! She is, after all, only a *suspect* and
England is not a police state. I fully expect to have her
released in my custody before this day is out. You don't
expect me to let her stay locked up in that awful place,
do you?" he exploded. "Then I suppose we'd better think
about what to do next. What do you think? — Brighton?"

"Alex has already booked us in at the Royal Albion for
the day after tomorrow. I believe the Scotland Yard
inspector now in charge, an Inspector Grey, is already
down there," she said with a certain smugness.

"By Jove, that was very enterprising of Alex," Toby
approved, and spoiled it by adding, "There may be hope
for him yet. Well, in that case, I'd better get busy on the
phone. Mind if I use yours?"

"Be my guest — you know where it is."

He did not make a move but remained for a moment
staring down at her in popeyed fashion. "Do you know
what Sonya said to me first off?" he said in an injured

tone. "She looked me up and down from top to toe and then said it was all my fault she would never be a prima ballerina! Just because I'm tall! Imagine! The nerve of it!" he gobbled indignantly.

For the first time in a day Penny laughed.

Chapter 4

"What you are witnessing and, I suspect, will continue to witness is the 'Old Boy' network in full cry," Penny said a little wearily. "Although I am against it in principle, let's hope that in this case it works."

It was the following day, and Toby's sanguine hopes about getting his daughter out the previous night had been initially thwarted. He had departed, his chin thrust out like a bulldog's, to continue the fight from his home base, and was keeping Penny posted on a blow-by-blow basis. The phone, in consequence, had been ringing off its hook.

"I still think a blood test would be a good idea," Alex murmured. He was sprawled in an easy chair, his feet on the coffee table, and sipping with lively appreciation some of old Thornton's "good hard cider."

His mother looked at him in some surprise. "Then you're not convinced she *is* his daughter? He seems so positive of it, and, after all, he should know."

"On the face of it, yes, but from what you've related to me—even granted the physical likenesses—it still could be a 'plant,' a setup. Think about it. . . ." He took his feet off the table and sat up straighter as he warmed to his subject. "The Russians are great at keeping dossiers on people, and I'm sure if their affair was as hot and heavy as Toby states it would not have gone unnoticed. So *they* have always known. Suppose they did want to set him up—they find a girl, a dancer, with some of the right physical characteristics, give her Danarova's name and instruct her what to do when the murder occurs—after all, *they* may have bumped Litvov off themselves."

"But *why*?" Penny cried. "That makes no sense whatsoever. Toby is not in the least political or even involved in any aspect of government. And if the setup was potentially for blackmail that makes no sense either because—rich though he is—he's still in a perfect Wellingtonian 'Publish and be damned to you' position. I mean he obviously *does* give a damn, but they could scarcely have known or counted on that."

"Well, I don't know why," Alex confessed. "But the Russians can be pretty devious—must be the fruit of living with the Mongol horde all those centuries and coping with the Oriental mind."

"I'm sorry, I'm afraid I can't buy it," Penny retaliated. "You've been reading too many spy thrillers. I believe she is who she says she is. What mainly worries me is whether she is as innocent as she claims to be. What I said about Litvov before applies equally to her—what was *she* doing in the kitchen during the Pavilion reception?" The phone rang again and she snatched it up and listened intently as Toby rumbled on and on at the other end.

"I see," she said at length. "That is good news. She is going to give a statement and then you'll come on here? Fine!" She hung up and looked over at Alex. "Well, Wynken and Blinken could not oblige, but Nod seems to have come through in fine style and they are springing Sonya into Toby's custody — on payment of a huge bail, I might add."

"Who is Nod?" he inquired.

"Oh, one of his many cronies high up in the Home Office. Toby may have had a limited circle of women in his life, but he sure has one hell of a lot of men friends," she said admiringly. "So they'll be coming here soon — I'm dying to hear what she has to say, and I suppose she'll be joining us in Brighton. We'll have to book another room."

"She could always share mine," Alex grinned at her, getting up.

"None of that!" Penny said severely. "This is strictly business." And she handed him the phone.

Toby and Sonya turned up on the doorstep within the hour; he looking smugly triumphant, she smugly relieved and a little wide-eyed. She inspected the cottage with a lively interest before sinking gracefully into an armchair. "This is very nice, very . . ." for a second her English failed her and she switched to German " . . . gemutlich."

"Have some cider," Alex urged. "It's very good."

She look at him reflectively. "Cider? That I do not know. Is it like vodka?"

"No, but try it. If you've a yearning for a snort of your national disaster, we could slope off to The Dog and Dragon and I'll treat you to a jolt or two."

"The Dog and Dragon? — what is that?" she demanded. "A zoo?"

"No, a pub — you must have heard of those."

"Oh, yes, I go to one in London. Very nice. Much noise and jollity."

Alex laughed. "Well The Dog and Dragon is not

much on noise and jollity, but high on atmosphere and sturdy rustic types. Shall we go? It'll be closing time soon."

Penny intervened. "Whoa! Before you go romping off, I'd like to know what's happening." She looked inquiringly at Toby.

He cleared his throat. "Er—if it's all right with you, we should start for Brighton first thing tomorrow morning. Inspector Grey is going to assemble the dancers in the Pavilion for a run-through of what they recollect on the night of the murder. He has to have them back in London by performance time in the evening. I think we should start by seven, which should get us there by noon and we can all fit in the Rolls."

"Better take my car as well," Penny said promptly. "Best that we both have wheels if we're going to stay there. And, yes, we're expecting to go."

Alex moved restively. "If we're going to make the pub before it clangs its shutters until six, we'd better go."

Sonya looked at Toby. "May I, father—is that all right?"

Toby's face was a study at the unaccustomed word: part glow, part terror. "Er—yes, but no roaring around the countryside after." He gave Alex his usual glare. "Come back here when you're through."

As they departed hastily, he heaved a relieved sigh and helped himself to some cider. Penny looked at him with some amusement. "I'm very anxious to see her statement," she remarked.

"Of course." He fumbled in his inner pocket and handed a typed sheet over without comment.

Penny read it, her eyebrows rising slightly as she did so. When she finished she looked over at him. "Hmm, short and scant. Got bored with the party, decided to explore, got to the kitchen, saw the frying pan on the floor, picked it up and replaced it on its hook, and did not see the body. Returned to party and saw no one on the way. Not too good, eh?"

He did not look at her. "No, not very. The part about not seeing the body is especially troublesome. Until we see the layout ourselves we won't know how feasible that is."

"As I recall, those copper pans had very burnished bottoms," she muttered. "If a man had been beaten to death with one, you'd think — er — some marks would be visible and she'd have noticed that."

"Yes, you would," he said stiffly. "But she says not." There was a small silence before he went on. "Last night she did talk to Corbett and myself, off the record, and gave some pointers that may be of some help. It appears that Litvov contrived very directly to get himself on this tour. The usual tour manager remained in Leningrad and — perhaps more importantly — the usual KGB man who keeps an eye on them did not come along either."

"Sonya have any idea why this was?"

"She felt he was after some possible defectors from the troupe — after all, there have been so many of their athletes and artists who had done so on similar tours that it must be an ongoing concern of the authorities. Yet it is odd that Litvov came along without a backup."

"But that's awful! The defector in this case being Sonya trying to get to you, I presume. It gives her one whale of a motive!" Penny exclaimed.

"No." Toby looked at her for the first time and there was pain in his eyes. "Sonya says she had no idea of contacting me or of defecting, and I believe this to be true." He paused, then, "I think I'd better tell you everything she told me in camera yesterday and you can judge for yourself. If I seem to ramble, bear with me, for I do it with a purpose."

"Sonya grew up not knowing who her father was. Natasha apparently cultivated her 'Bohemian artiste' image to a marked degree; there were many 'uncles' in and out, but no one in the least permanent. Whenever the question of paternity cropped up, Natasha would drop heavy hints that Sonya's father was someone very important in the Soviet and so she was 'protected.' She never married and, from the faint picture I get of her in later years, was a good if overly possessive and demanding mother. Early she ordained Sonya should follow in her footsteps, and the rigorous training of the ballet world — which I gather is every bit as demanding as that faced by their athletes — meant that there was very little of what we call 'home life' anyway. And since her mother was away so much, Sonya never felt the lack of a father to any marked degree. Then, five years ago, Natasha fell very ill with pneumonia. She was normally so healthy that she was convinced she was about to die, so it was then she summoned Sonya to her bedside, ostensibly to nurse her but to tell her before she died the true facts of her birth. . . ." He paused and visibly struggled for control, his voice cracked and hoarse as he continued. "She was very dramatic about it. Said I was the one true love of her life, but that she realized it would have doomed us both if she had carried out her plan and that, though she loved me, she loved 'her' — Russia — more and could not betray it. So she ran away, and it was only after she was back in Russia beyond my reach and, for that matter, any hope of escape — that she discovered she was pregnant. Since she had been having a sporadic affair prior to this with a young, up-and-coming member of the Politbureau — a married member I might add — she managed to convince him that the child she was carrying was his, and so established the protective 'cover' that stood her in good stead for the rest of her life, although I gather the Politbureau member hastily broke off any further contact in the interest of his own career."

Penny's heart sank, for it all seemed so glib and well-thought-out that her own doubts soared. "So how did Sonya take this news?" she managed to get out.

"Well, she was a little shocked and very intrigued, but did not really believe it," Toby said to her surprise. "Especially when her mother recovered and bade her forget everything she had said in her 'delirium' and swore her to secrecy. She thought it was just another of Natasha's fantasies — to which, apparently, she had long been inured. . . ."

"What made her change her mind?" Penny demanded.

"I was getting to that," Toby said with a sudden return to his usual testy self. "I think she told you that Natasha was killed four years ago in an air crash?" Penny nodded. "Well, in going through her mother's things after the funeral, she came across this small box of mementos from that summer of '59, together with her own birth registration — father not given. Er — the contents were enough to convince her that her mother had been telling the truth for once."

"What were they?"

His ears went pink. "Oh, some letters and — er — poems from me in English, a ring, inscribed, some odds and ends of jewelry I had given her, she described them to me and I remembered . . ." he said in a choked voice.

The thought of Toby writing love poems struck Penny speechless, as he hurried on. "Anyway, she started to do some research on me. For some odd reason the affair of Zadok's treasure and its aftermath received quite a large play in Russia. . . ." He cleared his throat vigorously. "She even began a scrapbook of all our various doings —

41

says she'll show it to me if ever she gets the chance. So that's all it was then — a sort of academic curiosity. I was nothing to her but a name, a face in press photos and a list of achievements. Even when she knew the tour was coming to England she claims she had no thought of contacting me. She felt I would not wish to know of her; that it would be an embarrassment to me, a reminder of something long forgotten. . . ." His voice died away forlornly.

"And yet she made a beeline straight for you after the murder," Penny said, her voice suddenly hard.

"Scarcely a beeline," he murmured. "When she learned of the murder and knew that the investigation would turn up the fact she and Litvov had been on bad terms, she claims she panicked. She did not know what to do, so she ran out of the Pavilion down the road to the bus station on the Old Steine and got the first bus out — to Bournemouth of all places! Checked into a B and B there under the name of Glendower, because she felt they would be after her under her own name. Using my name put her in mind of me and our murder investigations, and the more she thought about it, the more she became convinced I was her only hope. And you know the rest . . . they were watching for her and she got picked up by the police at the station when she arrived." He stopped abruptly.

"And doesn't *that* strike you as damned odd?" Penny's tone was sharp. "I mean, I'm not decrying our police forces, but why, in the name of Heaven, should they have even been on the *lookout* for her in Oxford, of all places, *unless* someone had tipped them off to the fact there was a connection between you and her? Which indicates to me that, despite Natasha's assertions, Sonya's parentage was known all along. The *someone* in the company knew; that someone so informed the police. Unless *Sonya* herself had confided in somebody else?"

"I had already thought of that. She says not." He said simply. "I even thought of the scrapbook as evidence of a link, but that's not even here. It's in Leningrad. And to answer our next question, she shares an apartment there with two other girls, one a set designer for the company, who is not on the tour, and one a computer programmer who is not connected with the ballet."

As usual, he had thought of everything. Penny changed tack. "What was the cause of her bad relationship with Litvov?" she demanded.

"Oh, that. Yes, well that *is* unfortunate," he muttered maddeningly.

"Well?"

"Litvov appears to have been a very nasty character indeed: an official bully boy. Liked to show his power. He considered all the ballerinas fair game, and if they dared to say no to his advances made life very unpleasant for them. He's been working his way through the company — married ones as well, apparently, and had got to Sonya. She said no and in a very public fashion, in front of the British organizers. They had a *very* public row. He tried to get back at her by taking some of her featured roles away, but the people here put a stop to that and that just made him even madder. He was threatening her with all sorts of retribution once they returned home."

"Uhm, bad, yes, but could be worse. It means that a lot of the other females *could* have a motive. The very murder method indicates a spur-of-the-moment killing, so that would fit a murderer goaded beyond endurance," Penny mused. She cocked an eye at him. "You don't suppose, after all, Sonya . . . ? I mean, if he had cornered her and was attacking her, it would be a good

43

case of self-defense. I'm sure any British court would let her off."

"She denies it. Besides, it wasn't just the women. He gave the men an equally hard time. They all hated him." Toby glanced impatiently at his watch. "Where the hell have they got to? It's well after closing time."

"Oh, Alex is probably just showing her around the village." Penny soothed. "They'll be along. Did Corbett give you any indication of where the police are heading on this?"

"He doesn't appear to know a great deal. I'm hoping Grey will be more helpful tomorrow. One thing for sure, they are working against time — as are we — because there's no way they can keep the company from moving on to Madrid unless they come up with something very solid."

The front door suddenly burst open and Sonya came flying in. She held out a slim arm to Toby triumphantly; a very small Band-Aid marred its ivory surface. "See!" she said, "now we prove all legal like that we are of the same blood. You too must give a sample. Alex will do it and then we will be all set and right."

Toby started to get very red in the face and glared at Alex, who has sauntered in after her with his medical bag. "How dare you presume to do such a thing! "he thundered. "I have already acknowledged Sonya to be my daughter. Who the hell do you think you are? The nerve of you!"

"An interested party," Alex said calmly. "And if you will simmer down and listen, even you should see the sense of it. I don't think you've thought this thing through at all. In the first place, by coming to you Sonya has very effectively burned her boats. If she returns to Russia now, I imagine life for her will be very unpleasant — maybe impossible. But she *is* a Russian citizen, and you can tell them until the cows come home that you are her father, but you will have to prove to them *and* the Brits that you are, before you can take any legal steps to keep her here. They aren't — they can't — just accept it as fact on your say-so and, so far as I can see, you don't have any kind of tangible proof. Not that the blood test will be *absolute* proof, but the process has been refined to such an extent now that it is *almost* a certainty if the match is there, and that, plus your own testimony, should be enough for the Brits. To be on the safe side, I had them take hers at the Radcliffe Infirmary, and they'll get the results by this evening. I got Ada to pull your medical records with your blood work, but a fresh sample, also attested to by Radcliffe, would be even more valuable. So, what about it?"

Sonya was looking wildly from one man to the other. "Oh, why must you two be so *angry* at each other?" she cried, and burst into a flood of tears.

As Penny anticipated, the flood brought about instant surrender on Toby's part. He looked helplessly at the sobbing girl, then bared his arm. "Oh, very well!" he said gruffly. "Get the damn thing over with, and be damned to you, too."

Chapter 5

The Royal Pavilion of Brighton is one of a kind: if the tiny watering place of Brighthelmstone had been chosen as the unlikely Xanadu of the Prince Regent, then the mini-palace he had constructed there could certainly be construed as his "stately pleasure dome," with its fantastic green domes and turrets, its Arabian-by-way-of-India pillars and elaborate traceries, all incongruously set in an almost prosaically English garden. From the outset, public opinion had been sharply divided over it; many hated it, others loved it, still others found it endlessly amusing. Penny fell into this last group, and when American friends asked her "what to see in England" it always ranked high on her "must see" list, after the Tower of London and before Windsor Castle. Not surprisingly, Toby was a dedicated pavilion-hater, but then he was hard to please, since his yardstick of architectural beauty never veered far beyond Classical Greek. Thus his daughter's statement, "Oh, I *do* like this building—those onion domes, just like Kiev!" drew from him a disapproving sniff, as they hurried towards it under the watchful eye of a plainclothes policeman, who had been awaiting them in the lobby of the Royal Albion hotel just a short walk away.

Sonya was very keyed up; spots of hectic color flaring on her high cheekbones, and she had been talking at fever-pitch ever since their arrival. It was part anxiety and part excited anticipation, Penny surmised, for she was feeling much the same herself; her pulses stepping up their beat as they approached their goal.

Hordes of tourists, augmented by curiosity-seekers — for the English love a good murder — were roaming in hungry disgruntled fashion around the gardens and crowding around the main entrance to read the police notice that stated unequivocally that the Pavilion would remain closed that day but would reopen on the morrow. Their small party eschewed the main gate and were led by the policeman around to a side door, guarded by a uniformed officer, who quickly let them in, then turned to fend off a sudden flurry of determined tourists who had rushed hopefully at the opening. Penny was momentarily disoriented by coming in at this unexpected angle, but the policeman led them with silent authority through a narrow passageway that came out into the main foyer just beneath the grand staircase, where she saw a small group of men huddled in conference. The plainclothes man went up and muttered to them and a figure detached itself from the group and came towards them.

To Penny, a great reader of classic English murder mysteries, who had been expecting someone massive and solid along the lines of Commander Gideon, or tall and dominating like Superintendent Alleyn, Inspector Grey came as a great surprise. He was small — the bare minimum height, she surmised — slight of build and exquisitely neat, almost dandified in appearance. Her first impression was of youthfulness, but as he came closer she saw that his dark blond hair was silvering at the temples and there were deep laughter lines around his shrewd gray eyes. He shook hands politely all the way around, but when he came to her gave an engaging, rueful grin, as he looked up at the other three figures towering over them. "Ah, Dr. Spring, I have read much about you," he said. "Let us hope you and I, at least, can see eye to eye on this matter." Her heart rose perceptibly — could it be that at long last she had found a policeman who didn't hate her at first sight?

He stepped back and inquired, "Well, shall we get on with it? First I should like a statement from Miss Danarova as to her recollections and movements the night of the murder. I have already taken the statements of those others present. Then I would like her to show me where she went and what she did that evening."

"I wish to accompany my daughter — in fact I insist upon it," Toby said stiffly.

The inspector cocked an appraising eye at him. "It has yet to be established that she is your daughter, Sir Tobias. So, in those circumstances. . . ."

Toby cut him off. "It has been so established." He nodded grimly at Alex, who produced a sheaf of documents and said formally, "My name is Doctor Alexander Spring, specialist in internal medicine, currently in practice at 401 East Sixty-first Street, New York. Here are the results of blood tests sworn to by Dr. Tewson of the Radcliffe Infirmary of Oxford and executed in my presence yesterday. The close match of the two blood samples from Sir Tobias and Sonya Danarova, together with this accompanying sworn statement of Sir Tobias acknowledging his paternity and giving particulars, I have been informed, would constitute sufficient balance of proof in any English court." He sounded relieved. "I would be glad to elucidate any of the technicalities if you so desire."

The inspector studied the documents carefully, and then slid another amused glance at Penny. "Your son, I presume, Dr. Spring?" he murmured. "Well, yes, these documents certainly appear to be in due order, so in that case I have no objection to your being present, Sir Tobias. However . . ." he looked quizzically at Penny.

Here goes, she thought. Now we'll see how fast my welcome wears out. "As you probably know," she said, "Sir Tobias and I work as a team. So where he goes, I go, and in this particular instance we are here to stay. However, I have no intention of intruding on your deliberations, but I wonder if it would be possible, while you are so deliberating, for Alex and me to meet the other members of the company? We are going to sooner or later anyway."

"Yes, I can see no objection to that," he agreed with a suspicious alacrity. "They are all gathered in the Music Room. Sergeant Dicks here will show you the way. Er, do you speak Russian? I'm afraid you'll find that collectively they do not speak much English." And she got the definite impression he was laughing at her as they went their separate ways.

The Music Room, as they came into it through the great double doors, appeared like a study in still life, as under the stolid gaze of two uniformed constables, one at each of the entrances, a group of people sat in attitudes of disconsolate boredom on a series of small gilt chairs, ranged before an ordinary folding bridge table that, by its scatter of papers, had been Grey's center of operations.

While Sergeant Dicks muttered at the constable on the door, she cast a quick eye along the row. At the end was a roly-poly man, with a shiny bald spot like a monk's tonsure in the middle of his dark hair, whom she could not identify, and next to him a small mousey-looking woman with an anxious face, who was equally unknown. After her came a tall, thin, fair man with interesting, irregular features, whom she labeled quickly as Peter Gregorvich, and next to him a small fair woman, who was gazing blankly up at the ornate ceiling—probably Mala Oupenskaya. Beyond her a couple, both small and dark, who were murmuring quietly, their heads almost touching—undoubtedly the Kupinskis. They were flanked by a stolid man in a black suit, who moved restlessly on his small chair and watched the newcomers with a lowering brow. Beyond him were two empty seats, then another pair of men, who had their heads together and were literally turning their backs on the rest of the company: one large, soberly dressed in a three-piece suit and sporting a pink-striped Harrovian tie, and, rather amazingly, a pair of white cotton gloves on his large hands. The other was slighter and taller, dressed in a blue denim suit, a silk scarf knotted with casual elegance in its neckline. He stopped talking abruptly as they entered and twisted around to look at them. Penny's pulse quickened as it came to her that in all probability among them sat the murderer of the appalling Litvov. For a second she was tempted to turn tail and run: this was one murderer, she felt, who may have done the world a good turn.

"Got the murderer spotted, ma?" Alex's voice in her ear caused her to jump. "Want me to take notes and play Watson?"

"Oh, don't be absurd, Alex!" she said, but felt a surge of relief at his large, reassuring presence; she was a little at a loss, for Segeant Dicks, his charges delivered, had disappeared again, and she could think of no graceful way of making herself known to the people before her, still less of questioning them. Her problem was quickly resolved when the denim-suited man, after a meaningful grimace at his large friend, got up and swiftly crossed the room to them. "Something I can help you with?" he inquired in a light, pleasant tenor voice. "Since you arrived with a policeman, you can't be stray tourists who wandered unwittingly into this lion's den, so you have to be someone connected — official or suspect? For the life of me I can't place you, although you do have a familiar look about you." He looked at her quizzically. "I'm Selwyn Long, by the way, official British liaison to the ballet company and responsible, I'm afraid, for the arrangements that got us all into this mess. Now *everybody* hates me." He sighed tragically.

"I'm, Dr. Penelope Spring and this is my son, Dr. Alexander Spring," Penny said, half-nettled, half amused by him.

His eyebrows shot up. "Good Lord? Don't tell me you're shrinks! I hope you are specialists in the Slavic mind. I could use some pointers; just about at tether's end I am."

She laughed. "No, not shrinks, but if you know everyone here we would appreciate an introduction to them. We will be very much around from now on." He looked expectantly at her, but she did not elaborate, so with a little petulant grimace and a toss of his head he turned and flapped a languid hand in the direction of the large Harrovian. "Well, that's my friend Herbert Spence of the Foreign Office, who's just *livid* with me for getting him mixed up in this. I've been staying at his place just outside of Alfriston." In good Watsonian style Alex made an entry in his heiroglyphic doctor's scrawl in a small, black notebook.

"Good Heavens! Notetaking yet! Shouldn't you give me a warning or something about anything I say being used in evidence against me?" Selwyn Long said archly, but eliciting no response from Alex went on, "But to proceed . . . the somber-clad gent glaring at us is someone called Korkov from the Russian embassy, keeping an eye on all of us, as well as his own little darlings. Next to him, Olga and Mikail Kupinski from the ballet, then Mala, who is their star turn and, of course, Peter, ditto ditto — *gorgeous* dancer, just gorgeous," he gave an ecstatic sigh. "Then that's little miss — er — what's her name, Miss Rogers. She's the interpreter we laid on to smooth their path. Not a raging success, I'm afraid. And finally Boris Borotov, their assistant manager, who has taken over for poor old Litvov — a nice chap."

"And that is *everyone* who was here from the company on the night of the murder?" she asked. "There were no other Russians among the guests at the reception?"

"Oh, perish the thought!" His voice was a little shrill. "No one but the *crème de la crème* of Sussex society, headed up by the jolly old Duke himself. The nobs like to comingle with the arts from time to time, you know. Makes them feel cultured and — er — democratic." The sneer was unmistakeable. "But we do have one glaring omission here," his voice dropped to a dramatic whisper. "Sonya, the *suspect*. Once the police get their hot little hands on her, they'll probably have all this tidied up in no time and we can all go home again with loud cries and paeans of joy."

"She should be here very shortly," Penny said, and watched his reaction.

His jaw dropped and he gazed at her open-mouthed. "Sonya? *Here?* So she didn't make it to the States?" That jolted her.

"Why? Was that where she was heading?" she said quickly.

"Well — we assumed . . . with Litvov dead . . . I mean. . . ." he stuttered.

"Who are 'we'?" she pressed, but his answer was cut off by a dramatic interruption — the double doors flew open and Sonya entered, flanked by Inspector Grey and a grim-looking Toby with two other policemen bringing up the rear. The still life erupted into sudden chaos, as Peter Gregorvich, with an incredible bound that over-turned his chair, leaped towards her, arms extended, and more chairs overturned as the other dancers hurled themselves after him. Borotov and the Embassy man exchanged alarmed glances and surged to their feet. Sonya was submerged in a second by the tide of dancers, all hugging and kissing, laughing and crying, at one and the same time; the lofty ceiling echoed to the sudden babble of Russian voices all talking at once, as Sonya, tears of joy running down her own face, hugged and kissed and babbled back. Only the interpreter, looking more frightened than ever, and the astonished Herbert Spence stayed rooted to their seats as the demonstration went on and on. Selwyn Long, after a soft exclamation, added himself to the throng.

Penny, feeling very Anglo-Saxon in the face of all this Slavic exuberance, watched the watchers. Grey was observing keenly and a little helplessly, for it was evi-dent he did not understand a word of the babble. Toby's face was blank, but she knew he was absorbing every detail of the uproar for future replay. Glancing up at her son, she found him gazing fixedly at Peter Gregor-vich, who was kissing Sonya passionately for the fifth or sixth time; his expression was enigmatic. Suddenly, the Russian diplomat, who had stationed himself on one side of the central group, while Boratov came up on the other, roared out a stream of Russian, and the group froze and fell silent. They turned towards him slowly,

Peter Gregorvich keeping his arm tightly around Sonya's shoulders, a wild, defiant light in his dark eyes.

But with order restored, Inspector Grey was not about to let the Russian hold the stage; he said with quiet authority. "Well, now that we are all here, I would like you all to the best of your ability to both show and tell me your movements during the reception on the night of the murder — who you talked to, what others of your party you noticed here and so on. . . ." He beckoned Miss Rogers with an imperious finger, but before she could answer the summons, Toby quietly repeated his statement in Russian and the group turned to him in surprise and curiosity. Sonya said something in a low voice and the curiosity was replaced by blank astonishment. Selwyn Long suddenly turned and favored Penny with a long, hard look, while Grey placed himself in the middle of the group and began to ask questions.

Feeling curiously weak at the knees, Penny headed for one of the gilt chairs and sat down, while Alex strode over to the long French windows and stood gazing moodily out. She noticed Herbert Spence gazing reflectively at him, and after a moment he got up from his chair and joined him. The gloved hand was proffered, shaken, and they started to talk in low voices. She felt totally inadequate and at a loss. Patience, she told herself fiercely, patience! Though she was dying to know what had transpired from Toby, she knew he was in the thick of it and could not be disturbed. She closed her eyes and tried to sort out her impressions from the chaos of her thoughts. After a while the squeak of a chair beside her signaled company, and she opened her eyes to see Toby gazing somberly at her. "You all right?" he inquired.

"Yes — and you?" He nodded and glanced over at the

central group. "This is going to take some time. Grey's a bright chap, thorough too. He's obviously looking for holes, and he is going to let me have the notes on all this later — very cooperative. Want to visit the scene of the crime? — we can talk more easily there."

"Yes, but will they allow it?"

"No problem, Grey has given me a police pass." He fumbled in his pocket and produced a small card. He nodded towards the far door. "Easier that way." She followed him as he showed the pass to the constable, who let them out into the long drawing room, which she had always thought to be the pleasantest room in the palace, with its delicate Regency furnishings and colors, and its own collection of harps, spinets and harpsichords. From there they gained the dining room, the huge table still set for a ghostly gargantuan Regency banquet, and at length gained the kitchen where Toby stopped and drew a long, shuddering breath, as he looked around it.

"Well?" she demanded anxiously. "How did her story hold up?"

"She claims she came in by this door," he said carefully. "And was enchanted by all the pots and pans and knick-knacks, and was equally taken by the palm trees." He pointed up to where the iron painted pillars supporting the high ceiling branched out into stylized still green palm fronds at the top. "As she walked down this side looking up at them . . ." he demonstrated, "her foot struck something — the frying pan. She looked down, saw it, noticed the empty hook at the end of the row . . ." he pointed to where the hook on the wall was again empty of its sinister burden, ". . . and being a 'neatnik', as she puts it, picked it up and replaced it. She was continuing on around this side of the room . . ." again he demonstrated, ". . . when she thought she heard someone approaching the other door. She was frightened that she would be discovered by a guard and ticked off for being out of bounds, so she ran back the way she came. . . ."

"And the body?" Penny interrupted anxiously.

"The body was lying face down on the far side, close to the other door, but partially hidden from this side by the big table. If her movements were as she has claimed, it is possible she did not see it." Toby said without expression.

"And what do you think?" she said with misgiving.

"I think she did see it. I don't believe she *did* it, but I have the feeling she knows — or thinks she knows — who did," he went on quietly. "I believe she is shielding someone. I have no idea why, but I'm damned sure I'm going to find out. She might bamboozle everyone else, but she certainly isn't going to bamboozle *me*."

Chapter 6

Night had fallen and peace had returned to the Royal Pavilion. The hungry hordes of tourists had finally departed from the shadowed gardens to seek more rewarding excitement, and the Music Room, its chandeliers now casting a dim mellow light, had a melancholy, deserted air about it that caused its three remaining inhabitants to huddle closer to each other around the bridge table. The only sound was the faint crackle of paper, as they silently read and handed on sheaves of sheets to each other.

Inspector Grey ran a weary hand over his face, on which the travails of the day had etched deep lines of fatigue. "Damn it!" he said, leaning back in his chair with a sigh. "I had hoped this run-through would at least clear the field a little—rule out some of them and point a clear trail, but, as you can see for yourselves, it has done nothing of the kind. All of them, with the possible exception of Long and Spence, had strong motives; the means was evidently spur of the moment and to hand, and this run through has clearly shown they *all* had the opportunity, though some of them did lie about that. . . ."

Penny and Toby looked at him with wary expectancy as he continued, "You see, we've been fortunate in having among those distinguished guests a very expert witness — the Chief Constable of Sussex, Sir William Frere, who had been dragged unwillingly to this affair by his wife and who spent his time, since he was bored, people watching. And we already have had a very detailed account from him about the coming and goings of the group, against which we can compare their own statements. He is a trained observer of the best kind. As you have seen, they were all rather careful to corroborate each other as to their presence, or even short absences, from here. But they *don't* all match up with his recollections. Strangely enough, your daughter, apart from her own admitted absence, was the one most continuously in view. She spoke the best English of the group and so was much more 'talked to' by the notables. The Kupinskis — especially Mikail — also speak some English, but Gregorvich and Oupenskaya only a few phrases — their main second language is French. So they huddled together most of the time, and indeed, left together for a while. The same holds true for Spence and Long who, according to them, were always in each other's sight, but Sir William says he saw both of them leave separately and at different times. It was from him we got the departure time of Litvov, who went out by the same door your daughter later used . . ." he nodded his head towards it. "That was about forty minutes after the reception began, around ten o'clock. He did not return and his body was discovered by the night guard an hour later at eleven. So some time in that hour he was struck down, but the autopsy could not pin the time of death closer than that. Your daughter's statement was not much help on that either; she could not give us a time, and Sir William, who did notice her leave, could not be more specific than that he thought it was about half an hour after Litvov's 'departure'."

Toby cleared his throat uncomfortably. "There is, however, the problem of the fingerprints."

"Ah yes, that. If it weren't for that we'd have a far stronger and simpler case against Sonya," Grey sighed. They looked at him in blank amazement.

"Yes, I thought that might surprise you," he said, and groped in a cardboard box under the table from which he produced a large copper frying pan in a clear plastic bag. "I want to show you something." He put the pan down on the polished parquet floor, bottom up, so that its angled handle lifted it at a slight slant from the wood. "Now, according to her story, it was lying like this when she stumbled over it and she picked it up with her right hand. The position of her fingerprints agree with that statement. Would you pick it up in the same way, Sir Tobias?" With a doubtful glance at Penny, Toby did so.

"Now, the dents in the bottom indicate that that was the surface which rained the blows of the head of Litvov with enormous force, sufficient in fact to dent it even though it is of very heavy construction." Grey went on, "Would you then, gripping it in the same way, demonstrate how you would hit me over the head with it?"

Toby made a tentative swing and his face lit up. "It's impossibly awkward! It should be facing the other way! I should be holding it like this," he twisted it around.

Grey nodded. "Exactly."

"You mean she's *not* a suspect after all?" Penny cried.

"On the contrary, she's very much a suspect," Grey snapped. "Perhaps not of the murder — for to suppose that we'd have to assume she had used it one way, carefully wiped her fingerprints off of it and then put them on again the other way. Which is so complicated as to be absurd. But I am virtually certain she knows a lot more than she has told us, and as such is an accessory to murder and so equally culpable under the law. This is why I have told you all this—which, by the way, is strictly confidential. I am hoping that you may get her to open up to you in a way that she would never do to the police. Until she does and clears herself, the *official* view is that she is the prime suspect."

Toby's face clouded. "You may have to have a lot of patience, Inspector. You must remember that up until two days ago I was unaware of her very existence. She is a stranger to me, as I am to her—it may take time. You must have seen where her loyalties *do* lie. . . ."

There had indeed been another very emotional scene when the dancers and their entourage had been shepherded aboard the mini-bus to take them back to London and their evening performance. Again there had been much hugging and kissing and crying, and Sonya had broken down completely in tears and desolate despair after they had driven off. Toby and Penny had been helpless to comfort the sobbing girl, and it was Alex who had taken the situation firmly in hand, had calmed her down and then had insisted on taking her back to the hotel to complete the process.

"I appreciate all that, but time is something we have very little of," Grey returned. "There's no way, unless we have a very strong case against someone, that we can delay the departure of the company for Madrid. Already the Russians are starting to mutter that this is an affair they can take care of themselves, and that pressure is going to build with each succeeding day. In fact, it may well come to the point, Sir Tobias, when you yourself will *want* me to arrest Sonya as the only means of keeping her here, which I presume is what you would want."

Toby gazed at him with troubled blue eyes. "It may be what I would want, but I'm not at all certain it is what *she* would want," he muttered. "But I'll do my damnedest, I assure you."

"Why does Herbert Spence wear those gloves? Does he always do so?" Penny, who had been following her own line of thought, asked suddenly.

Grey gave her a tired smile. "You are thinking about the absence of other fingerprints on the weapon? Well, I'm afraid his explanation is far from sinister. He suffers from a painful and disfiguring form of psoriasis, which for both medical and esthetic reasons has to be kept covered. He's had the condition for several years and the cotton gloves have become almost a trademark of his. He even carries a couple of spare pairs around with him. Unfortunately, nowadays everyone is aware of the importance of fingerprints, and that handle was undoubtedly wiped before it was left. I'm surprised myself that it was even left where it was—it may indicate that the murderer was panicked and in a hurry, or possibly was interrupted by the arrival of someone else." He favored Toby with a long look.

"It seems to me that if all this effort has left us no better off than before, we had best look in another direction," Penny said tartly. "Namely Litvov—we know he was a grade A stinker, but what kind of stinker? What or who was he after? If it wasn't Sonya, who was he suspecting of defecting? It is obvious to me that he slipped away from the main party to meet someone and in a place at farthest remove from here where they were not likely to be disturbed. And another thing, since such force was used in the murder, surely the women can be ruled out? Litvov according to his description was a fairly tall and burly man. Surely, if a

61

woman had donged him one with a frying pan, he would just have wrestled the thing away from her by brute force, but if it were a man. . . ."

"I wish that were true," Grey interrupted, "but it just isn't so. According to the coroner's report, the first blow was from behind and caught him on the lower occiput in an area which would not only have stunned him but partially paralyzed him. He fell face down on the floor and then, by the direction of the blows, the murderer straddled his body and proceeded to beat his brains out at his or her ferocious leisure. Granted, one thinks of a man primarily, but a sufficiently motivated woman— and don't forget ballerinas tend to be in great physical shape—would have been capable of it. As to the rest of it: yes, we have to find out more about Litvov, but that isn't all that easy to do. Naturally the Russians aren't being very forthcoming about him—and if he *is* a KGB man it's easy to see why. We've got MI5 working on it and also our embassy in Moscow, but it will take *time*. No, first and last, it is Sonya we have to go after." He pushed back his chair with an angry, nerve-grating scrape and stood up. "Well, there's no sense hanging about here any longer. We haven't been able to narrow our list of suspects and since—bar Sonya—they are all in London, I may as well return to the Yard and keep digging from there."

"There is no possibility that an outsider could have got in and had this rendezvous with Litvov?" Toby queried.

"None. Security was very tight that night—the guests all entered by the main door and were accounted for, having presented their invitations. They came in a group because they had all attended the performance at the Stables, and after they were all in the main doors were again locked and guarded. So no one could have got in within our time framework and got out again. The first thing the Sussex police did was to search every nook and cranny of the Pavilion for an intruder or signs of one—without result. No, we've been looking at our murderer, but *which?*"

Penny and Toby got up slowly, both drooping from the long day. "We do appreciate your frankness, Inspector," Toby said wearily. "Am I to understand you have no objection to our pursuing our own investigation? As you yourself have indicated, there may be avenues open to us that would be closed to you."

"Normally I would be dead against any such thing," Grey said with devastating honesty. "I don't hold with amateurs—however well-intentioned and successful—but this is not a normal situation. In a sense I am depending on you for help with Sonya. I will share any information that I think may be of help to you and ask, no, insist that you are equally open with me. As long as that is clearly understood—go ahead!"

They went out to where a night guard was in low-voiced conversation in the main foyer with a uniformed policeman. "We're all through in there," Grey announced. "See that the things are put in my car, will you? And tell the driver I'll be heading back for London tonight. You'll be staying on here?" he asked, as they went out into the cool night air that held the omnipresent tang of the sea.

Toby looked at Penny. "No, tomorrow we'll go on to London ourselves."

Grey gave a brisk nod. "Right. Well, let me know where you're staying, and I am afraid I must insist that one of your party accompany Sonya at all times, otherwise I will have to put a man on her, and I don't think you really want that, do you?"

"I understand," Toby said, and Grey, with another

polite handshake, took himself off. "So what do you think? — What next?" Toby asked gloomily.

"I'm too tired to think," Penny said. "Let's go back to the hotel and turn in. Sufficient to the day is the evil thereof et cetera. After a good night's sleep and a solid breakfast we'll be in better shape to consider our options." And they trudged in weary silence back to the Royal Albion.

But Penny's day was not destined to be over. As she let herself into her room, her mind dwelling with pleasant anticipation on a long, hot bath, she suddenly froze as she saw a figure sitting in the dark in the room's sole easy chair pulled up to the window overlooking the Promenade. "Alex?" she queried, flipping on the light, but the head that turned towards her was dark: it was Sonya.

"I am very confused," Sonya announced in a flat voice. "I need to talk to you. There are things I need to know, need to understand."

Her hopes of an early night fading, Penny flopped wearily on the edge of the bed. "Well, I'm not at my best, but go ahead — what's troubling you?"

"Many things," Sonya said, but appeared in no hurry to communicate them.

"Then I think I'll need some coffee and sandwiches," Penny said. "Would you like some?"

Sonya shook her head. "No. Alex took me out to dinner. Very nice. Then we quarreled, so I came here to you. The chambermaid let me in."

"Oh!" Penny said blankly, and called down her order, wondering what this was all about. "Er — did something about what happened today upset you?" she queried.

"No — yes." Sonya contradicted herself. "Since I did not do this thing, it has to be one of them, doesn't it?"

"I'm afraid so," Penny said and waited, her hopes rising. But Sonya's next remark confounded her. "My father is very rich, isn't he? My mother did not tell me this." Her tone was angry.

"Well, at that time he was well-to-do but not *very* rich. His father died in 1961 and it was then he became a millionaire." Penny said cautiously. "Why? Does the idea of him being rich upset you?"

"I do not believe that some people should be very, very rich when others are so poor, but it is not his fault he is so rich," Sonya conceded. "And money can be useful, very useful. Would he let me have some, do you think?"

It shocked Penny. "Well, if you needed it for something, I think he would," she managed to get out.

"Good!" Another silence fell.

"Er — what did you quarrel with Alex about?" Penny hoped to start things off again.

"Oh, that!" Sonya sprang up and started to stalk angrily up and down. "He infuriated me. He said silly things about me and Peter, stupid things. He does not understand us at all. This I tell him and he shouts at me and I at him. Peter is like brother to me. Since five years old we have known each other. We do not make love, it is not like that at all. Besides — how do you say it? — Peter is on both platforms?"

"Bisexual?" Penny hazarded.

"Yes, that's it. Poor Peter, the men are always after him, but I do not think he minds it too much, though I think he likes women better."

"But he did object when Litvov went after you?" Penny prodded hopefully.

Sonya looked at her in surprise. "Not especially. After all, Litvov had had his turn with him, so why not me? I knew it would come and Peter knew that I knew what to do about that pig. Litvov was of the old regime. In the time of Stalin and Beria I could not have done as I did

65

and got away with it. But now things are different in Russia. Even in the old days you *could* do it — my mother showed me how. Someone comes after you that you do not want, then you make big stink in public and let them know someone else more important than they are wants you too. She did it all the time. Which is why I don't." Sonya gave Penny a defiant glare.

"You have never had any lovers?" Penny said softly.

"Oh, yes, some — but not many." Sonya confided. "When I was seventeen I had my first grand affair, but I soon tired of it. I am not promiscuous like my mother. It is not that important to me. Maybe if ever I really fall in love, but so far . . ." she trailed off wistfully, then, "My father and you, were you ever . . . ?"

"Lovers? No, never." Penny was definite. "Our relationship — close as it is — has never been on that basis."

Sonya looked at her doubtfully. "Then I don't see why Alex and he are always at each other's throats. Why are they always fighting?"

Penny sighed. "Well, in the first place, they are both very definite personalities and they have always tended to clash. In the second, I'm afraid it's — well — a question of attention. They are both jealous of the attention I give to the other one — it has always been like that and there seems to be nothing I can do about it. It's not that they don't like or respect one another, they do, but when we are all together, well, you've seen how it is."

Sonya gave her a wan smile and sat down again. "Now I understand and I am glad of that. Life is very difficult, isn't it?" The coffee and sandwiches arrived and interrupted them. Having tipped the waiter and closed the door upon him, Penny returned to the attack. "Did Litvov put sexual pressure on many others of the company?"

"Oh, yes. First this one, then that one. He was like a

stud in heat. Some did like me and fought him off, but others were too afraid or did not care."

"How about Mala and Olga?" Penny persisted.

"Both. Mala—she does not care. She is like a cow, that one, so bovine—not like a prima ballerina at all. If a man wants her, she goes to bed with him, but it means nothing to her. All she cares about is the dance—once she is on stage she is a different person. She even looks different! With Olga . . ." Sonya's expressive face tightened. "Poor Olga was afraid to say no. She is Jewish, you see. It was very difficult."

"And how did Mikail take that?"

"Oh, he was furious, just furious, but there was nothing he could do, and it was only for one night in Paris," Sonya exploded, then checked herself and sprang up. "I think I go now, you must be very tired, so I leave you." At the door she turned and said earnestly. "In the morning I ask my father for money. You will help me with that, yes?" And on that surprising note went out, leaving Penny gazing thoughtfully into her coffee cup.

Chapter 7

Penny was very relieved, when she descended to the Royal Albion's pleasant dining room, to find her son had already breakfasted and had departed for his daily jog along the Promenade and that there was no sign of Sonya; she badly needed a tête-à-tête with Toby. Her late-night coffee had so stimulated her that she had had trouble sleeping, but her over-active mind had spawned several ideas that she was aching to try out on her partner. She was still at the bacon-and-egg stage, which she was attacking with gusto, when he joined her, the bags under his eyes indicating a kindred restless night. "I've been thinking . . ." they said simultaneously.

He waved a resigned hand and took up the coffeepot with the other. "You go first," he muttered.

"Well, Sonya came to see me last night. I'll give you the details later, but her state of upset and concern set me thinking and I believe I've come up with a couple of ideas that may calm her down and possibly open her up. You can tell she is worried now that it *may* be one of her fellow dancers. What if we start talking about and honing in on Long and Spence as likely suspects? Presumably she doesn't care a fig about them, and this may soothe her down and start *her* thinking seriously. The other idea I had is even more important. Do you think you could wangle it so that Sonya is allowed to go back to the ballet company, provided one of us is with her at all times? I think that would be useful on two counts— one, we would observe her interaction with the others more closely, and two, we could get to see them at closer hand ourselves."

Toby ingested coffee and pondered. "Sounds reasonable. I have several contacts in the Foreign Office who probably could give some info on Spence. Not that I consider him at all likely, but I see your point. And if I can get Grey to agree to Sonya's return presumably we could keep an eye on Long as well as the others. However . . ." and he paused. "If we do that, I should warn you that the brunt of watch-dogging will fall on you and Alex, at least for the next few days. I am going to be tied up with Pontifex—the legal business of recognizing Sonya as my daughter and heir and completing all the financial arrangements are a lot more complex than I thought, and I am desperately trying to get the protection of British citizenship in case the Russians try to pull anything shady, and *that* is going to require a minor miracle to be done at all speedily."

"That's all right—Alex and I can cope. And talking of financial arrangements, Sonya asked me about money last night." She rapidly related the conversation verbatim. Toby, whose riches had always been more of a burden than a blessing to him, chuckled grimly. "Spoken like a good socialist I see—well, I'm glad she doesn't blame me too much. Any idea why she wants the money?"

"None, but it may be very interesting to find out what she does with it. If what she wants is at all within reason, I should give it to her. Could be for any number of things—bribes, hush money, maybe just buying stuff." She cocked an enquiring eye at him. "I gather you *do* want to keep her here."

"Yes, I do," he said simply. "But not if it is against her will. I lost her mother; I don't want to lose her, now that I have found her. I don't think. . . ."

But they were interrupted as Alex came racing into the dining room, clutching a bunch of newspapers, which he threw down on the table, and breathing hard, panted out, "I think we should get out of here—fast! The press has got hold of the story. They'll be on us like a pack of wolves." He pointed at the banner headlines— DISTINGUISHED ARCHAEOLOGIST RUSHES TO RESCUE OF COMMIE DAUGHTER screamed one; MILLIONAIRE 'TEC GLENDOWER INVOLVED WITH BRIGHTON MURDER SUSPECT trumpeted another; STARTLING DEVELOPMENTS IN BRIGHTON RED MURDER *The Times* stated in more sedate fashion.

Toby winced as he read them and Penny looked at him anxiously. "It was bound to happen sooner or later," she admonished. "I know it's hateful but you can't let them intimidate you, Toby."

He favored her with a haughty stare. "In this case I have no intention of so doing."

Alex was dancing up and down with impatience. "I think the Clarendon is out, so let's split forces. Ma, why don't you get Sonya out of the sack and I'll drive her up to London in your car? You and Toby can come on later in the Rolls. We'll rendezvous somewhere in town and try to figure out where to go."

"I'll go to the Athenaeum," Toby said with visible relief. "They'll have a damned hard time getting at me there."

"Yes, your club is a good idea, but any hotel will be just as bad as the Clarendon for us," Penny fussed, thinking furiously. "Where on earth can we go with Sonya?" her face cleared. "I know! Mrs. Walker . . . I'll see if she can take us in."

"Great idea!" Alex exclaimed.

"Who on earth is she?" Toby asked plaintively.

"She used to look after Alex up until the time he went away to school, remember?" Penny said. "An Oxford war-widow? She inherited her parent's little news-agent's and tobacconist shop in Fulham and went down there. We've always kept in touch and she adores Alex, I'm sure she'd take us in — though God knows if she'll have enough room for three of us."

"If she hasn't I can always go to the Clarendon," Alex said quickly. "They may come after me, but as long as I act like a tourist they won't get very far and will soon get fed up."

"Or you could come to the Athenaeum with me," Toby offered.

Alex looked at him in surprise. "My, that would be going up in the world! Anyway, let's move it."

Penny sprang up. "I'll get Sonya and phone Mrs. Walker from her room. You'd better bribe the telephone operator here to keep a tight lip with the press about our calls, Toby."

"Certainly. As soon as I've finished my breakfast," he said with amazing calm, and helped himself to more toast.

"I shall never understand that man, never!" Penny muttered crossly to herself, as she scuttled upstairs and proceeded to pound on Sonya's door. The very mention of publicity in times past had been enough to reduce Toby to a gibbering, incoherent wreck, who had fled before newsmen in complete and craven rout, usually leaving her to cope as best she might. Now he was calmly finishing his breakfast!

Her pounding brought a sleepy-eyed Sonya to the door. "What is it?" she said, yawning. With her long black silky hair falling in charming disarray about her creamy shoulders and with the faint flush of sleep on her cheeks, she looked very exotic, and Penny realized for the first time how sexually alluring she was. "Time to get up and go," she said, prodding the girl back into the room. "Someone has leaked the story to the press and we've got to get you out of here fast. Hurry up and get dressed and packed, while I do some phoning. Alex is driving you to London and we'll meet you there later."

"But it is so early, and I am not talking to him!" Sonya complained.

"Well, in that case you can finish your sleep on the way up there, but we've got to *move* it," Penny retaliated, diving for the phone.

"What about my breakfast?" Sonya demanded, languidly making for the bathroom.

"Alex will feed you on the way up."

"I shall not talk to him" Sonya declared, and shut the bathroom door with a bang.

Mrs. Walker was contacted, and went into mild ecstasies at the thought of seeing "her" Alex again, this apparently taking precedence over the startling import of the rest of Penny's message. "I'll be that glad to see you again," she declared happily, "and I'll fit you all in somehow, don't you fret. A Russian girl, did you say?"

"Yes, I'll explain it all at length when I see you, and I don't know exactly when that will be," Penny said. "But we'll be there sometime today. And, Mrs. Walker, it is *very* important you say nothing of this to anyone. We want to hold off the press as long as possible."

"Oh, yes, dear, don't you worry about that," Mrs. Walker assured her comfortably. "I'm looking forward to it — real bit of excitement for a change!" And on that rather ominous pronouncement she hung up.

Penny bustled around packing Sonya's things, and when she finally emerged from the bathroom, dressed but still half asleep, Penny zoomed downstairs to find out what was happening, then hustled the faintly complaining girl out through the kitchens to the tradesmen's door of the Albion, where Alex was waiting in the loading zone with her car. "We're meeting you at Pontifex's office, Mallard Court, just off the Strand at noon," her son informed her. "See you later," and sped off towards the London road.

Feeling somewhat limp, she hustled back to pack her own bag and, this done, sought out Toby in his room, where she found him in deep converse with the anxious-looking manager. " . . . there's quite a crowd of reporters in the lobby already," the latter was saying. "I've told them you have checked out, but I don't think they believe me."

"If you'll have my car brought to the rear entrance, we'll slip down the back stairs," Toby said. "Thank you very much for your cooperation. Don't worry, we'll be out of here before they can create any disturbance."

"Delighted to be of help, Sir Tobias," the manager said, visibly relieved.

They were not, however, destined to escape unnoticed, for when they went out the kitchen entrance, several enterprising reporters and a photographer were circling the Rolls, in which a wooden-faced garage hand sat at the wheel, like sharks in a feeding frenzy. "Damn! Don't say anything, just leave this to me," Toby said with calm authority and stalked towards the car, Penny following in increasing bemusement. The reporters zeroed in and rushed towards them, shouting questions as they came. Toby smiled pleasantly at them, tipped the driver a five-pound note as he sprang out with alacrity and held the door, slipped behind the wheel, as Penny scrambled in beside him, and said sweetly, "No comment — none at all, gentlemen. And that's my final word." He put the car in gear and inexorably nudged a reporter, who was desperately trying to stop the car and shout questions in at the window at one and the same time, out of the way. The reporter leaped aside at the last moment, and the car shot out onto the Promenade and turned left along it.

"Well, that was impressive," Penny said drily, when she had recovered her breath. "But where exactly are we going? You're heading towards Dover, not London."

"Just to confuse them a little. We've plenty of time. I'll head inland when we get to Newhaven." His face was serene.

"I just can't get over you!" she exploded. "You're a changed man."

"I am indeed," he smiled faintly. "I came to terms with this last night, though I confess I did not expect them on our trail quite so soon. I'm working on a valuable bit of advice from the long past. When I was a student digging Tell Atchana, Sir Leonard Woolley, who was heading up the dig, was going through a particularly scarifying divorce — really scandalous 'News of the World' stuff. This was back in the days when that sort of publicity could really hurt a man's career, too. From first to last he never said a word about it — not to the press, not to his colleagues; to no one. He was perfectly pleasant and calm at all times, but never broke his silence. He never explained or complained — and it worked like a charm. Afterwards, when all the fuss had died down, he said to me, 'Never try to explain your personal business to anyone else, my boy, because it is none of theirs. Deprive the fire of fuel and it will soon go out.' This to me is very personal business, so I intend to follow his advice."

"Let's hope it works," Penny said doubtfully. "I wonder how it got out so fast."

"I called Grey about our change in plans, and he was duly livid about it—as is the Russian embassy, by the way," Toby rumbled. "According to Grey, all the papers he talked to reported the same thing; an anonymous caller, male and *English*. He is certain it isn't any of the police involved, so feels it has to be either Long or Spence or one of their cronies. He is *not* amused."

"But why should either of them do such a thing?" Penny queried. "Knowing how stuffy FO types tend to be, you'd think the last thing they'd want would be to focus the public spotlight!"

Toby grunted. "Long is anxious that this Russian tour should be a success and I suppose the notoriety would increase public interest and stimulate sales. Struck me as rather an eager-beaver type. Grey thinks they are both gay. What did you make of them?"

"I didn't get to talk to Spence at all, but Long certainly could be. Spence talked to Alex and when he found out he was a doctor, started to pump him like mad about AIDS and the extent of it in the US. Long seemed eager to impress as being 'one of us,' as it were. At one point in those long dreary proceedings yesterday, he cornered me and went on about how he was a Magdalen man himself, so appreciated how painful all this must be for you, and then pumped away about our murder investigations. Seemed harmless enough."

"A Magdalen man, eh?" Toby said with distaste. "Know what he read?"

"Philosophy, Politics and Economics, I think he said."

"Might be useful to check with the dean," Toby mumbled. "Memory like an elephant old Reed has. Might turn up something on him. Though what good that can do . . ." he sighed heavily and they fell into a companionable silence as he turned away from the coast northwards and expertly threaded his way through back roads to the main London artery.

They fought their way through the usual tangled congestion of city traffic and by a quarter to twelve had turned into the little cul-de-sac off the Strand that was Mallard's Court. Her car was already parked on its cobbles outside the eighteenth-century building that announced on a discreet brass plate, "Pontifex, Pontifex and Fisher, Solicitors at Law." Penny could see a fair head and a dark one close together inside and apparently in deep conversation: the quarrel had evidently been resolved, and by the smug expressions on both their faces as Alex and Sonya emerged from the car to greet them, very happily so.

"Well, we are certainly out of the public eye here," Toby observed with satisfaction. "I asked old Pontifex if he'd lay on lunch for us in his private dining room here. Sonya and I can do some business first and eat at about one-thirty, if that's all right with you?" He looked inquiringly at Penny and Alex.

"Oh yes, I'm sure we can amuse ourselves till then," Penny said, with a grin at her son.

"Father, I must speak with you before we go in there." Twin spots of color flared on Sonya's cheekbones. "There are things I must understand. Alex tells me that I cannot go back to Russia, that I must stay here with you. Do *you* want me to stay here? This I must know."

Toby glared at Alex. "He has no right to say any such thing. If we can clear up this present mess there is no reason you cannot go back to Russia, if that is what you wish. To answer your second question. Yes, you are my daughter and heir, and I would very much like to have you stay here—but only if that is what *you* want. Late though it is for both of us, I would like to be the father I have never been, the father you have never had."

Blue eyes searched blue eyes. "Then I think I stay." There was a touch of defiance in her tone as Sonya continued. "But all my things are in Russia and I will need money to replace them. May I have some—now? In cash?"

Penny could see Toby tense slightly. "Of course," he said, fumbling in his pocket and producing his checkbook. "I don't have much on me, but I can write a check and perhaps Penny can cash it for you while we see Pontifex. How much would you like?"

A calculating look came into Sonya's eyes. "Three thousand pounds? Would that be too much?" she hazarded breathlessly. "I need things, many things."

She's lying, Penny thought, as Toby said, "Not at all," and calmly scribbled out a check and handed it to her. "We'll set up a regular account of your own as soon as possible."

Sonya looked at both of them, her eyes glowing with delight. "Oh, thank you, thank you very much! And now we see this old Mr. Pontifex?" And she tripped lightly up the steps.

Toby and Penny exchanged a long look. "Well, see you later then," he said, and followed his daughter.

Chapter 8

Penny watched her charge with all the attention of a proud parent at a school recital, as Sonya's lithe figure dipped and swayed at the bar in unison with her fellow dancers at the crackling commands of a little gnome-like ballet master, who reportedly had been one of the "greats" and who in his extreme youth had partnered the legendary Anna Pavlova. Their images in the mirrored wall of the practice salon enhanced the strange puppetlike effect of the scene and increased her feeling of having indeed entered a Looking-Glass World every bit as strange as Alice's.

Three puzzling and frustrating days had passed since their precipitate flight from Brighton. Sonya and she had settled snugly, and so far, safely in with Mrs. Walker, and Alex and Toby had been doing some expert reporter dodging at the Athenaeum. But this respite they realized would soon come to an end, for Grey had sanctioned Sonya's return to the company under due supervision and tonight would mark her reappearance on the stage. After that, perforce, they would again be in the public eye.

Penny was already prey to raging doubts as to

whether this had been such a good idea after all. Far from opening Sonya up, as hoped, her return to her peers had had the opposite effect. It was as if an invisible curtain had dropped between them. Sonya was pleasant and polite, but there was no sharing of thoughts and she had quietly blocked any of Penny's efforts to get closer to any of them: nor had she shown any disposition to spend any of the money she had been so eager to obtain. A second frustrating factor was the language barrier, for although Penny could observe who Sonya talked to and when, often the entire substance of those fast-paced Russian exchanges was entirely lost to her. She had tried to enlist the services of the mouse-like Miss Rogers, but found her of small help. She was so timorous that she never translated unless asked directly, and Penny was getting extremely tired of prompting "What are they saying now?" She longed for Toby and his expertise, but he was still enmeshed in legal technicalities from which there seemed no early respite. To complicate things still further, her own watching was watched, either by Borotov or by the somber Korkov, and this she found unnerving.

All she had garnered for her pains up to now was the gut impression that Sonya was up to something, but what and with whom she could not put a finger on. The Brighton group were sticking close together, that at least was evident, but it seemed that no sooner had Sonya drawn her attention to her conversations with Peter and Mala and her eyes were fixed on them, and their interaction, than she would find Sonya in equally deep converse with Mikail and Olga. She felt she was getting absolutely nowhere.

"The relief column has arrived. Want to take a break? I'm all set to take Sonya out to lunch after rehearsal." Alex murmured in her ear as he sat down beside her on the wooden bench. Miss Rogers on the other side of her cast a languishing glance at his handsome profile, sighed and went a little pink.

"Oh yes! Fine," she breathed thankfully. "I could do with a breather. You're sure you don't mind? This is certainly not much of a vacation for you."

"Not to worry. It's a pleasure — honest!" he grinned at her. "I'll bring Sonya back to Fulham, so no need to worry about that, and we'll go together to the performance later, right?"

"Right," she said, and slipped out under the watchful eye of Korkov. As she emerged into a London drizzle and put up her ever-ready umbrella, she almost cannoned into a burly figure that was sheltering in the doorway of the rehearsal hall. With a muttered apology she went on by and started along the empty pavement in the deserted side street, only to hear heavier footsteps behind her matching her own. A little prickle went up her spine and she deliberately slowed her pace; the footsteps also slowed. She felt a spurt of anger. Were the Russians actually having her followed? The nerve of it! If so, she'd out a stop to that right her and now.

She swung around, her umbrella cocked aggressively, then gasped with shock as a big, burly figure came towards her. The man doffed his soft tweed hat politely, unmasking a mane of shaggy dark hair; from the middle of a fuzzy black beard a grin flashed, revealing a gold tooth. "Ah, Doctor Spring, I was hoping to catch up with you. Remember me? Gregory Vadik?" he announced. "I was wondering if we might have a little talk."

"You!" she stuttered, her pulses pounding. "What in heaven's name are you doing here? What do you want with me?" Voices from the past echoed in her mind,

"Gregory Vadik is strictly bad news," "Wherever Vadik is there is trouble," Vadik the mystery man.

"I was in Paris when I read of your latest trouble. I came to offer my help," he said softly.

"Why?" she exploded.

The grin faded from his face. "Because I owe Sir Tobias a debt — twice in Israel he saved my skin when he could have thrown me to the wolves, and I could do nothing in return then. I am a proud man, I do not like to owe debts. I want to clean the slate. Besides, Vashti would wish it so. A very soft heart my wife has — for you both."

"She's here?" Penny said hopefully.

He shook his large head. "No — far away, and safe." His voice lingered on the last word. "So I am entirely at your disposal."

"There has to be more to it than that," she stated, eyeing him with deep suspicion. "What are you up to? How did you find me here?"

His answer took her breath away. "Very simple. I asked Inspector Grey of Scotland Yard who, I believe, is in charge of the case — and he directed me to you." His dark eyes studied her. "My offer is a genuine one, and I think I can be of help. Why don't we go somewhere and talk it over? You see I knew Litvov."

That decided her. "All right, Where?"

"There's a cab stand on the corner. Let's go to the British Museum," he said to her further amazement, and taking her firmly by the elbow steered her towards it. "We will not talk of this in the taxi," he directed, and when they were settled and on their way, completed her befuddlement by producing his wallet and saying with great pride, "I think you do not know that Vashti and I have a son now — Stefan. He is three years old." And this notorious man of international intrigue and sinister reputation, began to show her endless photos of a sturdy little boy taken from every conceivable angle, to which she found herself responding with the usual idiotic exclamations of admiration.

The taxi dropped them before the massive iron railings of the museum and Vadik stalked off towards its heavy classical portico like a man with a fixed purpose. The inner foyer was its usual crowded bedlam. Penny looked around dubiously. "This is hardly the place for a talk of this nature, is it?"

"On the contrary, it is exactly the place, if you know where to go. Come!" he commanded, and shepherded her with unerring steps to the gallery housing the Elgin marbles. It was completely empty. "See!" he said, and they sat down on a wooden bench that commanded views of both entrances. "We can talk freely here."

"So you knew Litvov — KGB was he?" She started the ball rolling.

"Very much so. One of Beria's boys — of the old Stalinist regime and hard line. The last time I saw him he was very unhappy about how things were going in Russia, and I think he had reason to be worried. He was involved in some things back in the 50s and 60s that did not sit too well with his new bosses."

"Disaffected?" she murmured.

"More like scared for his skin. He was still very hard-nosed. Hated Americans and so on." Vadik looked at her, "So tell me about the murder and the persons involved. I only know what was in the papers. It takes a lot to surprise me, but to think Sir Tobias was one of la Danarova's conquests positively flabbergasted me." He grinned widely at the thought.

"Did you know her?" Penny said quickly.

"No — only of her. She had quite a reputation. But I

did see her dance several times — she was very good. What's the daughter like?"

"As a dancer? — I haven't seen her perform yet," Penny evaded. "I gather she is not much like her mother. And she did not murder Litvov."

He continued to grin at her. "I'll take your word for it. No need to be defensive — until I hear all you can tell me, I won't know how to help. If it helps *you* at all, I think Litvov was up to something and what exactly that was I would very much like to find out."

"Right." Penny gave a quick and admirable precis of the setting, the people involved and the murder method. "If the KGB was involved and they wanted to get rid of him, do you think they'd do anything like that?" she queried.

"No, it's not a KGB killing," he said positively, "They're a damn sight more subtle than that. But you've told me two things that confirm my own suspicions, One, that Litvov finagled his way onto the tour in the first place, and two, that he was working alone. That is very unusual — particularly if they were on the track of a possible defection." He ruminated for a moment in silence. "Something *must* have been important about that gathering; something that made it imperative to silence him *then*. What, I wonder? There seems no indication from what you have told me. You're sure you are holding nothing back? He did not, for instance, make an appointment with one of the important people there that he did not keep?"

"Not that I know of, but . . ." she began, and suddenly Vadik held up a warning hand as there came the soft pattering of many feet. From the left entrance came a single file of camera-laden Japanese tourists, all holding little red pennants, shuffling silently behind a red-tagged guide; almost simultaneously from the right appeared another line of Japanese bearing little blue pennants high. Before their amazed eyes, the two groups criss-crossed and circled in a silent ballet, and at the rapped commands of the leaders, they lined up, pennants still held high, and gazed obediently up at the Elgin marbles. The guides began a high-pitched spiel in Japanese, then, on another rapped command, the two groups changed sides and the same performance began. At the end of this there was a communal sighed 'Hai,' another command, and the red pennants went silently out the right door, the blue pennants the left.

Vadik gazed bleakly after them. "Have we just seen the future of our world?" he murmured, and Penny got the distinct impression he was talking to himself and not to her. Then he looked at her. "What were you about to say?"

"Well, nothing important. I have told you everything," she said, a little at a loss. "So what do you think Litvov may have been up to?"

He hesitated. "He may have been trying to get out himself. But for that he would have needed money — a lot of money. The KGB has a very long arm. To escape them he'd have had to set up a new identity, find a new country — probably South American — and with enough money to allow him to keep a low profile in it. He may have been blackmailing someone; someone over whom he had a tight hold."

"But *none* of the people involved is rich!" she exclaimed. "So what bearing does that have?"

"Sir Tobias is," he murmured.

"But Toby didn't even *know* of Sonya's existence," she cried. "And anyway, you know him. He would never have submitted to blackmail."

"Ah, but would Litvov have known that?" Vadik queried.

"I am convinced Sonya did not do it," Penny stated.

"Are you equally convinced that someone did not do it on her behalf?" he said silkily.

"No one is that close to her," she said with far more conviction than she felt. "No, you're barking up the wrong tree. There has to be another motive."

To her great surprise, he nodded his head. "Yes, let's assume you are right. The question is where to start." He debated with himself. "I have something I have to finish up in Paris, so I may as well start sniffing around there to see if I can pick up a lead. It was their stop before coming here, so it may yield something. Then I'll be back. How do I get in touch with you and Sir Tobias?"

She shifted uneasily. "Er—I think for the moment we might leave Toby out of this. This will be just between us, until things are clearer."

"Meaning he would not appreciate my sudden interest in his affairs," he said with a chuckle, and got up. "Well then, how do I contact you?"

She thought quickly. She was still not sure how far to trust him and was not about to disclose her Fulham hideaway. "You can get in touch with my son, Dr. Alexander Spring. He'll be at the Athenaeum Club, and he'll set up a meeting when necessary."

"Your son, eh? Another anthropologist?" he asked.

"No, a medical doctor."

"Ah, good, very good," he approved. "That would be a good profession for my Stefan, I think." And on that amazing note took himself off, leaving her gazing dazedly at the frozen elegance of the ancient Greek marbles.

"Damn!" she muttered after an interval. "I hope I've done the right thing." But made up her mind to keep the curious developments of the morning from her partner:

Toby, she knew, would not take kindly to the news they were being assisted by a man with such a bloodstained and dubious reputation. However, she did need to see Toby, so deserted the marbles and went in search of a pay phone. On her second try she ran Toby to earth. "How about lunch? — I need to see you," she said hopefully.

"All right. Can you get to the Aldwych easily? If so, meet me at Giovanni's in an hour. I'll be through by then," he announced; he sounded worn.

She was there ahead of him and had fortified herself with a couple of drinks before he dropped into the seat opposite her. He was looking as worn as he sounded. "Anything?" he inquired, absentmindedly scanning the menu.

"Damn little." She poured out her meager store of information and the greater store of frustration. "So far as I can tell she hasn't spent any of that money yet," she concluded. "Have you got anything?"

"Yes, a little — and it's very puzzling." Toby groped in several pockets before he came up with his little black notebook. "Not a lot on Spence. He's had a rather mediocre career in the Foreign Office; a few European assignments — Finland, Sweden and a tour in Paris, also a couple in the Middle East — Syria and Turkey. Not overly ambitious, and is padded by a private income. Collects antiques."

"Rich?"

"Not very. Just comfortable. Never married; he may be gay, but, if so, is very circumspect about it."

"How about Long?"

"Well, there's where it gets a bit interesting." Toby proceeded to light up his pipe with maddening slowness. "I got on to old Reed about him, and he was very excited when I told him I was involved in the Brighton affair. Said he'd been wondering if he should contact the police. You see Litvov contacted him at Magdalen."

Penny gasped. "About Long?"

"No, that's what is so odd. About a fellow called Carstairs. Edmund Carstairs. Was an economics lecturer at Magdalen for a while—I knew him slightly. Then went off to the Home Office, where he is now quite a big wheel. Litvov wanted to find him — didn't or wouldn't say why. So Reed gave him Carstairs' Home Office number."

"Have you contacted Carstairs?"

"Yes, but only spoke with his secretary to set up a meeting. Haven't actually talked to him yet." Toby shifted uneasily in his seat. "Apparently he's on leave. Has a big place down in Sussex."

She pounced on that. "Sussex! Is he rich?"

Toby looked at her a little popeyed, "You seem to have money on the brain. Yes, as a matter of fact he is. Inherited a bundle. That's when he left Magdalen and moved to higher spheres. They say he has political ambitions, but he's Labour, so the climate hasn't been right for him to make his move yet."

Penny was getting excited. "He wasn't at that party by any chance?"

"No, and that's another odd thing, he apparently *was* invited, but according to Grey's list never showed up. I'll have to ask him about that."

"Any connection between him and Long?"

Toby shrugged. "Not so far as I know. Reed didn't have too much recollection of Long—who, by the way, is a lot older than he looks. He's fifty. I must say that surprised me. Took a rather dismal Third in PPE and was a bit of a hell raiser when he was up. Nothing too scandalous — practical jokes on blue bloods and that sort of thing. Reed had no idea what he had done since." He peered at her. "This mean something to you?"

"It might," she said cautiously. "Try and see Carstairs as soon as possible will you? I would love to know if there is any connection between him and either Long or Spence. Anyway, this will be something to tell Sonya to show her we are looking in other directions besides the ballet company. It might help."

"How is she bearing up?" His tone was a little wistful.

"Oh, a little keyed up about tonight — which is only natural. You're coming, aren't you?"

"Of course," Toby said haughtily. "You don't think I'd miss my own daughter's performance, do you? If she is only half as good as her mother was, she will still be wonderful."

Chapter 9

The touring program of the Leningrad Ballet relied heavily upon the tried and true — if they experimented with newer, more daring modern ballets on their home turf, they certainly were not about to reveal this fact to the world: thus the program for the evening commenced with Chopin's *Les Sylphides*, with Sonya dancing the lead role in this short ballet, and continued with Tchaikowsky's *Nutcracker* with Mala in the lead role, and in which Sonya was dancing as the Sugar Plum Fairy. That their choice was dead on the mark so far as the general public went had been evidenced by the good audiences up to now, and word had come from the box office that the added spur of notoriety had resulted in "Sold right out" notices until the end of the tour.

Unlike Toby, Penny had never been a fan of the ballet. Now, of course, she understood his unlikely addiction to it, but for her the ballet of the Western cultures had always made her faintly uneasy. Drilled as she was in the importance of the dance as a cultural expression, expert as she was in the significance of the dance in more primitive cultures, she had always felt that the ballet exemplified the more woolly-minded aspects of

Western culture; a romanticism and an idealism that were too far removed from the realities of life to have much validity, even if they were pretty to look at. Hence she was no expert on the quality of the dancers, but it seemed to her uncritical eye, as she peered down from the upper box from which they had deemed it wisest to spectate as a group, that Sonya was very good indeed. Despite her height — which was eye-catching — she was elegant, stylish, and expertly precise.

As *Les Sylphides* came to its romantic climax with the two lovers clasped in each other's arms at the apex of the triangle formed by the corps de ballet, Sonya's head bent lovingly towards the fair head of Peter, Penny braced herself. She did not dare look at Toby, on her left, for she was acutely aware of the white handkerchief clutched tightly in his right hand that surreptitiously mopped at his glasses, and of his many subdued throat clearings, his head turned away from her. For him a dam of past and present emotions had burst; a dam he was vainly struggling to contain. Much as her heart ached for him she knew the only thing she could do for him was to let him be.

As the curtain swept down and the applause began, she did look at Alex on her right, and the expression on his face twisted her heart with new pain. It was the same expression he had as a little boy when opening an especially coveted Christmas present or contemplating his favorite banana split — an expression of yearning joy. He was applauding madly and had risen to his feet. He looked down at her, his face alight, "She was great, wasn't she?"

The two principals appeared through the curtain, bowing and smiling; the inevitable flowers were thrown and bouquets appeared from both sides of the stage and were laden upon the arms of the smiling, curtsying

Sonya. With an incoherent gobble, Toby made a dash for the door of the box and was gone, before the applause had died away and the dancers had taken their final bow.

"What's with him?" Alex demanded, settling in to his chair again, as the full houselights went up for the interval. "Didn't he like it?"

"Too much," she murmured. "Just a little overwhelmed, that's all. Don't say anything, Alex, when he gets back."

"Well, life is just full of surprises," he remarked as he studied his program.

"Yes, it is," she said eying him thoughtfully. As any mother with an only son, she had gone through countless throes of anxiety over the years about a too-early marriage, an unsuitable marriage, and of late, whether there would be any marriage at all: all the time knowing full well that there was nothing she could, or probably would, do to alter the situation. But now some of the old anxiety was back. Was he becoming emotionally involved with Sonya? If so, it was not only Toby who was headed for emotional torment. Sonya was still an unknown factor: if not a murderer, then at the least, very much mixed up in a murder. An equally sobering thought was that, while she might be Toby's daughter in many ways, she was also the daughter of the notorious Danarova. These troublesome musings kept her occupied and silent throughout the interval, and it was not until the lights had gone down again that Toby reappeared quietly by her side.

The Nutcracker was a ballet Penny knew well; a staple of the Boston Christmases of her childhood which stirred many warm memories. Peter was excellent as the Nutcracker-soldier hero, but when Mala came on stage it was electrifying. It was hard to equate that ethereal, magical, brilliant figure with the slightly dumpy, stolidly placid creature of the rehearsal hall. Mala, as Sonya had predicted, was transformed. As the ballet proceeded even Penny could see the difference—the rest were very good; Mala was great. She dominated the scene and drew the eye, even when she wasn't dancing.

Penny noted that Mikail Kupinksi played a double role. He was the magician-maker of the Nutcracker and also partnered his wife in the amusing Chinese dance. Similarly, Olga was also the featured dancer in the Waltz of the Flowers. Evidently the Leningrad Ballet made its principals work hard for their privileged position.

At the finale, when the entire company came forward to take the first of many bows, Toby sprang up. "Let's go," he said huskily. "We have to make it backstage before the ovation is over. There's a door in the Grand Circle level we can slip through without being noticed." Apart from a suspicious redness about his eyes he was back to normal. As they followed him down, he elaborated, "Borotov has been very cooperative. The idea is to stay backstage until the crowd has gone and then, while the main body of dancers go out the stage door, we'll go out by the front, where the car will be waiting; it should minimize the press onslaught."

"What's on tomorrow?" Penny asked, as they made their way unnoticed through the passageways.

"*Spectre de la rose*, Gregorvich's *pièce de résistance*, and *Sleeping Beauty* I believe," Tony mumbled. "Although they have done a bit of rearranging of schedules with Sonya being absent. However, with the Sunday's break coming up they should be back on the usual track with *Swan Lake* on Monday."

Their arrival behind the scenes coincided with the first arrivals from the corps de ballet straggling off the stage, where the principals were still collecting plaudits and bouquets from the audience. They brought with them a "morning after" atmosphere of exhaustion as they drooped tiredly by with the peculiar flat-footed gait of the ballet. The intruders flattened themselves against the wall and looked vainly around for further direction; it came in the form of Selwyn Long who emerged from a dressing room and inquired brightly, "Oh, hiding out, are we? How's the amateur snooping going? Off duty or on?" He seemed elated to the point of hysteria and it crossed Penny's mind that he might be "on" something. "Went well, didn't it?" he rattled on. "Were you impressed by your darling daughter, Sir Tobias? Good, wasn't she — even in a tired old thing like *Les Sylphides*."

"I wonder if you could show us to her dressing room," Toby said edgily. "Then we can get out of your way."

"Here she comes now and she'll take you," Long chirped, as she came off stage with the Kupinskis, leaving Peter and Mala still receiving the plaudits of the crowd.

Sonya encompassed them in a tired smile and beckoned, but Penny lingered behind. She was interested to see how long the magic of the moment lasted for Mala, who was now alone in the spotlight and blowing her final kisses to the audience. Peter brushed past her, his face still sheened with sweat, then the curtain closed for the final time and Mala turned towards her. It was as if an internal switch had been suddenly flipped off and it was the dull-eyed stolid figure of the rehearsal hall that shuffled off the stage. "You were magnificent," Penny said in French.

The dark eyes gazed mildly at her, the fair head nodded and with a timid smile Mala went on by without a word. Penny followed her and was interested to see that both Borotov and Long were waiting outside her dressing room, then she turned into Sonya's just beyond it, where Toby and Alex were propped on opposite sides of the door in the tiny room and Sonya, still in costume, was seated before the lighted mirror wiping off her stage makeup. "I'm hungry," she was complaining. "I may have a whole pizza to myself, yes? And with beer, lots of beer — I am very thirsty also."

Toby looked slightly pained. Alex grinned, "To take out or eat in?"

"Either, so long as it is quick." She flashed him a brilliant smile and disappeared behind the dressing screen, on which the pale pink tutu and pink tights shortly appeared, and after another short interval Sonya emerged in a pale blue linen long-jacketed suit with toreador pants that accentuated her shapely legs, and a black turtleneck silk blouse. "You like?" she said, twirling like a model. "I get this in Paris — on sale at the Galeries Lafayette."

"Terrific!" Alex exclaimed. "Too good for any pizza parlor, my girl."

"We could go the Savoy Grill. That stays open late," Toby said hopefully.

"But that would take so long!" Sonya wailed, "And I die of hunger. There is a good Italian restaurant near here, let's go there."

Toby cleared his throat. "Before we go, there is something I would like you to have now and this seems to be an appropriate occasion." He groped in his pocket and produced two cases, one long and thin in maroon leather, the other in much-rubbed blue velvet. He handed them over to her. "The pendant was my mother's — your grandmother — and the others, well, one day I expect you will have use for them."

Sonya's reaction was strange. All the exuberance in

her died and she looked uneasily from him to the cases. Hesitantly she opened the leather case and emitted a little gasp, for in it nestled a single, solitaire-cut rose diamond of some twenty-five carats on a heavy gold chain, that twinkled rosily in the harsh light of the dressing room. She snapped it shut abruptly and opened the smaller box: in it lay two platinum and gold wedding bands chased with elaborate Celtic designs. She studied these, her head bent, then said in a muffled voice. "You kept them all these years? You were going to marry her then?"

Toby looked highly indignant. "Well of course I was!"

Her long slim fingers clasped the blue velvet case tightly. "Then these I would like to keep, but . . ," her head went up and there was a flash of defiance in the blue eyes as she handed the leather case back to him. " . . . this other, not now. It is too valuable, much too valuable. Maybe when all this is finished; when we know if there is to be a future for us and what that might hold, maybe then you will still feel like giving it to me, and then I will take it gladly — but not now." She sounded a little desperate.

Toby studied her face for a long moment, then took it. "Very well," he said calmly. "As you wish. Shall we go?"

"Something to be said for the stiff upper lip, I suppose," Alex murmured in Penny's ear as they followed the two tall figures out through the empty darkness of the theater. "And here was I thinking of bestowing upon her my very best Johns Hopkins Medical School T-shirt. Scarcely in the same class, but I don't think she'd turn that down, do you?" His mother punched him in the arm.

The crowded Italian restaurant was evidently a favorite rendezvous of the ballet company, for as they wound their way to a table in the rear Penny spotted Peter at a table with Selwyn Long and the inevitable and sullenly silent Herbert Spence, and the Kupinskis by themselves at another, as well as several chattering groups of the corps de ballet: the new Russian longing for pizza and beer seemed to be omnipresent.

The sight of food restored Sonya's spirits and she chattered gaily about the performance and the performers, fascinating her male audience with all the expertise of a snake charmer. Penny tucked into her pizza with gusto, wondering where Mala was and how her unlikely partner was getting on in Paris. She kept a quiet eye on the other tables: Peter seemed to be restive, and at one point got up and went over to the Kupinskis where he chatted and laughed for a few minutes, during which Long and Spence began an argument in fierce undertones until he reappeared, whereupon Long was once more wreathed in smiles and Spence relapsed into angry silence. Peter certainly seemed to be having a disturbing effect all around, she noted, for no sooner had he left them than Olga Kupinski dissolved into tears, and Mikail, with a furtive glance around, was evidently chiding her, and in a short while was bustling her out of the restaurant. What, Penny wondered, could that be about.

Suddenly, Sonya, who had been eying her, addressed her directly. "What did you think of Mala? Do you see what I meant?"

Penny tore her eyes away from the departing Kupinskis. "She was magnificent, and yes, I did. Quite an amazing transformation. But where is she? I don't see her here."

"Oh, Mala never goes out after a performance. She will have gone back to her hotel and had a tray sent up to her room. She is changing into Aurora for tomorrow, you see. Just like she will take Sunday off and then on Monday will have changed into the Swan Queen. It is always like this. She is never Mala for very long. It is the price she pays for greatness," Sonya explained earnestly. "The rest of us dance for a living, and live in spite of that. Mala lives only to dance. Perhaps she is fortunate, but I do not think so."

The tables were emptying and their own dinner finished; Sonya sprang up. "Now I must get to bed. I am tired and rehearsal is at eleven tomorrow and with two shows. I shall sleep late — very late." She stretched luxuriously.

"Lunch after rehearsal?" Alex said before Penny could get a word in. "And then some sightseeing?"

"Yes, lunch would be nice, but there is a matinee tomorrow, so no time for the other. Sunday perhaps?" Sonya asked.

"When would you like to go shopping?" Penny put in.

"Oh, some time. There is no hurry," Sonya evaded. "Maybe next week sometime. I think I go to the ladies'." And she dashed off. Again she was being evasive, Penny thought with a twinge of unease.

"I'll be seeing Carstairs tomorrow morning and then will check in with Grey," Toby murmured. "Want to come along?"

She was tempted, but resisted it. "No, I think I can be more useful doing some heavy telephoning. Now we know when Long was up, I think there are several people's memories I can tap in Oxford — I may even pop up there for a few hours, since we aren't due to go to the theater until evening, and Alex is going to look after Sonya. When you do see Grey try and tap him some more about Spence as well — he wasn't Oxford, was he?"

"No, Cambridge — King's College. Modern Languages."

"Russian?"

"No—French, German and Italian. I'd already thought of that."

"Humpf! Well, anyway, I'll leave a message for you at the club when I get in and you call me."

"Right." They went their separate ways; Alex and Toby in the Rolls to the Athenaeum and she and Sonya in her car to the humbler glories of Fulham.

Before she went to bed, she made a list of all the people she intended to contact and called Ada Phipps—avid for news—at her Oxford home. She cut short Ada's curious enquiries and acquired a list of telephone numbers from the Oxford directory to go with her names, then, satisfied, went to what she felt was a well-earned rest: it had been quite a day.

Penny descended to the pleasant smell of coffee and frying bacon, to find Mrs. Walker fussing happily about her tiny kitchen. "I'm afraid I'm going to have to tie up your telephone most of the morning," she told the elderly woman. "But I'll be charging all the calls to my own phone, so don't worry about that."

"Oh my, as if I would!" Mrs. Walker exclaimed. "I'm that glad to be of help. Is there anything else I can do for you?"

"Well, if I do get tied up on the phone, maybe you could give Sonya a call about ten? She has to be at rehearsal at eleven."

Mrs. Walker looked at her in mild surprise. "But she's up already. Up and gone. Real early too. I was just getting up myself—about seven that was—and I heard the front door go, so I said to myself, 'Now who could that be, so early like?' and so I peeked into your room and then into hers. Very neat she is for a foreigner, I must say that. Bed all made up and everything."

Penny turned to ice, then made a dash for the stairs

and flung open Sonya's door, her heart pounding. She calmed a little when she saw Sonya's clothes and luggage were still there, then turned to Mrs. Walker, who had followed her up the stairs, a worried expression on her amiable face. "Is something the matter then?" she quavered.

Penny controlled herself with an effort. "No, nothing, Mrs. Walker — nothing for you to worry about. It is just that she did not say anything to me last night and I was a bit surprised, that's all. There were no phone calls during the night were there?"

The old woman shook her head, looking puzzled.

"I have to call Sir Tobias," Penny said, and made a dash for the phone.

Chapter 10

"It's no use blaming yourself, there's no way you could have stopped her, but where on earth could she have gone — and to do what?" Toby had rushed right over and was now pacing the floor in Mrs. Walker's tiny sitting room.

"I had some time to think while you were on your way over," Penny said, "And the way it looks to me is this: I don't think it was any accident we ended up in that restaurant last night. I believe Sonya was hoping for a private word with one of the group there and for some reason did not get the chance to have it. She hasn't done another bunk by the look of things, but there is someone she has to see alone. On this basis I think we can rule out Mala, but it could be any of the others. I rather favor the Kupinskis myself, for Olga is the only logical one Sonya could have been sure of a *private* word with in the ladies, and they did leave in rather a hurry after Olga had an emotional upset."

"But what should we *do*?" Toby exploded. "Grey is going to be furious if he hears she got away from us. He could pull her in again."

"Then don't tell him. I suggest you go on with your

original plans to meet Carstairs and then Grey, and I'll go over to the rehearsal hall and see if she turns up there. Call me there about eleven thirty, and if she hasn't appeared, well, I suppose then we'll have to push the panic button, but there's no sense doing it prematurely."

"I suppose you're right." He stopped pacing and looked at his watch. "In that case I had better get going. I feel as if I'm running around in circles in a dense fog."

"Join the club!" Penny murmured, as she went out into the little shop to tell Mrs. Walker of her change in plans and to take a hasty skim through the daily papers. She was thankful to see that other world disasters had driven the Brighton murder off the front pages, and that Toby's steadfast stonewalling of the press had begun to pay off, for all she found were some small paragraphs on the inner pages, all playing variations on the theme of "Brighton ballerina murder suspect rejoins cast of Leningrad ballet," but with little additional substance. The yellow press had her fellow dancers cowering away from her in fear and suspicion, the more sober journals speculated on Scotland Yard's next moves and on the future of "glasnost."

She hurried off to the rehearsal hall and was relieved to see Alex already in attendance and immersed in a morning paper. "Oh, thank Heavens you are here — we have a crisis. Sonya disappeared at seven this morning," she burst out.

He looked at her in utter amazement. "But she's here! Getting togged up for rehearsal."

Penny slumped down with relief. "Was she here when you arrived?"

"Well, no, actually she got in about ten minutes ago."

"Was she with anyone? Did you notice who came in before and after her?"

"She was alone. And I didn't take much notice — I

thought you'd just dropped her off. Let's see. Mala and Peter were already here, I think. And, yes, the Kupinskis arrived a bit later—about five minutes ago."

"Then I'm going to have a word with her and give her a piece of my mind," Penny said tightly, for the first dancers were already at the barre limbering up. "Not that I imagine it will do one bit of good."

It didn't. Sonya was all wide-eyed injured innocence. "But why the fuss? I woke early—I ate too much last night. I could sleep no more and wanted some exercise, so I take long walk. I walk here."

"From *Fulham*?" Penny said in disbelief.

"Yes. Walking is very good for you," Sonya said firmly. "And I did not want to disturb you so early."

"Well you did. You had your father and me worried to death," Penny snapped. She did not believe a word of it, but there was no way of breaking down the girl's obstinacy.

"Then I am very sorry, but I am not used to being looked after, being prisoner," Sonya snapped back. "I am used to going my own way. I must go now."

"Are you indeed? Then you better watch out that your way doesn't land you right back behind bars," Penny called after her, as the monotonous tinkle of the practice piano started up.

Before returning to Fulham and her delayed telephone calls, she again sought out Alex. "Don't let Sonya get away from you today, not for a minute. And, one other thing, a man named Vadik—Gregory Vadik— may be contacting you at the Athenaeum. If he does, set up a meeting for me, but don't tell him where I am. And don't breathe a word of it to Toby—this is important."

Her son eyed her askance. "Curiouser and curiouser—

set up a meeting with a strange man, eh? What are you up to, ma?"

"I'll fill you in later, but just for the present this is strictly between us. Oh, and Toby will call about eleven thirty for me here. You take it and explain all is well."

Penny supplied the anxious Mrs. Walker with Sonya's "walk" explanation, whereupon that good lady exclaimed. "Isn't that just like the young ones! — never a thought do they give you. So much energy too, they don't know what to do with it, and that's a fact." She went happily back to her storekeeping, leaving Penny a free field with the phone.

Several hours later she looked at the meager store of facts she had garnered and wondered if it had been worth the time and effort, for none of it seemed to have much bearing on the present situation. The general impression she had got from a spectrum of people, ranging all the way from an ex-University Proctor to the retired "scout" who had looked after Long's rooms when he was up, was that he was very anti-establishment and had delighted in twisting the tail of the authorities. He'd been active in the Oxford Union as a Socialist — a very *in* thing in his time — and had been pro all the many *anti* causes of his day: anti-bomb, anti-American bases, anti-NATO and so on. That he was noted for an explosive temper, and that the practical jokes that had earned him a brief notoriety when he was up, some of which had exhibited a vindictive, destructive streak, had been aimed at a group of conservative lordlings, who had all been concerned in a humiliating public "debagging" of Long early in his Magdalen career. No one seemed to have any idea what he had done since he had gone down from Oxford. "Much ado about nothing," she sighed, and put in another call to Toby. She was fortunate to catch him just as he returned from the Yard, but he sounded every bit as doleful as she was feeling, and they agreed dismally to rendezvous back at Giovanni's for lunch.

There Penny laid her slim harvest before him; he listened with marked attention. "Make any sense to you?" she asked.

"It might," he said cautiously and went on to give his own news, starting with his interview with Grey. "They've got nothing new on the murder itself. The British Embassy in Moscow has confirmed Litvov *was* KGB, but have nothing else on him. The Russians won't even admit that much."

For a second she was tempted to pass on Vadik's deeper knowledge, but decided this was not the moment. "And what did you get from Carstairs?"

"Not much. He always was a bit supercilious and age has not improved him," Toby rumbled. "His story about Litvov was straightforward enough. Said Litvov contacted him and asked for a meeting because he had some information 'of great personal interest and concern' to him, but he wouldn't commit himself further on the phone. Carstairs was down in Sussex and did not feel like coming back to town just to meet 'some damn Russky ballet dancer' to quote him. Litvov mentioned the Brighton bash and he agreed to meet him there at the reception." Penny's interest quickened. "But then, on the night, Carstairs had some friends from overseas drop by unexpectedly. He only had the one invitation, and so decided to skip it at the last minute. Said that if it was that important he was sure Litvov would contact him again."

"But neither Litvov nor his murderer could have known that he wasn't going to show up!" Penny said eagerly.

Toby nodded. "Exactly."

"And did he know Long or Spence?"

"Spence, no. Long, yes." Toby paused and ruminated. "Again he seemed straightforward enough, but I'm not entirely satisfied that he wasn't holding something back. He was Long's economics tutor at Oxford, and he thought that Long had had a raw deal. Said the authorities were 'down' on him, and that he was a good deal brighter than his degree result indicated. So when Long came down, Carstairs gave him a helping hand with introductions and references and so on."

"To do what?" she demanded.

"Ah, there he became studiedly vague. He said they kept in touch sporadically for a number of years, but that he hasn't seen him for the past ten years or so and has no idea what he's been doing."

"And you don't believe him?"

"I don't *dis*believe him," Toby said thoughtfully. "It's just that all the time I was with him, everything about him — the way he talked, the way he acted — kept reminding me of someone, but I could not remember who until I came away. It was Tony Blunt."

She was puzzled momentarily, searching her memory for the name, then gasped. "You mean Blunt, the fourth man of the Burgess, Maclean, Philby team? The spy? Did you know *him*?"

"Slightly. Blunt was a member of two of my clubs — the Athenaeum and the Winetasters," Toby murmured. "A very cultured, erudite man — and a damn dangerous one."

"And you think Carstairs might be in the same mold?"

"I think it's something that warrants further investigation," he said heavily. "It is certainly not an accusation you hurl casually out of the blue at a man as powerful as Carstairs unless you have some damn good proof. I'm walking on the razor's edge on this one, for if I am to keep Sonya here it is the Home Office that will have to give its approval — and he could easily scupper that. I'll have to be *very* discreet."

"Well at least it gives you something to work on," Penny said with a sigh. "I seem to have run out of things to do."

"Maddening as it may be, keeping an eye on the Russians is the most useful thing you can do at the moment. Oh, if only Sonya would *trust* us," he exclaimed.

"Unfortunately, it's too soon for that. Don't forget she has been raised in a culture where suspicion is the order of the day. It takes time — which we have not got," she said glumly. "All we can hope for is a break."

But no such break was immediately apparent. The rest of Saturday went by without further incident. Sonya was all sweetness and light for the remainder of the day, dancing in the undemanding role of the girl to Peter's Spectre of the Rose, and then as the good fairy who mitigates the evil fairy's spell in *Sleeping Beauty*; Olga being the evil fairy. After two performances she really was exhausted, and submitted meekly to being shipped back to Fulham and a hasty dinner at a local restaurant there.

There was a slight dispute over dinner when it came to plans for Sunday. "Sightseeing time," Alex announced, "I thought a run into the country to see Windsor Castle, and then I'll wine you and dine you to your heart's content. How about it?"

"Oh, but I thought we might go with Peter and Mala and the Kupinskis," Sonya protested. "They go to Southend for the day — a big pier and many amusements, yes? With many funny things to see and do."

Toby uttered a faint groan of horror, and Alex, after a swift glance at his mother, said, "Southend is the pits! And if you think I'm going to spend the entire day as a fifth wheel while you all gabble unintelligibly to each other, think again. I'm open to any other suggestions, but Southend is definitely *out*."

Sonya pouted and protested for a minute or two, but finally gave in. "All right then we will go to your Windsor castle—but me, I have not much use for these kings and queens of yours. Me, I am of the proletariat and these I wish to see."

"They're not my kings and queens," Alex pointed out with a grin. "If you remember, we Americans had a revolution too—in fact we started the trend. But if you crave the proletariat, I will whisk you back here and we'll finish the evening at Battersea Amusement Park— that's about as proletarian as you can get!"

"Such a bully!" Sonya complained. "But yes, that sounds all right."

But before he came to pick up Sonya the next morning, Penny received a cautious phone call from him. "I can't say too much because Toby is hovering around, but the call you were expecting came in. Says to meet at the same place in the BM. Two o'clock. That okay?"

Penny's spirits rose. "Fine. See you later, and good thinking about Southend."

"Yes, I didn't think that would be wise in the circumstances—I didn't have a chance to tell you this yesterday evening, but she no longer has the money. I'll fill you in later," he muttered and rang off, leaving her with yet another item to worry about.

She went off to her rendezvous torn between hope and dismay; she still had great doubts about Vadik's motives in offering a helping hand. She found him peering studiously at the Parthenon frieze, but this time they did not have the gallery to themselves. After shaking hands with her, he said in a loud voice, "Ah, Dr. Schmidt, now that you are here, I would value greatly your opinion on a certain piece of sculpture," and led her firmly away to the remoter recesses of the Assyrian gallery, which was unpeopled. They sat down on a bench opposite an enormous "seraphim" statue from Nineveh. "A fine piece, I think you'll agree," he boomed for the benefit of the few who were hurrying through the gallery towards more exciting goals.

Damn it!, she thought crossly to herself, he is really enjoying this; probably getting no end of a kick out of seeing us squirm. "Well?" she demanded.

"It is as I thought," he murmured. "Litvov was running scared. So scared he was not covering his tracks very well. I turned up a bank account in Paris under one of the aliases he used in former days when he was operating abroad. He may have another in Switzerland – which one might expect – but I have no means of getting at that. Anyway the activity in the Paris account is enough. It shows that over the past few months he has been making regular and fairly substantial deposits. He was bleeding someone – no doubt about it. But the total was nowhere near enough to make a break and start over, so I think he was here for the final, big kill. And got killed himself for his pains."

"Did you get any line on the possible source?"

"Only that the deposits were always in cash and in pounds sterling."

"Which would rule out all the dancers," she said quickly.

He hesitated. "Probably. But then anyone can change currency these days. Tho' I don't think any of them could have consistently come up with that kind of money."

"So that points a finger at either Long or Spence. But what possible hold could he have on either of them?"

"Ah, that is where it all gets very interesting. Did you know that Herbert Spence is quite an authority on an aspect of Russian art? On icons? What is more, I found he is the silent partner in an antique shop run by a rather precious young man on the Left Bank; a precious young man who is disgruntled and so was persuaded to talk with the minimum of persuasion." He grinned at her slyly.

"Well, there's nothing illegal in that," Penny said. "I don't see where you're heading on this."

"Just this—for some time the Russian authorities have been trying to crack down on the smuggling of their antiques—particularly, of smaller objects like icons. There seems to be an organized pipeline out of Russia which they have not managed to track down. Paris appears to be the end of the line, and from there most of the stuff gets to America. What if Litvov had discovered how it works, and that Spence was involved? That would be enough to put the pressure on. It warrants looking into. What can you give me on him?"

She could see no harm in it, and so related what little she knew.

"Alfriston, eh? Well, I think that may be my first port of call," he said, making notes in some language totally unintelligible to her. "But you say he is not rich? Then there *has* to be someone else."

She was torn: should she tell him about the Carstairs episode? Would that jeopardize Toby in any way? She could not see how, so she told him. "It may not have anything to do with it," she concluded, feeling a little desperate. "But Carstairs is a rich man and he does tie in with the Brighton reception, although his links with the other two seem very weak or nonexistent."

"It most certainly demands further investigation." Vadik's beard positively bristled with energy as he scribbled on. "I have never heard of this Carstairs — but he is an important man you say? This may be the link I have been looking for."

She looked at him in alarm, her heart sinking. God, he *was* after something! What had she done? Her alarm was compounded when he sprang to his feet and said abruptly, "I must be on my way. I expect I shall be much occupied in the next few days, but if you need to reach me for any reason, leave a message at this number." He tore a page out of his notebook and handed it to her. "Leave it for Varoli — Guiseppe Varoli." And with another savage grin was gone.

Penny was in such an agony of doubt that she could not face going back to Fulham, so she wandered the streets of London until she was exhausted. Her wanderings having taken her as far as the National Theatre, she bought a ticket to some avant-garde concert to which she listened in an unheeding daze and rested her aching feet. It was dark when she got out and, too worn to face public transport, she treated herself to a taxi back to Fulham. As she went in the front door, Mrs. Walker pounced on her. "Ah, there you are! I'm that glad to see you. Sir Tobias has just called up — very urgent he was. You're to call him back as soon as you can."

With a terrible sense of foreboding, Penny dialed and was put through to Toby. His first words sent her spirits plummeting. "There's hell to pay," he rumbled. "We're to be in Grey's office at nine tomorrow morning. The Kupinskis have disappeared — they've run for it. Grey

thinks they did the murder and that Sonya covered for
them. We're in a mess."

Chapter 11

To both Penny and Toby it was evident that, despite his cool, collected air and his usual impeccable appearance, Inspector Grey was rattled and in a furious temper. His men had been made fools of. Worse, he had been made a fool of. And worse yet, in circumstances that a finger could be pointed at Scotland Yard for laxity of effort.

If indeed it had been planned with that much precision and forethought, and was not sheer happenstance, the psychological daring of the Russians had been masterly. Two officers had been detailed for the unwelcome chore of following the Russian quartet over the weekend. One of them, whose mother lived near Southend, decided to pay a quick visit when the Russians had all trooped onto Southend pier and appeared to be safely corralled there for several hours. The quartet had emerged before he returned from this filial duty. According to the lone remaining detective, the Kupinskis had gone to a restaurant close to the pier and settled at a table in the window. Peter and Mala, on the other hand, "had acted suspiciously" — glancing furtively around and then making a beeline for the outskirts of town. He had decided to follow them. They led him on a long circuitous walk and then had doubled back to the pier and went on it again. In the meantime the second officer had returned and taken up his former station, and it was only upon the return of his foot-weary colleague that he had gone off in search of the Kupinskis, only to learn from the restaurant owner that they had not eaten there at all, but had had a quick cup of tea and then had gone out by the rear entrance. There had been a further delay in raising the alarm while the by-now anxious officers had debated what to do. By the time they had got around to alerting the Southend police of their problem, the Kupinskis had disappeared without trace in the horde of day-trippers. A belated search of their rooms in the hotel where the company was staying revealed that all of their luggage was gone as well. There could be no doubt that they had taken flight.

Peter and Mala had been picked up when they came off the pier, but there had been another delay because of the language problem: no Russian interpreter could be found at a moment's notice on a Southend Sunday. They made do with a local sergeant who spoke some French. Peter, who had been spokesman for the remaining duo, expressed surprised outrage. They had no idea where the Kupinskis were, they said they were going to have a meal. He and Mala had not been acting suspiciously, they merely had wanted some exercise and had taken a long walk to see the town before returning to the heady delights of the pier. Mala's sole contribution had been emphatic nods to everything Peter said and not even threats of arrest "for impeding the police" could budge them an inch. It was a well-thought-out conspiracy and there was nothing the British police could do about it — a fact they were sure the Russian dancers were well aware of.

Now Inspector Grey had them all gathered before

him: the three Russians sitting in an uneasy, wooden-faced row before his desk. Toby, Penny, a police interpreter, and Alex — who had insisted on being present — sat ranked behind them. A slight trembling in Grey's hands when he picked up a sheaf of police reports indicated what a tight rein he was keeping on himself, as he cleared his throat and began, "Miss Danarova, I hope I can impress upon you the very serious situation you are in. I put it to you that you have known from the start that the Kupinskis were guilty of Litvov's murder; that you were aware of this and that you not only attempted to cover up this fact by drawing suspicion upon yourself but that you did willfully assist them to escape, along with your colleagues here. That makes you an active accessory to murder, for which you can be charged, sentenced and imprisoned for a long period of time. Your one hope is to assist us now, by telling us all you know and helping us capture the fugitives. I may point out that it is only a matter of time before this happens. If they are still in England they will be caught. Interpol has been notified and so if they have reached the continent they will also be found. Your own authorities will be after them. For your own sake I urge you to tell us everything, and then perhaps the courts may find mitigating circumstances for leniency."

There was a small silence and Penny found she was holding her breath as she gazed at Sonya's rigid back. Sonya said in a high clear voice, "This is quite ridiculous. I know of no such things. The Kupinskis did not kill Litvov, any more than I did. If they are gone from Southend, I know nothing of that. Yesterday I was away all day at Windsor in the company of Alex Spring — ask him and he will tell you that."

"That's right, Inspector," Alex broke in blandly. "She was with me the entire day at Windsor and the vicinity and during that time did not make so much as phone call. Apart from that she has been constantly in the company of either myself, my mother or Sir Tobias since we returned from Brighton—even at the theatre, I might add—so I really find it hard to follow how she can be implicated in the Kupinskis' escape. Or should I say defection?"

Oh Alex! Penny thought in dismay, as Grey glared at him and then looked to them for confirmation. "Yes, that is so," Toby said firmly; she managed a nod, and prayed that the police were not now questioning the innocently unaware Mrs. Walker.

"After all, wouldn't that make more sense?" Alex went on, digging their graves a little deeper. "That the Kupinskis simply took a chance and defected?"

"And giving them also an excellent motive for removing Litvov, should he have been suspicious of their intention," Grey said tightly. "We are already aware that they had another strong motive for killing him—namely the forced seduction of Olga Kupinski."

"Then you must also have discovered that on those grounds we all had an equally strong motive, and yet none of us did it," Sonya said.

"I am well aware of it," Grey snapped. "But despite your reiteration of communal innocence, in the face of the circumstantial evidence it becomes increasingly hard to believe. So *tell me what you know!*"

"I have," she cried. "You look in the wrong direction—*that* I know. I have nothing more to tell you."

Mala was twisting uneasily in her chair and muttering at Peter and the interpreter who interrupted, "Er, Inspector, Miss Oupenskaya here is getting very anxious. She says they will be late for rehearsal and can they go."

Grey gave a disgusted snort. "Oh, very well, they can go for now. But tell them that from now on their every

115

move will be watched until they leave this country, and God help them when they get back to theirs if they have helped the murderers of a KGB agent to escape." He turned to Toby. "I'd like a further word with you and Dr. Spring."

The interpreter rattled on and Mala surged to her feet, but as she did so Penny caught a glimpse of her expression. Mala was perplexed and a little angry, the placid brow wrinkled in unaccustomed thought. As the group, shepherded by Alex, moved towards the door, she turned back to the inspector and looked him anxiously in the face. She shook her blond curls at him. "Kupinskis—no kill," she muttered and went out still shaking her head.

Grey slumped back in his chair with a faint groan and waved Penny and Toby to the vacated seats. "Sir Tobias, I sincerely hope you have been honest with me, because I do not know if you realize how serious the situation is. The Russians are far less concerned about the death of Litvov than they are about the escape of the Kupinskis. They have already canceled the ongoing trip to Madrid and will return the troupe to Russia at the end of this week when their season ends. If those young fools have aided the Kupinskis, they are going to be in big trouble when they return. *I* feel like shaking the truth out of them myself, and you can be certain that the Russians *will* shake it out of them sooner or later. I cannot save your daughter. My hands are tied. If she would only do what I begged her to, I might be able to arrest her and delay things a bit. That would be all I *could* do. I have no doubt you have been bringing your considerable influence to bear in certain quarters to keep her here, but you must realize that the British government is not likely to put themselves in an invidious position on this."

"Of all that I am only too well aware," Toby said heavily. "And all I can say is that I will bring to bear whatever small influence I may have on Sonya to do exactly what you suggest. Other than that I am as helpless as you are."

Penny had been debating furiously with herself during this exchange, but the risk she would be running in being premature seemed to be worth it in view of this present crisis. "Inspector," she said, "if it could be proved that another person involved had a very good motive for killing Litvov, wouldn't that take the heat off a bit? Sonya may well know more than she has admitted, but she *has* hinted that you are not looking in the right direction, and I am inclined to agree with her. You see, another person may well have had a very *urgent* motive for killing Litvov. I would not have said anything at this juncture because as yet we lack proof, but a colleague is already working on this, and proof may shortly be forthcoming."

The two men looked at her in blank astonishment. "Who are you talking about?" Grey asked.

"Herbert Spence," she said, completing their amazement, and hurriedly went on to sketch the theory of Litvov's impending flight, the blackmail money, the smuggling ring theory and Spence's possible involvement.

Grey seemed to swell as she proceeded. "Why did you not inform us of all this before now?" he burst out angrily.

"Because I only learned of it myself yesterday, and, as I said, I was waiting for more proof," she hedged.

"And who is this colleague who seems to know so much more than the British government and the collective police forces about this?"

"At this juncture I would really rather not say," she

117

said desperately. "He is doing this as a personal favor and I don't want to jeopardize or impede him in any way."

"Dr. Spring, I must insist," Grey roared. "If you expect us to go haring off after a respected member of the Foreign Office just on your say-so, I can only tell you that is not the way we operate."

"Well, it was *you* who directed him to me," she said with spirit. "I assumed you were well aware of him and his credentials."

Grey gaped. "Good Lord! You mean this chap Vadik? Gregory Vadik?"

The cat was out of the bag: she sneaked a peek at Toby, who was glaring at her as if she had suddenly grown two heads. "Yes. He was involved in another of our cases and considers himself greatly indebted to Sir Tobias. He offered his help and since the offer seemed genuine I accepted. He has access to sources that could be extremely valuable to us."

"Evidently," Grey said faintly.

"If Litvov was on the run himself and collecting money in the form of blackmail to help his escape— someone who paid off in pounds sterling, I may add—it opens up a whole new range of possibilities, doesn't it?" She pressed on. "The dancers would not have had that kind of money. You have not looked at either Spence or Long very closely as yet, because of their apparent lack of motive—but neither of them had good alibis for the Brighton reception either. It certainly is worth looking into."

"Yes. How can I contact Vadik?" Grey growled.

"You can't," she said quickly. "I'll have to wait for him to contact me. It's the way he operates."

"Indeed?" Grey looked at her searchingly. "Then for your own sake I insist you keep me informed." He stood up. "In the meantime, the hunt for the Kupinskis goes on and I hope for everyone's sake will be successful."

"Do you think they are still in this country?" Toby broke his glowering silence.

Grey sighed. "I doubt it. Southend airport has a lot of rinky-dink airlines that specialize in day-trips or package deals to the continent. They could be anywhere— France, Belgium, Holland, Spain. . . . If this defection was planned—and I think it was—you may bet on it that they went armed with fake European travel cards, which is all you need in these Common Market times. It's not going to be as easy to pick them up as I made it sound to those young idiots. Our main hope is still Sonya—you have to put pressure on her, Sir Tobias. It's up to you now. If you'll excuse me, I have to get on with it." He showed them out.

"Why didn't you tell me?" Toby said, the moment the door closed behind them.

"Because you'd have blown up in a sheet of flame. Just as you are about to do now, and would have refused out of hand," she retaliated. "Look, Toby, people do change and I think Gregory has. He's quite the family man now, and I believe he does want to repay his debt to you. I was certain he could be of help to us and so far he *has*. And I was going to tell you as soon as I had something really substantive."

"Damned good of you!" Toby snorted in outrage. "But people don't change that much. If Vadik wangled himself into this, you can be certain there must be something in this for him. He's after something for himself."

"Well, what if he is?" she cried, tormented by her own growing fears. "Our main object is to save Sonya, no matter what, and if he can help us to do that, I for one don't *care* what he's after."

119

"There's no point in discussing this further now," Toby said tightly. "Whatever the damage, it has already been done and it can scarcely make things any worse than they already are. I'm going back to the Athenaeum for a drink — several. I'll have to tackle Sonya again at lunch. Care to join me? You look as if you could use one."

"I most certainly could," she agreed.

They were no sooner settled with their drinks in the only lounge where the female of the species was admitted by the die-hard club, when they were interrupted. An aged man, clutching a copy of the London *Times*, came hobbling up to their table. His pate was completely bald, but its lack of hair was compensated for by exceedingly bushy white eyebrows over a pair of bulbous blue eyes, and an enormous white moustache set under a large nose that trumpeted by its color that its owner was well-acquainted with the port bottle. "Ah there you are, Glendower!" the old man barked. "Been meaning to have a word with you for days — need a bit of help on something."

Toby got up. "Happy to be of service, Lord Dunraven — won't you join us? This is my colleague, Dr. Penelope Spring."

"How de do," Lord Dunraven nodded and settled ponderously into a club chair. "And don't mind if I do. Chota peg, boy!" he thundered at a passing elderly waiter, who grinned slightly and returned with a whisky and soda. Dunraven took a long contented slurp, wiped his moustache and sat back. "Well, it's like this. Hate to get mixed up in things at my age. Infernal nuisance the authorities can be, forms to fill in and all that rot. But it's about that Brighton reception — damn dull affair it was too — though, mind you, that little fair gel who danced was a smasher." A faint gleam of ancient lechery appeared in the bloodshot blue eyes as he took another slurp. "By the way, she's not your — er — is she? Dam fine gel that."

After a quick glance at Penny, Toby shook his head. "The Brighton reception — you were there?" he prompted.

"Well of course I was there — that's what I'm telling you about, am'nt I?" the old man said testily. "This fellow came up to me and said he'd met me when I was ambassador to Switzerland. 'Course I didn't have the faintest recollection of him — all that time ago, imagine! — how could I? Spoke quite passable English though for a foreigner. Asked me if I knew who Carstairs was and would I point him out for him? Well, of course I know Carstairs by *sight* — pinko bounder that he is I wouldn't pass the time of day with him. Naturally I didn't tell this foreigner that. Just said he wasn't there yet, but that I'd let him know if he came in. Damn persistent the fellow was. Said it was very urgent, matter of national security he said. Thought he was just trying to make himself important, y'know? Anyway, then this pansy fellow who'd been hovering around came up and dragged him off and that's the last I saw of him. But thought I ought to mention it to you. Didn't mention it at the time when the police came around — too anxious to get home to m' bed."

"But who was this man?" Toby said in a strangled voice.

"Oh, didn't I say that?" Dunraven mumbled. "The fella who got himself killed. The Russian bounder. Can't remember his name." He finished off his drink and got up. "Anyway, be a good chap and pass this on to the man in charge, will you? Don't want to get mixed up in it, y'see." And he toddled off leaving them gazing in consternation at each other.

Chapter 12

The Dutch courage with which Toby had so fortified himself turned out to be completely redundant since it was Sonya who went on the attack. No sooner were they seated at their table in a secluded corner of the Athenaeum's dining room — the only place Toby felt secure enough to go through with his inquisition — than she burst out, "This cannot go on. I have been very bad, very selfish. I should never have involved you in my troubles. Now I think it is time for me to go back and — how is it said? — face the music with the others. You tell the inspector, who is so angry, that I move back in with the rest of the company and then he can watch me all he chooses." She gazed desperately at her father. "You see I was very wrong about you — from my mother, from my own fantasies I do not get the truth. I did not expect you to be so . . ." she searched frantically for the right word, ". . . so *real*. You are a good man, an honest man, a generous man — and yet I drag you into this and you lie for me, you protect me. I am nothing but trouble and it cannot go on. I must go back to where I belong. I have no right to do this to you, or to Alex, or to Penny, who give up their precious time together to take care of

122

me. This is all my fault and I will not burden you further. You must forget me, you must forget this and go on as you were before."

A quick glance at Toby showed Penny that this passionate outburst had brought him to the edge of another emotional breakdown, so she said icily, "Are you trying to tell us that you did kill Litvov?"

Sonya gazed at her wild eyed. "No, I did not kill him. That is not why I say this."

"But you know who did," Penny went on in a hard, flat tone.

"No!" Sonya cried. "I do not know—that is the truth. I swear it."

"Then why won't you tell us what you and the rest do know? It is no use telling us that you don't know anything for we know better. If you are all as innocent as you claim then you have nothing to fear," Penny pressed.

Sonya slumped in despair, her eyes filling with tears. "I can't," she whispered. "I just can't. I'm sorry. It is best that I go—for us all."

"Oh, cut the dramatics, Sonya!" Alex broke in, his voice harsh and impatient. "Is that what you really want? If you go back with the rest of them, you know damn well the Russians are going to whisk you back to Russia in double-quick time. And then what? Prison, Siberia, a nut house? Is that what you want to happen? We don't have to be Einsteins to figure out you must have had a hand in the Kupinskis' disappearance. Maybe you don't know for certain who killed Litvov, but you must have a damn good idea. So why the hell don't you tell *us*, so that we can help while there is still time. Not one of us would be here if we didn't *want* to help, and I don't for a second believe you yearn for a prison camp and martyrdom. If you don't give us or the

British authorities something to work with, they'll have no choice but to turn you over to your own people."

Sonya shook her head miserably. "All this I well know, but I can't, I just can't."

These respective tirades had given Toby time to get himself under control. He had been staring in pop-eyed fashion at the nerve-wracked girl, now he said quietly, "Sonya, listen to me. If you really want to return to your friends then I will arrange it, but what Alex has just said is the truth. It will be well-nigh impossible for us to control what then happens. And you have to realize something else. I am your father, and I want to be your father. To ask me to forget you and to forget this is an impossibility. I have been more alive in the last week or so than I have been in the past thirty years. I want you here, I want to do all the things that I have never been allowed or had the chance to do—to look after you, to protect you no matter what. If you will not help us to help you then *I* go on as best I can. There are other possibilities, other motives for Litvov's murder that at this very minute are being looked into: these I shall pursue. But the important thing is to be absolutely honest with me on this one, vital, question—do you want to stay? For if you do not, I have no right to keep you."

Sonya looked at him, her lips trembling, "Oh, I do, I *do*! At first I was not sure, but now I am. I would so like a new life, a fresh start."

"Then that is all I need to know," he said and looked challengingly at the others. A waiter, who had been hovering at a discreet distance but with increasing impatience, seized the opportunity of the small silence to approach the table. "Dr. Spring?—a note has been left for you. It is marked urgent, so. . . ." He handed her a small envelope, then whisked out a bunch of menus and handed them around.

Penny tore open the note which was written in a spiky, flamboyant hand. It said tersely, "Litvov booked two air-passages London to Chile. Open dated. Need info on who second person was. Will be in touch." It was signed with a squiggly G. Just what I needed, she thought drearily, yet another complication! Now how the hell do I go about this? She realized they were all staring fixedly at her. "Nothing important," she said, tucking the note into her shoulder bag. "Let's eat, shall we? I have things to do."

On the way back to the theatre she shared the back seat of the Rolls with a subdued Sonya and began to probe gently but relentlessly about Litvov's sexual involvements in the company. After an initial and puzzled hesitation, Sonya began to chronicle his conquests since the tour had begun, with apparent frankness. "But was there anyone in particular he seemed attracted by, whom he singled out?" Penny probed.

"Well no," Sonya said. "Unless you count Mala."

"What about Mala?" Penny's interest quickened.

"Mala baffled him. As I think I told you, she didn't put up a fight, didn't give him any hassle at all, and yet remained totally indifferent to him. He just could not understand her and she fascinated him. He was always fawning over her with flowery compliments, giving her little presents, flowers and all that. *Trying* to get her to notice him, but she never paid him any more attention than she does to anyone else, except perhaps her dance partner for the performance of the moment."

"I see," Penny said thoughtfully, as a whole new scenario opened up before her: Mala, the single-minded; Mala who only lived to dance; Mala, the obdurately unaware. What if Litvov, in his late-blooming infatuation, had, with his plans for escape finally in place, made his plea for her to flee with him to parts

125

unknown—far from the world of ballet? She could just see the stolid Mala's surprise, her growing anger at the very idea, and then, when the cajoling Litvov had become the threatening Litvov, the final blaze of fury that would remove this pest from her path. She could just see Mala swatting him with no more compunction than she would swat an irritating fly. This made a lot of sense! Somehow or another she would have to corner the girl, preferably with Vadik to interpret, for she knew Toby would have no stomach for this. She would have to get hold of Vadik quickly.

They arrived at the theatre to find things in a state of more than normal confusion, for an extra rehearsal had been called to rehearse the substitute dancers for the missing Kupinskis in *Swan Lake*. It had also been decided to substitute Sonya in *Les Sylphides* again in place of the *Company at the Manor*, a short ballet that had featured the Kupinskis. They came in in the middle of a shouting match between Borotov and Selwyn Long who, as soon as he spotted them, rushed over. His normally pale cheeks were red with rage, he looked raddled and every one of his fifty years. "I wish to God I had never got involved in this damned tour," he shouted. "All of these damn Russians are off their rockers. Poor Herbert is in a terrible state and I have to get down to Alfriston right away—he's been robbed! But this ass insists I stay for this nonsense and the show tonight. As if it matters a fuck whether I'm here or not—I can't understand what they say in any case and the bloody interpreter isn't even here, so what the hell does he think I can do?"

Penny felt as if she had been hit in the stomach. "Robbed?" she said weakly. "What was taken?"

"His whole precious collection of icons!" Long shrilled. "He's *prostrate* with grief." He turned back to

Borotov. "I'm going, that's final, and you know what you can do with your precious ballet." He whirled back to the group, "Whoever is responsible for this, it'll be the worse for them," he said with venom. "I have connections too, you know." And he rushed off.

Toby eyed Penny. "Odd coincidence, wouldn't you say?"

She was flustered. "Er — yes. I have a lot of things to do — are you holding the fort here for a bit?"

"Can't," he said gloomily. "Have to see Pontifex to estimate the damage done to our cause by this latest catastrophe, and then I think it is high time I investigated Long's career since Oxford. Very hysterical type, I'd say."

"Very," she agreed. They looked expectantly at Alex, who in turn was gazing loweringly at Sonya in deep conversation with Peter. His mother prodded him. "Can you stand the thought of more guard duty?"

He tore his gaze away and looked down at her. "Oh, all right. See you at the performance tonight?" They nodded in relieved unison.

As they left the theatre, Toby said, "Does it strike you that Alex is becoming — er — emotionally involved with Sonya? I've noticed he seems very unhappy whenever she gets together with Gregorvich."

"Yes, I've noticed it, but have far too many other things to worry about at the moment to concern myself with that now."

"Why should you have cause to worry? Surely *I* am the one to worry about that," he said loftily, and stalked off to the Rolls.

"Oh, really!" she muttered, but the urge to find Vadik was so imperative that she made a beeline for the nearest call box. It did nothing to soothe her agitation when it proved vandalized and out of action. It was not until

127

her third try that she found one in proper working order and got through to a heavily-accented and wary male voice, who agreed with her cautiously that Signor Varoli could indeed be reached at that number but that he was not there. Her message would be passed on.

"I can't wait for that. It's vital that I meet with him. Where can he be contacted?" she insisted.

The voice was apologetic. This was just not possible. Signor Varoli had had to make a quick trip abroad. He had no idea how long he would be away. But Varoli had sent her a message.

"If you mean the message to the Athenaeum, then that I have already received, which is *why* I must talk with him," Penny said, stretching the truth.

"No—another; a small packet," the voice soothed.

"But where did he send it?" she cried, and to her amazement the voice reeled off Mrs. Walker's Fulham address. Damn it! How does he do it? she wondered crossly, more than ever convinced he was toying with her in some game of his own. "Well tell him this is *very* urgent," she snapped and slammed down the phone.

As she hurried back to Fulham her thoughts became progressively gloomier. She had little doubt that Vadik had been behind the theft of "poor Herbert's" icons. But to what purpose? Had he just become a common thief? Or was he acting for the Russians to recover what they considered to be theirs? Or was there something much deeper and darker involved? Toby, damn him, was undoubtedly right—Vadik had to have another motive for his dubious "help." If only she knew what side he was really on.

Penny fairly hurled herself into the little shop and at the surprised Mrs. Walker in attendance. "Oh, Mrs. Walker, has a small packet arrived for me?" she cried.

"Yes, and I was ever so surprised, because I didn't

think anyone knew you were here," Mrs. Walker twittered. "Ever such a polite young man brought it — Arab, I think, or maybe a Paki, I never can sort them out." She was fumbling under the small counter. "Drove ever such a nice car, he did — here it is!" She handed it over triumphantly and Penny pounced on it. "Thank you so much, you're a real treasure — now I'll have to make some more calls, I'm afraid."

"Quite all right," Mrs. Walker called after her. "Oh, and by the way, the police were here." Penny froze in her tracks. "Course I didn't tell them anything," Mrs. Walker said comfortably. "Just said everything was normal and you and the young lady were always together like a pair of Siamese twins. That all right?"

"Bless you, Mrs. Walker, you're a *real* treasure," Penny repeated and went on her way.

The contents of the packet initially surprised her, for they consisted of several photos and some photostated press clippings. This time there was longer note attached. "Think Herbert may be a false lead, but have to check this out in Paris," Vadik wrote tersely. "Other items of interest though. No doubt of Long's sexual preference. Frequent habitue of gay bar and cafe, The Purple Pigeon in Shoreditch [see enclosed photos]. Liaison with Herbert only about two years old and a cut above his usual tastes. Long a jack-of-all-trades [see clippings] but I have my own ideas. Ask Toby to check with his pal Barham Young re Long. Think answer might be very interesting. Will be in touch on my return. Happy hunting!" And it was signed with another squiggly G. There was an added P.S.: "Don't check out The Purple Pigeon by yourself, wait for me."

She studied the photos, which were all rather dark and evidently taken surreptitiously. They showed Long with several men — one, a big black man, another squat

129

and burly, with the look of a prizefighter about him. Yet another, big, very blonde and Scandinavian, and a young man with a girlish face but a startling Mohawk haircut that the color print showed as purple and green. They all ran heavily to black leather clothing and multitudinous chains. She found she was not overly surprised.

She turned her attention to the clippings, which she read with growing puzzlement: she could not figure out what Vadik was trying to convey. One was some fifteen years old and noted an incident at Munich airport of an attempted hijacking; on the list of liberated passengers was Selwyn Long "a diplomatic courier." A ten-year-old clipping was of a historical tour group "seeing the sights of Yugoslavia," who had been involved in a bus accident that had sent several of them to hospital. The conductor and guide of the group had been Selwyn Long. Most of the others were snippets along the same lines, indicating he had worked for a while for American Express, and the most recent — dated some three years ago — had him as "manager" for a British String Orchestra touring Europe under an Arts Council Grant. Certainly Long had not had a very steady or illustrious career, but it all seemed above board and innocuous — almost dull. Still, she was impressed and amazed at Vadik's vast sources of information, and somehow felt cheered. Maybe Toby could make more sense of it when she passed him the message about Barham Young.

She ran him to earth in Pontifex's office and read him the note over the phone, but was taken aback by his reaction.

"So I take it Vadik was behind the theft of the icons," Toby rumbled.

"It looks like it, but let's hope it clarifies something. This stuff about Long I don't quite get. Who is this Barham Young? I've never heard you mention him."

There was a perceptible pause at the other end before he replied. "He's a longtime friend. We were at Winchester together, and we've kept in touch sporadically ever since."

"But what does he do?"

"He works for the government," Toby evaded. "I'll get right on to it, but I have to go now." And hung up on her.

She waited all afternoon for him to call back, but he never did, so, feeling markedly irritated, she went back to the theatre for the evening performance. Belatedly, she remembered her desire for a tête-à-tête with Mala, and wondered if she could manage by herself in French, but evening traffic was heavy, and by the time she got there it was almost curtain time and obviously too late to do anything about it. She hurried to the box to find Alex already there but no sign of Toby, and it was not until the overture had begun that he slipped silently into the seat beside her.

"Well?" she hissed.

"Not now, not here. Later," he murmured. And to madden her further added, "A very interesting development — very. Long is not what he seems."

She fidgeted through *Les Sylphides*, but with *Swan Lake* Mala's magic reached out from the stage and captivated her, and as Mala fluttered in her throes to the immortal strains of "The Dying Swan," she found herself moved to the point of tears. As the curtain came down and the house rose in a standing ovation, Toby led the way in their by now usual dash backstage. There was no sign of Long, who evidently had carried out his threat, nor, for that matter, of the hovering Korkov, but as they peered from the wings at the assembled company they could make out Borotov standing guard in the shadows on the other side of the stage. The corps de ballet came off, then the substitute dancers for the Kupinskis, then Sonya, who had been detained for an extra bow with the principals.

As she came flying off the stage, it was evident that something had happened—her face was radiant with joy. She hurled herself into her father's arms and kissed him on both cheeks, then turned, her eyes sparkling, and whispered. "Quickly, oh quickly, we must get out of here fast. All is well, the Kupinskis are safe! Now I can tell you everything, *everything*. Oh, I am so happy!"

Toby had been struck dumb by her spontaneous burst of affection, so it was Penny who managed to get out, "The Kupinskis—where are they?"

"Why, where they planned to be! Where no one can get them now," Sonya said in an urgent whisper. "They are safely in Brazil."

Chapter 13

They could hardly wait for Sonya to scramble into her
street clothes and make some hasty swipes at her stage
makeup. She was far too excited herself to make a good
job of it and so achieved a striped effect like a Red
Indian who had made a half-hearted attempt to put on
warpaint. As they hustled back to make their exit by the
front of the house, Mala was just coming offstage, an
anxious, perplexed look on her face. She called something in Russian to Sonya and beckoned, but Sonya
shook her head, waved goodbye and rattled something
back. "What was that about?" Penny said, as they hurried on, for Mala's unusual animation had aroused in
her a sense of unease.

"Oh, nothing—she just wanted to talk. I told her I'd
see her in the morning and we'll chat then. She's probably just as excited about the news as I am," Sonya said
gaily. "Let's go to the car and drive somewhere, I'm far
too worked up to eat. The call came in the interval—
Peter and I were so excited we could scarcely feel our
feet through the whole of *Swan Lake*. He nearly
dropped Mala at one point!"

"Won't the call be traced?" Toby said in sudden alarm.

Sonya shrugged, "I doubt it, but what if it is? All it said was the packets had arrived safely. I took the call and Mikail did the calling, and he even disguised his voice. And, anyway, there is no extradition from Brazil. We had that all checked out."

Toby, somewhat grim of countenance, steered the Rolls into the quiet evening deadness of Bedford Square and parked. Sonya immediately started to gabble at a hectic rate, her English becoming more and more garbled in the process, until he held up an admonishing hand. "Sonya, calm down! You are far too excited and it is important for us to understand, so take it slowly and quietly, step by step, from the very beginning."

She looked at him in hurt surprise, but took a deep breath and began again. As she talked a chill grew in all of them that had nothing to do with the damp evening outside the snug confines of the car. For as she spoke the cold realities of life under a communist regime reached out and embraced them.

It was not an uncommon tale she related, and this somehow made it all the worse. The crux of it was that Olga's Jewish family had for some time been trying to emigrate to Israel: a brother and a sister had already gone, but her parents and another sister remained. Just before the tour had started, permission had finally been granted for the rest of the family to go — Olga included. There was just one big snag — Mikail was a Russian, albeit a minority Russian from Latvia, and not Jewish. Olga could go, but he could not. And the Kupinskis knew from many similar cases that, once parted, they would never see each other again. They had only one recourse — to defect together. And this required careful planning.

"Peter and I were in it from the start," Sonya explained. "But when things started to go so wrong we had to bring Mala into it. You see it was initially planned for them to make their break in Paris. Then Litvov started to make up to Olga, and we all got scared because we thought he was on to us. So we canceled out on that and decided to try again here. This special Brighton thing seemed the ideal time."

"The people they had paid in Paris hadn't given them their money back, so funds were low. We pooled what we had and I helped Mikail hire a pleasure-boat captain who agreed to run them across the channel and drop them off at Dieppe that Sunday night. We had to pay him a lot too. From there they were going to get a train to Brussels or Amsterdam and take a plane to Brazil. Olga has cousins in Sao Paolo and they had agreed to take them in and get them a job there. Brazil is rich and can afford dancers, but they were prepared to do anything so long as they could stay together." She paused, as if at a loss as to how to go on. "Anyway, the boat man was supposed to come and get them at the Pavilion between ten-thirty and eleven. He was to meet them at the onion-domed gateway — you know the one? We had managed to smuggle most of their luggage between us all in the minibus among the props and our baggage, and we had stashed it among the bushes near the Stables where we danced . . ."

"What on earth did you take such a stupid risk for?" Alex broke in incredulously. "Carting around extra suitcases would have been a dead giveaway! Surely you realized that?"

"Oh you, you . . . rich American!" Sonya flared at him. "What do you know about it? As it was they were leaving practically everything behind in their apartment in Leningrad. Olga cried and cried about that. You do not realize how poor we are, how little we have, how precious are the things we do have. They had to take their clothes, there was no money to buy more. And they had to take a few mementos of their old life with them; Olga what few trinkets she had, Mikail an icon that had been in his family for generations."

"An icon!" Penny and Toby exclaimed simultaneously.

"Yes, what of it?" Sonya rounded on them "Mikail was Russian Orthodox. They had to have something, didn't they?"

"All right, go on, go on," her father said impatiently.

"Well, that night we were a bit worried when we came in and saw how well that door was guarded, as to how we'd get out again without being seen. We all had our parts to play in it. So we took it in turns to explore a bit when we could get away from the party. It was Mala's job to keep an eye on Litvov so that if he tried to follow any of us she would intercept him: we knew he would always stop to talk to her." Again Penny felt a trickle of unease. "In any case he seemed very busy with all the important people there, and then Peter came in and whispered he'd found a way to open one of the French windows in that long drawing room that led off the Music Room. It wasn't ideal, being so near to the party, but it was the best we could do. We were so intent on our own business that we did not notice Litvov was also gone. Peter had gone to fetch Mikail and Olga, while I slipped out to see if the long drawing room was empty. It was then I heard a noise — I think it must have been the frying pan being dropped. So I peeked in the kitchen just as the door at the other side of it shut, but I saw no one. I was frightened, so I stooped down and picked it up, and as I did so I saw something dark on the floor on the other side of the room . . ." she shivered involuntarily. "I went around and there was Litvov. He was dead and I did not know what to do. I ran back and hung up the pan and then I tried to shove him under the table, but he was so heavy, and then I thought I heard footsteps coming towards the door — it may have been a guard, I don't know. So I ran quickly back the way I had come and found the others and told them. Olga was so upset that she burst into tears and Mikail had to take her out and calm her down. I told them I would run away and draw the police off and that they should go ahead with their plans . . ."

"Sorry to interrupt, but how did it come about that Mala did not see Litvov leave the party?" Penny said.

"Well, she said some old bald man came up to her and was trying to talk to her in French, but that his French accent was so bad she could not make out what he was saying and got all flustered, until Peter came up and got her away from him. By that time Litvov was no longer there."

"Dunraven, the old goat," Toby murmured under his breath.

"The rest is as I told the police. I slipped out of the French window and went down to the bus station — and you know what happened after that."

"Not by a long shot," Toby rumbled. "What about the others, what did they do? And what about the rest of it?"

"Mikail got Olga calmed down, but they were both too frightened to go on with it. They were sure the police would come at any minute and go after them before they could get away in the boat. So Peter slipped out after me and got their luggage back on the bus with the other stuff. He came back in and managed to lock the door again. Then, of course, the body was found, and the police did come, and then all they could do was to cover each other and go back to London. There Borotov and Korkov really grilled them, but they had had time on the way back to work out a plausible story and agreed not to say anything at all beyond what they had already said. And this they have stuck to all along." Sonya drew another deep breath. "When we all got together for that reconstruction at the Pavilion, they managed to tell me—bit by bit—what had gone on. But by then we were worse off than ever. Our money was all gone and Mikail and Olga were in despair. So . . ." her tone became defiant. "I told them I would see to it. I got the money from you and then we made a new plan. I helped Mikail book the tickets from Southend that morning I went off, and we booked in a travel agency from Brussels to Brazil. There was even a little left over for them at the other end. Peter and Mala agreed to try and draw the police off—and we succeeded. They are *safe*!"

"But still under suspicion of murder," her father said heavily. "And you still haven't demonstrated to us how you can be sure that they, in fact, did not kill Litvov, if he had stumbled upon what they intended."

"But I *am* sure," Sonya cried. "I admit I was not certain of that at first. But after I got back and we compared notes, neither of the Kupinskis were out of our sight for more than a few minutes at a time—not long enough to do what was done to Litvov. Besides, when I heard that noise in the kitchen—which *had* to be the murderer I think—I had just left Peter and Mikail, and I saw Olga with Borotov talking to an Englishman."

"What about Mala?" Penny said quickly.

Sonya turned to her. "Mala!—you make a joke, no? Mala would not harm a fly."

"Not even if her whole future was threatened?" Penny

queried. "There is something you do not know. The Kupinskis were not the only ones to have South America in mind. Litvov was also planning to fly there—he had booked *two* passages to Chile. And by what you yourself have told me, Mala is the only one that second ticket could have been intended for."

"You are wrong," Sonya said positively. "It cannot be as you say. Mala would never have gone with him."

"What if he had threatened her? What if he said he would see that she never danced again?"

"Mala may be unaware, but she is not stupid!" Sonya cried. "It would have been an empty threat, and that she would know. Oupenskaya is an untouchable, she is famous. And she knows it. She would have no reason to kill him."

"And where did your little nugget of information come from, Penny?" Toby said, a dangerous edge on his voice. "Not from Grey I warrant."

"Vadik," she said flatly. "He asked me to find the other person Litvov was taking with him, and I still think I have."

"And again you only have his word for it, I take it," Toby retaliated. "In any case it is almost irrelevant now. We have to consider what steps to take to get Sonya safely out of this."

"I'm sorry I lied to you about the money. I'm sorry I could not tell you all this before. But, don't you see, I had to—until the Kupinskis were safe I had to. They were my friends," Sonya burst out.

"Oh, my dear, I understand all that. The money is of no importance whatsoever," he said wearily. "It's just that I am not sure how much of this story Grey is going to believe after so many lies have been told, but it is imperative that you and I go and see him first thing tomorrow morning to try and straighten things out as much as possible. There may be something he can do." He did not sound overly optimistic.

"Do you think that is really necessary?" Penny said. "Before you do that I think Sonya and I should have a talk with Mala first. Despite what Sonya has said, I still think Mala has something to tell us. She strikes me as a girl with something very much on her mind. If she did kill Litvov, as I think she did, she deserves a vote of thanks rather than censure and should be told as much. I feel that she is worried that the Kupinskis are being blamed unfairly, but even if they are—what odds? If they are beyond the reach of the law, what difference does it make now? They will not be found, so Scotland Yard, after a due interval, will have to give up on it. So why tell Grey all this?"

"But we can't do that! It's . . . it's illegal, it's immoral!" Toby spluttered. "Besides, it would still leave the rest of them as accessories to murder. No, we *have* to find out who did it. Even if the British authorities let it drop, the Russians will not."

"If Litvov was on the Russian hit list anyway and was on the run, do you think, if they knew it was Mala who murdered him, they would prosecute her—granting her national fame?" Penny appealed to Sonya. "Would it be possible that they would let the whole thing drop as well?"

"Yes, I suppose it is possible, but I tell you Mala is incapable of murder," Sonya said. She sounded exhausted. "But I will do whatever you think best."

"You know what I think?" Alex broke his tactful silence. "I think I would like to take an adorable, brave, obstinate, cloth-headed, quixotic ballerina out to a richly earned dinner. Having got all that off your chest at last, aren't you hungry , or do you want to go and tilt at another windmill?"

"I do not understand this about a windmill," Sonya said faintly, "but I am ravenous. I am so hungry I could eat a snake."

"There's an all-night joint I've found just off Piccadilly Circus," Alex looked at Toby. "Care to join us?"

Toby restrained a shudder. "I'll take you there, but no thanks. Your mother and I have to talk things over. I'll drop you off and you'll have to take Sonya back by taxi. I'll drop Penny in Fulham."

"Wait! before they leave us, we've got to decide about tomorrow," Penny said, as he started the car. "How about letting us have a crack at Mala before you contact Grey?"

"All right," he agreed. "But make it as early as you can. It's imperative I contact Grey as soon as possible; the longer we wait, the worse it gets."

As soon as their hungry children were dropped off before the neon-lit cafe from which raucous music was blaring, Penny said, "I've been trying to get hold of Vadik, but he's gone again. As soon as he comes back I will call him off. For what it is worth, I don't think he was lying about Litvov. But if it was Mala there is no sense in having him sniffing around any longer."

"You seem fixated on this idea," he grumbled. "I must say I agree with Sonya, Mala just doesn't seem to fill the bill. But, if your hunch is right, she may indeed know more than she has told. She may have some idea who the murderer is, so it is worth a try."

"Well, if it is *not* her, who are we left with?" Penny said with some asperity. "There's Herbert Spence, whom Vadik now seems to think is a false trail—and Selwyn Long."

"Who equally appears to be a non-starter," Toby put it. "I have not had the chance to tell you about my talk with Barham Young; a talk that explained much, including why Carstairs was so evasive. You see, all these years Selwyn Long has been an agent for MI5 — albeit a rather minor and unimportant one, but nevertheless an agent. He was along on the tour to keep an eye on Litvov."

Chapter 14

Penny did not sleep well. Far from soothing her nerves, the revelations of the evening had disquieted her and she felt a growing sense of urgency. Above all, the news that Selwyn Long was an MI5 agent had completely floored her. "I would have thought he'd be entirely unsuited to it," she exclaimed. "Are you certain?"

"Agents come in all shapes and types," Toby, at his most ponderous, had replied. "And from what little I have seen of them are *not* a very impressive lot. James Bond is a creature of fiction, remember? Long may have been very useful over the years—after all it never occurred to *us* he could be one, and we're a damn sight brighter than most. Young said the British Embassy in Moscow alerted them to the fact that Litvov was to be the KGB man on the tour and that Long, who was already doing something along the same lines in Paris, volunteered for this one to keep an eye on him."

"Another volunteer, eh?" she said thoughtfully. "And who is Young anyway?"

"A man who knows a lot about MI5," his tone was dry. "I've done one or two small favors for him over the years, but I've always made it very clear that I would never become deeply involved."

"You've never mentioned anything like that to me!"

"And how many things have you never mentioned to me?" he retaliated. They had left it at that.

Now she was fidgeting with impatience over her morning tea, as Sonya, looking bright-eyed and relaxed, worked her way through a large breakfast. Anxious as Penny was, Sonya had informed her that there would be no hope of raising Mala before ten o'clock, since this was a day when rehearsal was scheduled for after lunch and Mala always slept late on such occasions. "I'll call her at ten and we'll fix a meeting," Sonya said brightly, buttering a third piece of toast. "You will see then you are all wrong about her. Mala may be a tiger on stage but she is a lamb off of it."

Under Penny's restive gaze the hands of the mantle clock seemed to crawl from one minute to the next, and she only half-listened as Sonya prattled on about the good time she and Alex had had the previous evening. Shortly after nine the phone started a diligent ringing, and since Mrs. Walker was already installed behind the counter of the shop, Penny called out to her, "Shall I get it?"

"Would you, dear?" Mrs. Walker called back. "It's probably for you anyway."

A grim-voiced Inspector Grey was on the line. "Dr. Spring, where is Sonya Danarova?"

"Why, she's right here." Penny was puzzled. "We've just had breakfast together. Now she is upstairs dressing."

"And before that?"

"Before that she had a long bath—we both got up about seven-thirty. What is this about, Inspector?"

He ignored that. "Can you swear she has not been out of the house? Before that, I mean."

"Yes, I can." She was getting increasingly irked. "That is unless she knows how to bolt locked doors again from the outside. My hostess here, being old and alone, has a formidable defense system against burglars, so has old-fashioned thick steel bolts at the top and bottom of both front and back doors. I bolted the front door myself when we got in last night, and heard Mrs. Walker unbolt it when she opened the shop this morning. In any case, surely the man you've had keeping an eye on this place could vouch for that?"

"What man?" he challenged.

"Oh, come now, Inspector, my landlady may be old but she is extremely sharp. She says that for the past two days there has been a man — or rather several different men — keeping an eye on the shop. They leave their motorbikes in a nearby alley and just lurk — a bit obvious, I'd say. So, I repeat, why all these questions?"

There was a long silence, and she got the impression he had put a hand over the mouthpiece and was talking to someone at the other end. When he came back on his voice was grimmer than ever. "Can you tell me if Miss Danarova talked with Mala Oupenskaya either during or after the performance last night?"

"Why, yes. We were leaving just as Mala came off stage, and she wanted to talk then, but we were in a hurry so Sonya told her she'd see her in the morning. In fact, that's why we're hanging around here. We're waiting for ten o'clock — the time Mala usually gets up on a late-rehearsal day like today. Then Sonya is going to call her and set up a meeting."

"I'm afraid it is too late for that." His voice was doom laden.

The feeling that had been growing encompassed her in an icy grip. "Why?" she managed through dry lips.

"Because at seven-fifteen this morning Mala Oupenskaya's body was found floating in the Serpentine in Hyde Park."

Her worst fears were realized. "Suicide?" she whispered.

"Suicide be damned! She was murdered. Strangled with her own silk scarf and then pushed into the water. The body weighted. The murderers did a lousy job. As you probably know but the murderers evidently did not, the Serpentine is shallow, and a groundskeeper on his way to work spotted something colored — the scarf — under the surface. He fished for it, because people are always dumping stuff in there, and up she came. So, the Kupinskis must still be here and we'll get them now for sure."

The news had so shocked and stunned her that she was not thinking coherently. "But they're not!" she cried. "It *can't* be them — they're in Brazil."

"*What!*" It came like a gunshot.

Desperately, she grappled for control. "We only learned of this last night. Sir Tobias was going to come around with Sonya and tell you everything this morning. I'm surprised he has not already contacted you."

"He did," Grey snapped. "Last night he left a message to that effect and repeated it when I contacted him about this just now. But he said nothing of that. What the hell sort of game do you think you are playing?"

"Where is he now?" she parried.

"Probably on his way over to you. And I want you *all* here as quickly as possible. We have not yet informed the Russians, pending official identification of the body, but when we do there is going to be an almighty blowup."

She went on the attack. "I though you were having Mala and Peter followed! How come your own man was not aware that she had left or been taken from the hotel?"

A groan burst on her eardrum. "Another of those million-to-one foul-ups that have bedeviled this case. The two-man night shift went on after the performance last night; about midnight one of them got violently sick to his stomach — and, by God, if I find he'd been drinking, I'll break him," Grey said in a vicious aside. "Anyway, instead of calling in for a backup, the two of them agreed that he'd just go home for a few hours and get some sleep and be back at seven this morning. Both the dancers had gone to their rooms and the fools thought they were safe for the night. So the remaining man, knowing Gregorvich is usually the earlier riser of the two, stationed himself on his corridor. When his colleague returned about seven he took up his usual post, unaware that he was guarding an empty room."

"But didn't the night clerk at the hotel see her go?"

"No, she must have slipped out through the kitchen entrance — God knows when. She did not go through the main lobby, we have established that much," Grey growled.

"How about phone calls? Did she make any?" She was grasping at straws.

"No, there was nothing logged to her room. But she did receive two calls after she got back from the theatre. Unfortunately there is no means of tracking those. All the operator remembers is that they were not long distance."

"Male or female?"

"She couldn't say for sure — she wasn't paying any attention."

Penny felt an aching desolation — poor, unaware,

slow-thinking Mala had been lured to her own death by the murderer. By what means, she wondered? It would have had to be something very persuasive to have made the girl deviate so far from her usual patterns. She had been completely wrong: Mala had not murdered Litvov, but she had realized who had. It all made sense to her now; Mala's flat statement in Grey's office, her growing anxiety, her sudden desire to talk. If they had only taken the time to meet with her last evening she would still be alive! It was a burden of guilt that she would carry with her always, and she writhed now with the pain of it.

There was a sudden commotion outside in the tiny shop, and Toby came striding in, his face tight with concern. "Sir Tobias has just come in and we'll be around as quickly as possible," she said into the phone and hung up.

"Does she know?" were his first words.

"Sonya? No, she's upstairs putting on her makeup and getting dressed. Grey only just called."

"Then you'd better let me tell her."

"Where's Alex?"

"When I relayed the news to him he went off into a brown study and then said he had to go the American Embassy. Never have understood his thought processes and never will. Well, seems you were wrong, doesn't it?"

"Oh God, don't rub it in!" she said in a choked voice. "How do you think I feel?"

"I'm sorry. I shouldn't have said that," he mumbled. "My own guilt talking, I'm afraid. Should I go up to her?"

"Here she is now," Penny whispered, as Sonya came tripping in, radiant and looking as immaculate as a high-fashion model. "We call Mala now I think," she announced, glancing at the clock.

"Sonya, sit down!" her father thundered in his unease. "I have some very bad news to tell you."

Her reaction startled them both. A hand flew to her throat, her eyes searched desperately around and she went deathly pale. "Not Alex!" she whispered. "Nothing has happened to Alex?" She wilted into a chair and looked up at Toby with wide, pleading eyes.

Toby was disconcerted. "No, no, nothing like that. I'm afraid it is about Mala. She is dead."

"Mala? Mala!" she said on a rising note. "I do not understand, how can this be?"

"She was murdered," he said flatly. "Lured from her hotel by the murderer, strangled and thrown into the water in Hyde Park. We have to go immediately to Scotland Yard and make a full statement. So, I beg you, Sonya, if there is *anything*, anything at all you have not told us or have forgotten to tell us, now is the time for it. There may have been some grounds for shielding the murderer of Litvov, but there are *none* for Mala's killer. She did not deserve to die like this." His voice shook.

"But I *have* told you everything," Sonya cried. "If Mala knew more of it she said nothing to me, but I do not think she did. It must just have been something she did not understand. Oh Mala, my poor Mala!" She buried her face in her hands and burst into tears.

Her father decided to try Alex's tactics. "There is no time for tears now, no time for grief," he thundered. "That may come later, but now we are fighting for *your* survival, so come along. We must see if Scotland Yard can or will help us, because as soon as the Russians hear of this I am afraid they will bundle the whole lot of you back to the Soviet Union, and we cannot let that happen."

They hustled the still-sobbing Sonya into the back of the Rolls and Penny scrambled in beside Toby. "Well, despite all our previous conclusions it is back to Long and Spence," she said, a fierce anger mounting in her. "The trouble is which, and how the devil to prove it."

"It's not my first priority now." Toby was driving like a madman through the thinning rush-hour traffic. "My first priority is Sonya. There is no way the ballet can continue with its program without Oupenskaya, so my guess is that the Russians will try to pull them all out as soon as possible. Maybe tonight; tomorrow at the latest. All I've managed to accomplish thus far is to have her recognized as my daughter and heir, and the deed-poll papers will be ready today so that she will legally be called Glendower. But she still isn't *British*. And unless Grey can come up with some means of detaining her here, we have no leg to stand on if the Russians demand that she return with them."

"But surely Grey could stop them doing that?" she interrupted.

"On what grounds? The only other Russian suspects around are ruled out by this latest murder: Sonya by you; Gregorvich by the police themselves. How can Grey possibly detain them further? Our own government could not countenance such a thing."

"How about their aiding and abetting the Kupinskis to escape?" Again, she was grasping at straws.

"Since they also are ruled out as murder suspects and it is no concern of the British whether they have defected or not, the most they could throw at Sonya would be a misdemeanor charge, which would not hold up."

"Well maybe we should change our story and just leave the Kupinskis under some suspicion," she cried.

He threw up his hands to the imminent danger of all their necks. "Oh, Penny, there have been *enough* lies. What good would that do? It would only delay things for a day or two at most, and the Russians would be *more* furious at Sonya. No, if Grey cannot help, there is only one thing left to do. I must take Sonya away and go to ground, for as long as it takes to get the Russian authorities off our necks and until the murders are solved. I cannot let her fall into their hands." There was despair in his voice.

"But, Toby, won't that put you on the wrong side of the law? Won't it just make things worse in the long run?"

"I don't care." There was a desperate recklessness in him now. "Not even if it means spending the rest of my life in exile in some God-awful place like South America. It's what I have to do."

"Then for God's sake just don't fly off the handle. I tell you what. Don't do anything crazy, like trying to leave the country just yet. I'll stay here, get hold of Vadik and solve this damn case, if it's the last thing I do," she pleaded.

"Oh, I had no intention of trying to get out yet," he said loftily. "After all this will also take careful planning. My first step will be to disappear with Sonya — and that is easy. There is one place I can go that only you and Ada know about, and I know I can trust you not to disclose it."

"You mean the Folly?" she said, as they drew up with a squeal of brakes in the courtyard of Scotland Yard.

He nodded. "I don't suppose it will serve forever, but if we go there it may give you enough time to do what has to be done. Only don't *trust* Vadik. He may be useful but, by God, I wish I knew what his motive was in all this — who he is working for."

"So do I," she agreed dismally, as they clambered out of the car and assisted Sonya out. Her tears had dried, but she was still deathly pale, her eye makeup so smudged that she looked as if she hadn't slept for a week.

They were more than expected, for a uniformed sergeant pounced on them in excited anticipation as they emerged and escorted them smartly to Grey's office.

Grey was far from being his usual immaculate self; unshaven, his hair tousled, his suit crumpled. He looked up at them with grim, haggard eyes as they came in. "I am hoping the statements you make now will be of help to *us*, but I am afraid they will be of little help to you, Miss Danarova, Sir Tobias," he said abruptly. "We have just received official word from the Russian Embassy. The tour is ended and they are flying the entire company back to Russia tonight. They have asked for a police escort to accompany them to Heathrow. So I must request that after this statement is made, Miss Danarova return to Fulham, pack, and present herself at the hotel where the rest of the company have been staying by six o'clock this evening." He emphasized the hour slightly and gave Toby an unfathomable look. "There the Russian officials will check her in and they will leave under escort for Heathrow airport. I am sorry but this matter is completely out of my hands. I cannot stop this or even delay it."

"I see. Then let us get on with it, shall we?" Toby was icy calm. "And, by the way, the name is legally Glendower now, Sonya Danarova Glendower. Please bear *that* in mind, Inspector."

Chapter 15

It was misty on the Embankment; the Thames shrouded in a white woolly blanket that wrapped itself around the necklaces of lights outlining the bridges and marking the river's sinuous course through the city and reduced them to fuzzy blobs in the murk. Somewhere unseen a watercraft hooted in plaintive protest. But to Penny, hunched in a small depressed heap on a wooden seat looking out over the unseen river, it was but part of the misery that surrounded and permeated to her very core.

"Never again," she whispered to herself. "If I get through this one, never again. . . ." Their murder investigations, so unlikely begun, so strangely continued, she realized had always been a challenge, an excitement, a satisfaction — up until now. But this, this was far too close to home. Now everything and everyone she cared about was in jeopardy; her entire world in a state of imminent collapse.

It had been one hell of a day; a day of endless rows, arguments and surprises that had cut her to the heart. But she had been helpless to stay the ominous flood of events. "Stonewall — stall them as long as you can, but there is no sense in putting your own career in jeopardy, so stay put." Toby had been at his most stubborn and most peremptory self. "All my concern now is to get Sonya away to a safe place and to start afresh. Time has run out on us and there is no alternative now. Whether the murders are ever solved or not, the Russians are going to want their pound of flesh, and I'm going to make damn sure it's not Sonya's."

Things had worsened with the arrival of a determined-looking Alex. "I'm going with you two," he had announced to her horror. Stemming Toby's immediate protest, he'd gone on, "You'll need me, and I'm as interested in seeing the Russians don't get their hands on Sonya as you are. Think about it. You'll need a leg man to make the ongoing arrangements, and as of six o'clock this evening you're going to be a marked man. A very well-known marked man at that. You won't be able to show your face. They'll not be after me—I'm just an American tourist. Where I go is nobody's business, and I have a sneaking hunch that Grey isn't going to look too closely at my activities, because basically he's a nice guy and is on your side. I've already hired a car and parked it close by the Athenaeum. My suggestion is that when you and Sonya leave here in the Rolls that you go out the Great West Road, just as if you were heading for Heathrow as per orders. I'll wait for you in one of the outer parking lots—say parking lot ten. There Sonya will switch to my car and I'll take off. You hang around about twenty minutes then take off again, heading west. Then, if they have tailed you and stop you, they won't find anything and your story is that you dropped Sonya off. We'll rendezvous somewhere along the route and Sonya can switch back again and you head on to Wales, where I'll meet up with you later. I have to go into Oxford to pick up some of my stuff at Littlemore."

"And what about your mother?" Toby had boomed disapprovingly.

Alex had looked astounded. "Well, *ma* knows how to look after herself! She doesn't need me. She'll stay on here and try to sort things out, of course. After all, she'll have what's-his-name to help her."

This had done nothing to pacify Toby or soothe Penny's feelings. But after long argument and some intercession from Sonya, Alex's plan, somewhat modified, was adopted. Toby had seen the sense of not showing his face in Oxford, so, duly armed with a note to Toby's housekeeper, Alex was delegated to pick up some of Toby's things including a revolver, some personal papers and the file on the Folly from his archives. "They just might get a search warrant when it becomes apparent I have flown the coop," Toby had observed grimly. "There is no sense in taking chances. Also Alex is right. If the Russians do turn nasty on this and somehow ferret us out, it may be well to have some protection. Old Williams has a shotgun and a twenty-two for potting rabbits, but that won't take us very far against real heavies."

While they continued to plot ongoing strategy it had been her job to clue in the flabbergasted Ada and to swear her to absolute silence and professed ignorance about the Folly. She'd also had to soothe the now-agitated Mrs. Walker. "We'll not involve you any further, and I'll move on, too. I never imagined anything like this would come up or I would never have involved you in the first place."

"But where will you go?" the old lady wailed. "With that murderer out there and you so close to it all, where will you be safe?" It was a thought that had not even crossed the mind of her nearest and dearest, Penny reflected bitterly.

155

"Well, I don't quite know at the moment," she confessed. "But I'll find something."

"I've an idea! I've got a cousin in Camden Town: Clara Penrose, regular miserly old maid, she is. Never goes out, never sees anyone—bit queer in the head, I think—but if I ask her, she'll take you in. It won't be much, but whoever would think of looking for you there? *I* know how to keep mum, and so who's to know?" Mrs. Walker had looked at her with an encouraging nod. "Why don't I give her a call?"

So during the afternoon Penny had surreptitiously exchanged the warm coziness of Fulham for the musty bleakness of Camden Town under the myopic, suspicious stare of a fusty old woman surrounded by a small horde of cats, who added their own unmistakable aura to the little row house. One thing Miss Penrose did possess was a phone, and it was from there that Penny had finally contacted the elusive Gregor Vadik to set up her present uncomfortable rendezvous.

She had returned to Fulham to find Alex about to embark on stage one of the enterprise: he was to return to the Athenaeum to check himself out, but also book dinner for Toby as an added bit of camouflage. "Take care of yourself, ma," he had said with a final hug and kiss. "And don't worry about us—we'll be fine. I'll see Toby doesn't get into any trouble." It had done nothing to cheer her.

Then, just after six, had come the departure of Toby and a tearful Sonya. Belatedly he had said to her, "You'll be all right, won't you? You know I would not go off leaving you holding the bag like this if there were any other alternative." There was an edge of desperation on his voice. "Just don't put yourself in any jeopardy on our account—it's too late for that. God knows when or where we'll meet again."

"Just do what you have to do and don't worry about me, I'll be fine," she had lied, on the brink of tears. With an incoherent gobble he had dived into the Rolls and driven off into the mist.

She had waited another half an hour before taking her leave of Mrs. Walker. "When the police call — as they may do at any moment now — just tell them that Sir Tobias was running a bit late so left directly for Heathrow, that Alex has gone on a touring trip of England, and that I've gone too but you don't know exactly where — probably Oxford. Stick to that no matter what. And bless you for all you've done for us."

The old woman clasped Penny's hand between her own frail, work-worn ones. "Mum's the word. I'll deal with them, don't you fret. And you take care of yourself, my dear — and don't take any lip from Clara, neither. If she gives you any trouble, you just let me know and I'll sort her out."

She had driven aimlessly around the city until it was almost time for the rendezvous and then had taken up her vigil at the appointed bench. She stirred restively and peered at her watch in the gloom. Vadik — damn him! — was overdue.

She peered about her, realizing her own isolation and that this was not the best place to be with night falling. A burly figure loomed out of the mist and she looked up at it with quickening hope, but it was only a street bum, who loomed over her and muttered thickly, "Got the price of a cuppa on you, lady?"

"If I had, d'you think I'd be sitting here?" she retaliated in her best Cockney accent.

He continued to peer down into her anxious, attractively-ugly little face. "Sorry, mate," he rumbled. "Helluva life ain't it for the likes of us? There's a shelter dahn in Whitechapel got some beds left. Better there than aht here on a night like this. If I make a touch I'll come back and share the wealth, but don't count on it." He shambled off.

Another burly figure loomed up shortly, and this time it was Vadik. "Sorry I'm late," he wheezed, slumping down on the seat beside her. "It's been one hell of a busy day."

"Do tell!" she said acidly. "Make another good haul of icons or what? This all part of your new image?"

He glanced at her and sighed heavily. "Things not going too well with you either, eh? Well, all my efforts were largely a washout; my theory on Herbert Spence does not seem to pan out. Just got back from Paris a few hours ago. I thought it would be quicker if I lifted the lot and had them checked out by the experts over there. Trouble is that with one minor exception they are all as clean and as genuine as can be — thought I'd give a small fortune to know how he came by the icon that *isn't*."

"So Herbert is out one valuable collection and we're not one damn bit further forward," she snorted.

"Since I got back I've been packing the damn things up again and making certain arrangements to get them back to him," Vadik said with hurt dignity. "Minus the 'hot' one, of course — I thought that might shake something loose. I gather that while I've been gone the murder count has risen by one — too bad about Oupenskaya, she was a good little dancer. How the hell did that happen? I thought the police were watching her."

It was Penny's turn to sigh heavily. "They were, but. . . . Well the murderer seems to be ahead of us at every turn. I'd better tell you the whole dreary story . . ." and embarked on the series of events since their last meeting. In the middle of it, Vadik grasped her arm and gave it a warning squeeze, as a figure emerged from the mist. It halted before them. "You all right, mate?" it demanded of Penny, and she realized it was the street bum.

"Quite all right, I found a friend," she returned.

"Oh, that's all right then. Don't let him cheat yer, mind! And if things don't work aht, you come to the Whitechapel shelter. I made two touches of fifty P, so I'll treat yer. Bert's the name." The figure shuffled off.

"Who the hell was that?" Vadik exclaimed in astonishment.

With a little inward surge of amusement, she said, "That was my mate, Bert," and returned to her narrative. At the end of it Vadik ruminated in silence for a while, then said, "Well we seem to be running out of suspects fast: Oupenskaya is dead, the Kupinskis are out of it, Sonya ditto, and — if the police are to be believed — Gregorvitch is out of it too. So we're back to Long and Spence."

"One of whom is a British agent supposedly there to keep an eye on Litvov, and, the other a respected, if undistinguished, FO-type who is *not* an icon smuggler. Neither of them rich enough to be blackmailed and neither with an apparent motive for liquidating the Russian," Penny fired back. "I'm beginning to wonder if we're not up against the inevitable Mr. X, whom we haven't even considered."

Vadik shook his head. "I just can't buy that. The second murder stemmed directly from Litvov's, and his, when you think about it, occurred in what was a variation of the old 'locked-room' puzzle. It *had* to be one of the people in the Pavilion that night, and that brings us right back to Long and Spence. The problem is which, and how to prove it." He fell into another ruminative trance.

"So what now?" she demanded restlessly.

"I think, if you feel up to it, it is high time to pay a

159

visit to The Purple Pigeon and make some direct inquiries," Vadik said, rousing from his stupor. "I've had someone keeping an eye on the place since I've been away and they report that only one of the types in those photos I sent you has shown up during that time. I find that odd. You still have your car?"

"Which one showed up?" she asked. "And yes, it's parked two blocks from here." She sprang up, anxious for anything that might take her mind off what might be happening on the road to Wales.

"The black guy. And Shoreditch then it shall be," Vadik answered, and they hurried off into the increasing murk.

The mist pursued them, so that The Purple Pigeon manifested itself as a purple rectangle of diffused light that, without its present mask, would have been hideously garish. "Do you think it's a good idea for me to go in?" Penny said, hesitating on the threshold. "If it is a gay bar won't it look a bit odd? After all, it's not the sort of place that a casual tourist might saunter into."

"I don't think that matters. I'm banking on the fact that more goes on in this place than just a little male handholding," Vadik returned, gently propelling her in front of him. "We *want* them to notice us and to get their attention. I'll play private detective wanting to hire and you can be my client. If the help isn't helpful, maybe we can stir up something from the patrons."

They groped their way through the dimly lit foyer and a curtain of rattling beads into a room that was far longer and larger than the outside had indicated. Along one side ran a line of booths and small tables, along the other a well-stocked bar and a couple of lighted display cases. One held an array of pies, sausage rolls and quiches, the other replete with cakes and fancy desserts. Here also the lights were few and far between and muted, and as they peered around them it was evident that this was a slow night, for only a few of the booths were occupied and there were just two patrons sitting up at the bar. These looked at the newcomers in blank astonishment as Vadik helped Penny up on a bar stool and took one himself.

The bartender, clad in what appeared to be the regulation garb for the bar—black leather and multitudinous chains—came up to them, his pale blue eyes fixed in an unfriendly glaze. He had a mop of carrot-red hair that stood stiffly up in spikes, as if in continual terror at what was going on in the skull beneath. "What will it be?"

"Two cognacs—Remy Martin—and some information." Vadik ostentatiously pushed a ten-pound note across the bar. His voice boomed unnaturally loud, so that it carried to the farthest corners of the hushed room.

"Two Remy Martins coming up," the bartender repeated, his face expressionless. "But I think you're in the wrong place. You can find information booths at any of the big stations." He handed them the brandies and carefully counted out the exact change.

Vadik ignored this, and groping in his pocket came up with the four dark snapshots from which, Penny noted, Long had been airbrushed. He spread them out on the bar and said in the same loud voice. "I understand from this friend of mine who comes here that these men are patrons of yours and I want to hire them. Got a job to do for this lady here."

"And who might you be and who might your friend be?" There was an edge on the bartender's voice.

"Private enquiry agent—friend of Selwyn Long. He said these men were trustworthy and the pay will be good."

"Never heard of him," the barman said promptly.

For the first time Gregor Vadik looked all around him, an unpleasant smirk on his face, before fixing his black eyes back on the bartender. "That may not be the name he used—here," he said pointedly, and proceeded to give a vivid cameo description of Long.

The carrot-haired man shrugged his indifference. "Rings no bells with me. My job is to serve drinks not keep tabs on the customers. You're welcome to look around, if that's what you want."

"Maybe if I talked with the owner?"

"He's out of town." The barman ostentatiously turned his back on them and stalked to the other end of the bar. One of the bar-sitters slipped off his stool and casually sauntered to the exit. He was a tall, dark-haired, thin-faced youth, and as he passed them he slid a sidelong glance at Vadik.

Vadik drained his glass and spoke in the same loud voice. "I'm sorry Mrs. Stone, but I seem to have been given the wrong information—no sense in wasting our time further in this dump." The bartender swung around, an angry frown on his pale face. Feeling very conspicuous, Penny hopped off her stool and scurried in Vadik's wake. "What now?" she hissed, as they got beyond the bead curtain.

"I think we may have flushed our pigeon—just play along," Vadik murmured, as they went out into the mist.

A tall shape stood under a nearby lamp post: it jerked its head meaningfully and strolled away. They sauntered after it and turned into a side street. The figure had disappeared and Vadik tensed.

"Over here," a voice hissed from the doorway of a darkened shop on the other side of the street. "Eddy was lying in there. I know the bloke you mean. Let's have a dekko at those photos."

"Just stay behind me and if there is any trouble scoot back to the car. Not that I think there will be any," Vadik whispered, as they crossed the road. The thin beam of a penlight flashed in their eyes as they got to the doorway. "You paying for info, mister?" The voice was a shrill Cockney whine.

"Take that bloody light out of my eyes," Vadik said with quiet menace. "And yes, a tenner if it's useful; twenty if you can give addresses." The light snapped out as he got out the photos and then on again focusing downwards on them.

"Called himself Greg, he did. Splashed money around as if it was water." The Cockney voice was vicious. "That big black man's called Cannon. This one's Bob Edwards—used to be a boxer, he did. That's Anders and . . ." the voice grew tearful. "That's my Geoff that is. The perishing swine broke us up, he did—after two years together mind!"

Penny had been peering around Vadik's broad back. Geoff, apparently, was the girl-faced, Mohawk-haired character.

"Where can I find them?" Two ten-pound notes had appeared in the light and were wafted gently under the unseen nose.

"They've not been around lately." The voice grew uncertain. "Not like them, neither. Always hanging aht the Pigeon, they was. I can give you Geoff's address—he got a room somewheres else when he moved aht on me. Don't know about the others. I only saw them at the bar and with the Yamahas, see."

"The address," Vadik hissed.

The voice grew even more uncertain. "This is on the

level, ain't it, mister? You're not after them for anything are yer?"

"Just want to talk to them about a job," Vadik repeated.

"Well, this is the latest one I have for Geoff — we don't talk no more," the youth said mournfully, and named a street and number in the neighborhood.

An uneasy thought had just come to Penny. "These Yamahas you mentioned — who are they?" she broke in.

"Why our motorbike club, of course!" The Cockney sounded astonished at such ignorance. "We all got Yamahas, see. Real great times we used to have . . ." he trailed off with a gasp and the flashlight went out as footsteps echoed on the deserted street. Two shadowy figures passed them, talking quietly. After their footsteps had died away the youth said in a tight voice. "I'm off. Ain't healthy to be seen talking to strangers in these parts. You paying up, mister?"

The money changed hands and he slipped like a shadow away from them. "Well, it's too late to do anything more tonight," Vadik said, as they emerged from their shelter and hurried back to the car. "But I'll put some of my people on this in the morning. Now we've got their names and this address it should be easy to locate them."

"I certainly hope so," Penny murmured absently.

Vadik peered down at her. "Something he said seems to have upset you — what was it?"

"Well, it may be nothing, but the old lady I was staying with in Fulham reported some days ago that her place was being watched — by men on motorbikes. I naturally assumed it was the police keeping an eye on Sonya. But what if it wasn't?"

"So? No great harm done, is there? If Selwyn Long is up to something, he might have been keeping tabs on you too, for his own purposes. But if we locate these men I can cut that off in very short order." His tone was smug. "No need to worry about that anymore."

She opened her mouth, then closed it again. She could not confide in him the thought that now terrified her: if these watchers were also followers, Toby's secret destination would not remain a secret for very long.

Chapter 16

Toby opened his eyes, gazed up at the bare-board ceiling and groaned inwardly, as realization flooded in banishing the last remnants of the blessed Nirvana of sleep. He took a swift look around the little wooden hut and saw with relief that the sleeping bags of his two companions were empty. Hastily he unzipped his own sleeping bag and sat up on the canvas camp cot. Once upright he buried his face in his hands and tried to bring some order to his chaotic thoughts. Even though his watch showed him he had slept heavily and late, he felt utterly exhausted. It was not so much the tensions and alarms of yesterday's escape that wore upon him but what lay ahead. He was not a man of devious subterfuge. All his life he had been law-abiding to an unbending degree—a characteristic that had often caused him to clash with his more free-spirited and daring partner. What he was doing now, what he would have to do, went so against the grain that the stress of it was tearing him apart. "This won't do!" he told himself fiercely. "This won't do at all. You've got to get yourself together and get on with it."

The door of the hut opened with a protesting creak,

causing him to sit up hastily as Sonya's dark head appeared cautiously through the crack. "Oh, good! You are up," she pushed the door open and came in bearing a steaming mug. "See, I bring you some coffee—two lumps and milk, yes? And then there is scrambled eggs and bread and butter. I cannot make toast on a camp stove." Her dark hair had been plaited into two long braids that hung sedately on each side of her vivid face, making her look far younger than her twenty-eight years.

His heart constricted and he felt an overwhelming wave of emotion at the sight of her. "Well—er—thank you. That was very clever of you. How did you manage it so quietly?" he muttered. His eyes went to the small shelf for the primus stove, but it was empty.

"We took it outside so as not to wake you," she said, going out again and reappearing almost instantly with a plate of scrambled eggs and a thick hunk of buttered country bread. "It is a lovely day out there. I like it here—so pretty! What is this place called?"

"On the map this mountain does not have a name, so locally they call it after the farm below, Pwhelli Tor, but the mountain to our left is Myndd Mawr and the one to our right is Moel Herrog, and the big one you see to the northeast is Snowdon, the highest of them all."

"This Welsh," she said, sitting down beside him on the cot, "I never hear of it before, but it has such a pretty sound to it—like singing almost. You will teach me this one day? Like you, I am very good at languages," she confided.

This almost completed his devastation. "Of course . . ." he managed to get out. "One day—but for now. . . ." The door again opened and Alex's head peered enquiringly around it. "What's happening? I'd like to get cracking."

Sonya made a shooing gesture with her hands, "Go, go! Father has not finished his breakfast and we talk now." Alex snorted and withdrew. She turned back to Toby who was obediently wolfing down the eggs. "So restless!" she complained. "Always it is go, go, hurry, hurry! Are all Americans like this or is he just like his mother?"

Toby gave an amused grunt. "A little of both. But he is right — there's much to be done." He handed back the plate and mug. "So if you'll dispose of these and let me get dressed, we'll get at it." The little interlude had put fresh heart into him and he felt invigorated.

Sonya pouted and tossed her head. "Well, you send him on his way and then you show me over your cave, yes?"

"Later, I promise, but first I have to go down and have a talk with Williams, my tenant farmer. I must alert the locals to keep very quiet about our presence here."

"Can I come too?" she said instantly.

"No, you'd better stay here out of sight. If Williams does not actually see you, he can lie with better grace, if need be."

She sprang up. "Oh, I am nothing but a burden to you!" she cried, and stamped out.

Toby sighed and got on with his dressing. Although he had put up a stout opposition to Alex's being there, he was secretly thankful that he was. He hadn't the faintest idea how to handle his spirited daughter, and he was relieved to see that Alex — to Toby's amazement — apparently did.

Before Alex was ready to go, they had a brief conference over the map, for they had arrived long after dark and the network of small roads around the remote Pwhelli Tor was confusing. They had tentatively agreed

168

on a plan—proposed by Alex—the night before. "I think by far your best bet is by ferry from Liverpool to Belfast, hire a car there and drive to Dublin, and then fly from Shannon to Brazil, since we already know there is no extradition from there. They'll probably be watching all the airports and the southern ports at this point, thinking you'll be heading for the Continent. If they have no clue we're here, I doubt whether they'll get to the northern ports, as yet. I'll book the tickets as for my mother and myself—two Doctor Springs—and as far as Dublin that should present no problem to you. In Dublin you can change the airline booking by phone at the last minute to your own name. Spin some tale about an archaeological conference Ma cannot attend—after all, the *Irish* authorities won't give a damn."

"I hope!" Toby had replied heavily. "But how the hell are we to get Sonya by them without a passport? You'll have to try and buy one in Liverpool and that may take some time."

The young couple had smiled smugly at each other. "All taken care of—I was very busy yesterday," Alex said. He reached into his pocket and pulled out a British passport, flipping it open to reveal Sonya's photo with the name of S. Marie Glendower across it. "Fake, of course, but a good one; courtesy of the same guy who provided the Kupinski's with their documentation. I'm beginning to get good at this."

"It must have cost a fortune," Toby exploded, to cover his own amazement.

"Well, let's just say it wasn't cheap, but I figure you're good for it." Alex grinned at him. "I'll send the bill later."

Now, as they pored over the map, Toby said tentatively, "I would suggest—to be on the safe side—that you book the Liverpool-Belfast leg in Caernarfon and then go on to Bangor, which is a bigger center, to do the rest. I also suggest you book in as a tourist at a pub in any one of these little villages in the neighborhood. See, there is Penygroes or Carmel or Nebo or Nasareth — all within easy walk of this place, so when you have to make contact you just would leave your car wherever you settle."

"Why not Pen y Nai? — that's the closest."

"For one thing, it is off the beaten track for ordinary tourists. For another, it is just too close *if* they should trace you. The rest are either on or nearby A407 which is the main road between Porthmadoc and Caernarfon. No one would question you being there."

"I still feel we'd do better to stick together — I mean, if you send Williams away as you plan to do, how are you going to manage for supplies?" Alex was truculent.

"We have enough to last us three days, and that should be long enough — I hope," Toby said grimly.

Alex shrugged and gathered up the maps. "Well, anyway I'll report back in after dark to see how things are shaping." He paused. "One other thing — don't leave Sonya alone too much. She is putting a brave face on it, but she is very disturbed about all this. Yesterday, after she switched to my car, she tried to persuade me to turn back to Heathrow to give herself up to the Russians. Said she could not do this to you. Of course I squelched that, but just keep an eye on her, will you?"

"I see," Toby said forlornly. "Well, I'll keep that very much in mind"

"Until tonight then." And Alex was off, with an airy wave of his hand to Sonya who had just emerged from the hut. He strode downhill towards the distant farmhouse where his car, along with the Rolls, was discreetly hidden from view in the barn, together with Williams' sole milch cow.

Father and daughter were left staring at each other. "I've changed my mind," Toby said. "Why don't you come along with me to the farm? You won't be very much entertained because old Williams doesn't have much English, so we'll be talking in Welsh, but the walk is nice and it's a good day. And after, we can go and see what I've been up to here in the past twenty-five years."

Sonya's face brightened. "Yes, that I would like. I have tidied up the dacha and all is neat and proper now." And as they set off down the hill, added, "Twenty-five years — that is a very long time. You must love this place!"

"It has had its uses," Toby said somberly, not caring to think about the black moments in his life that had sent him to this particular refuge.

Their approach to the farmhouse was heralded by the barking of Williams' sheep dogs that brought the old man to his door. Toby pointed to the barn and made for it, and Williams came out, carefully closing the door behind him, an expression of devouring curiosity on his weatherbeaten, dark-skinned face. "Good morning, Glendower-bach," he said in Welsh as he joined them in the barn. "There is trouble I think. On the news you are. How may I help you?"

"Yes, there is big trouble, Williams-bach," Toby returned. "And it is of this now I must speak." Then in English, "But first I would like you to meet my daughter, Sonya Glendower."

The old farmer gravely shook hands with Sonya, not a flicker of expression giving away his inner amazement. "It is honored I am indeed, Miss Sonya-vach," he said.

Toby switched back to a rapid spate of Welsh as he explained, as best he could, their circumstances. Sonya curled up on a bale of hay and listened raptly as the two

171

men lilted at each other in this strange mellifluous tongue. "So you see, we must hide from everyone until we can escape from the country," Toby concluded. "If they find us before that, there may be trouble, big trouble, and I do not wish you to be involved. I would like you and your wife to go away for a few days. Have you not a daughter in Caernarfon? Perhaps a few days holiday by the sea? And before you go, I would like you to spread word in the village that it is their silence that is needed; that no one speaks of seeing anyone on this hillside. Do you think that is possible? It is much to ask, I know, for it is the law you'll all be breaking, but a few days is all I ask."

The old man ruminated for a minute, then said, with something like a twinkle in his dark eyes. "Many a month these hills sheltered your forefather, Owen Glendower, from the English, you recall, and not a man of Gwynedd betrayed him. Should we do less for you, Glendower-bach, who have done so much for us hereabouts? My wife, I will send away, but me, I stay. If there is trouble, you can use me and my dogs, for who knows the hills better than we do? Foreby, Tammy, my grandson, who is a bright lad, can be our eyes and ears in the village, and I will spread the word." Toby started to protest, but the farmer held up a commanding hand. "Those are my terms, Glendower. If you ask my help, I will give it my way."

There was nothing for it but to accept gracefully. "But I really must insist your wife leave," Toby added. "I should not know an easy moment if I thought I had put your family in jeopardy."

"Oh, there'll be no trouble about that: nattering at me for months she's been to go and see Gwendolen and the grandchildren. But with petrol the price it is and me so busy with the farm and the buses not running as they did and their fares such a terrible price, I told her straight that if it's our Gwenny she needs then Gwenny must come to us." Williams sounded fretful.

Toby suppressed a grin, for the farmer—like many a good Welshman—was notoriously tight-fisted when it came to parting with hard cash. "I would be most happy to pay for someone in the village to drive her over," he said, fishing in his wallet and extracting two ten pound notes. "In fact, I insist."

Williams brightened perceptibly. "Well, that's most kind, Glendower-bach, most kind! Then I'll set her to packing and be off myself to the village."

"There's just one other thing. I had an express package from my solicitor's sent to me under your name—it should be in the Pen y Nai post office by now. Would you pick it up yourself and bring it to me at the hut? It is rather important."

"Glad to, and if there is anything else I can do, just tell me. And I'll be bringing you up some fresh milk and eggs when I come." Williams carefully folded the money in a tight little wad and stowed it away in a deep inner pocket.

Toby looked over at the silently attentive Sonya, "Well, that's all settled," he said with relief. "Now shall we 'do' the cave?"

She uncurled herself and took his arm with a smile. "Lead on, o learned father!"

The old farmer stopped at the door and looked at them. "It is a grand thing to see you happy at long last, Glendower-bach," he said softly in English, and went out.

"Why did he say that?" Sonya demanded as they set off at a brisk pace up the hill.

"Williams has often not seen me at my best." He did not elaborate.

She looked at him questioningly. "And *are* you happy?"

Toby looked up to where a hawk was circling lazily over the grey rocky crest of the hill, outlined against a blue sky scattered with puffy white clouds. "Yes, in spite of all this, I think I am," he said simply, and began to talk about the cave. Wisely, she did not press him further.

The Spartan hut that was now their refuge Toby'd had erected some fifteen years previously, and had situated it in the shelter of a ridge of rock that curled around the mountain like an encircling arm. In this way it would not mar the landscape and, more importantly now, it was invisible to the lower reaches of the hill. Five years ago — as a guard against the vandalism that continued to sweep across the face of England like a scabrous plague, and had even reached its tainted fingers into the Welsh countryside — he had protected the hut with a steel mesh fence, and had put a similar barrier across the twin mouths of the cavern to protect the excavation. Short of breaking off the massive padlock that sealed the only gate into the cave, there was no way to breach the barrier, and for this too he was now thankful, should trouble arise.

As they drew abreast of the hut, he said, "You'd better put on a warmer jacket — it's chilly in the cave."

"What about you?" Sonya said promptly.

"Oh, I'm all right, I'm used to it."

"That is not good enough — you must be looked after. I bring you that old camouflage jacket I see in there. That you dig in, no?" She was firm.

"That I dig in, yes," he smiled at her, and while she disappeared into the cabin contentedly lit up his pipe.

"This place is similar to another Paleolithic site, Kent's Cavern down in Devon," he explained, as he carefully locked the gate behind them. "As you see, it has two entrances that interconnect within, but which run back in two long galleries to a great chamber at the end. Then there are several smaller galleries off of it." He bent down to fire up a Coleman lantern and handed her a large flashlight and a trowel. "I've sounded most of the cave over the years, but my main excavation has been in the great chamber. . . ." The harsh light of the lantern threw grotesque shadows on the encompassing grey rock walls as he rumbled on about the glaciations that had carved these tunnels in the volcanic rock of the area and of the ancient hunters who had used this handy shelter over thousands of years. As they wandered along, Sonya kept looking uneasily around. "To live in such a place," she whispered, awestruck. "And for so long! I can almost feel them around me now." She shivered.

He chuckled. "To them it was a cozy retreat, a safe home. And they are long gone, my dear." He led her into the great chamber, which was some sixty feet across and which he had bisected diagonally for his dig, leaving shelves of earth for the necessary ladders as he had gone deeper and deeper, "Careful on the ladders now, and don't look down. I'll go first," he told her, and they descended in silence until they reached bottom, some twenty-five feet below the present floor of the cave.

Sonya looked up in awe at the series of levels above their heads, all neatly tagged with white labels. "So much time!" she whispered. "So many lifetimes. And you did all this yourself? Why did you not get people to help you?"

He gazed up bleakly at the levels, thinking that each of those tags represented a particular moment of black, inner despair. "Because I wanted it that way," he said shortly. "This was where I could come to be alone—all alone."

Still looking up, she spread her arms wide. "But what did you do with all the earth you took out of here? There must have been tons of it!"

Again he chuckled. "Well, normally it would be carried out and dumped outside, but I did not want to mar the hilltop, so I early established that one of the little side galleries had nothing in it and it had a handy sinkhole at the end of it, so I've been dumping up there—it's almost full. I'll show it to you later. See, there is a simple bucket and winch arrangement at the top of the first ladder? All I do is lower the bucket down and when it is full, haul it up and sieve and dump it. Quite easy really."

But Sonya was now eagerly scanning the floor of the level they were on with her flashlight. With a little scream of delight she pounced on something that glittered dully. "I think I've found something!" She scrabbled it out of the grey powdery earth and held it up proudly to him. "What is it?"

Amused, he contemplated the greyish-black object with becoming gravity. "Good spotting! This looks like a broken segment of an Aurignacian backed blade—they used it something like a penknife. It is made out of the local obsidian, which isn't of very good quality. but its presence around here might have attracted the hunters in the first place because it makes such good tools."

She gazed at it like a prize jewel. "How old is it?"

"Oh, about twenty-five thousand years."

With a squeak of joy, she whipped out the trowel and started to dig feverishly around. "So old! Maybe I find the rest of it—that would be good, yes?"

"Whoa there!" he said, the archaeologist in him coming to the fore, "You can't go digging nasty little holes everywhere, you know! You have to go about this thing scientifically. We dig each level on the grid system, so that later we can reconstruct exactly where everything came from, and from that we can deduce what went on in this cave at any given period of time."

"Then show me how!" she cried, her face flushed with excitement. "This is fun. I want to find things."

"But not now! We've other things to do," he protested.

"What things? It is Alex who is doing things, and old Williams, and Penny—but what have *we* to do but wait?" she said, getting back up. "So why not show me how to do it properly?"

"Well, you have something there," he admitted fondly. "Why not indeed? Stay put and I'll get the rest of the equipment. . . ."

And so for the next several hours, round silver head bent close to round black head, showing, instructing, delving, they toiled happily away in the past—the twentieth century and its problems banished temporarily from their minds. Only hunger finally drove them to the surface and back to the everyday world.

"Can't we go back down after?" Sonya demanded, busily frying bacon and eggs on the camp stove. "I *like* doing this."

Toby contentedly sipped a glass of red wine and contemplated her. "Well, not today, maybe tomorrow. Williams should be back soon and I have to hear what is going on."

The old farmer did indeed arrive just as they finished their meal, bearing with him the packet and an assortment of food, including a shepherd's pie for their dinner. "The wife thought you might like this—fair tickled she was to be off to our Gwenny," Williams said. "And I

177

spread the word like you said. No sign of the police around, which is good, look you! Unless there is some emergency, no need to come down to me, I'll come up here same time tomorrow to check with you."

After he had left, Toby opened the packet which contained ten thousand pounds in large banknotes and a slim bundle of bearer bonds. Sonya gasped when she saw the contents. "I have never seen so much money!"

"Pontifex has done pretty well in such a short time. We'll need it to get away and get established in wherever we end up," Toby said grimly. "And God knows how long it will have to last us—it depends on how vengeful the British government is, after the dust settles."

"But surely they can't take what is yours?" she gasped.

"I wouldn't count on it in the circumstances—not even here."

"How much is there?"

He flipped quickly through the bonds. "A hundred thousand." He divided the money and the bonds into two piles and handed one of them to her. "Here, stow this somewhere unobtrusive in your things, and I'll look after the rest."

"I'd rather you kept it all," she said hesitantly.

"No—if we should get separated along the way for any reason, you'd need it to go on." He was firm. "Now, shall I show you how to write up what we did in the cave today?"

They looked at each other for a long moment. "Yes, that would be very nice," she said.

Darkness had fallen and they had finished their dinner before a rapping on the bolted door announced Alex's return. He came in looking somewhat windblown and carrying a flashlight and a bundle of newspapers. "Quite a hike!" he announced, sinking gratefully into a camp chair and grinning up at Sonya. "Well, you're booked on the Liverpool-Belfast ferry for the day after tomorrow. Best I could do, because all I could get on the Shannon-Brazil leg were two standbys for the day after that. But they told me in Bangor to come back tomorrow and that they'd probably have some cancellations by then." He produced the tickets and handed them over to Toby. "I didn't think you'd want to hang around in Belfast in the open."

Toby grunted and nodded. "Where did you settle?"

"I checked in at the pub in Nebo—nearest to this place after Pen y Nai. Not that it's all *that* near," Alex said ruefully. "I'm glad I told them I'd be visiting friends tonight, and I'll spend it here, if it's all right with you." Again he grinned over at Sonya. "All this exercise is killing a city boy like me."

"You hear any talk about us?" Toby asked anxiously.

"Well, the papers are full of it," Alex nodded at the pile. "But over dinner in the bar I didn't hear the locals give it more than a passing mention." He yawned. "Their main topic of conversation was a London motorcycle gang that's been roaring around the whole neighborhood raising a rumpus. Seems they're *really* up in arms about that. . . ."

Chapter 17

The step that Penny was about to take she realized was a perilous one. However, she could think of no other way to get the information that had now become vital to her: she simply had to come back out into the open. Hunched over the scattered pile of newspapers in her fusty little bedroom, she regarded their screaming headlines with a bleak eye SONYA AT IT AGAIN! trumpeted one; WHERE IS SONYA, WHO IS SHE THAT ALL THE COMMIES SEEK HER? parodied another; APPARENT THIRD DEFECTION IN MUR-DER-STRICKEN RUSSIAN BALLET COMPANY, *The Times* said cautiously.

The beleaguered Inspector Grey, she noted, had done his work well. In the raggiest of the papers there was no question that Sonya was being sought as a murder suspect, but as a Russian defector. At Heathrow there had been a scene the night before: Korkov and Grey in a public shouting match with the Russian yelling accusations at the English police for harboring a criminal and putting "glasnost" in jeopardy. This had touched British pride on the raw, and one feature writer, after emphasizing her eminent English parentage, had thrown down the gauntlet by concluding, "Good luck to you, Sonya, wherever you are. We hope you make it!"

While public opinion was now evidently swinging behind the refugees, it was also evident that the British government did not share in it: an official apology had already been sent to the Russian embassy "for the slip-up in police security arrangements," and the ominous pronouncement issued that "all ports and airports were under tight security surveillance and there was no possibility that the fugitives could escape from the British Isles." But in none of the pronouncements was there the slightest hint as to where the fugitives were, and it was this that now mainly concerned her.

Her fears, born the previous evening, had been fanned by a morning call from Vadik. "No doubt about it," he had reported grimly. "With the exception of the black, who is still around but not located, all of them and their bikes have gone. According to Geoff's landlady, he didn't come back for his tea last night—which is unusual—and she got a call from him later that he wouldn't be back for a while. He did not say where he was, but she thought it was a long-distance call."

So it seemed clear to Penny that Long had been watching them, but had not passed this information on to the police. To her that meant just one thing—that he, for reasons of his own, was either going after them himself or, worse, was going to inform the Russians. But she had to make sure of that: had to find out if the police *did* know more than they had revealed to the press; were in fact hot on their trail. If this were so, Toby would have to be warned, although she did not have the faintest idea *how* to do so. She sprang up and struggled into her coat—she could waste no more time thinking, she simply had to act—and hurried out to her car.

As she drove into the courtyard of New Scotland Yard, she was relieved to see the same sergeant who had been on duty the day before, and who looked suitably astounded at the sight of her. He made not the slightest quibble when she demanded to see Inspector Grey and positively bustled her on up to the inspector's office. His astonishment was equaled by Grey's, who looked up from the phone as she was ushered in. He hastily cradled it and got up. "You're about the last person I expected to see," he said tightly. "Where are the others?"

She managed to look equally astonished, "Why, that's why I'm here! — as soon as I saw the papers this morning I was dumbfounded, so I came right over."

"Where have you been?" he snapped.

"I went up to Oxford yesterday to take care of some business — didn't Mrs. Walker tell you? Now I'm back investigating the murders," she cried.

"Corbett tried to get you at Littlemore yesterday night and you weren't there." His tone was ominous.

"No, I didn't *stay* in Oxford. I came back last night for an appointment here," she said indignantly. "What is this? Of what am I being accused? I came here to exchange information about the murders, not to be treated like a suspect myself."

Grey looked unconvinced. "Where are they?" he repeated. "You realize that this is senseless, don't you? They are *not* going to get out of the country."

"The last I saw of Sir Tobias and Sonya they were in the Rolls heading for Heathrow," she said hotly. "Where they are now I have no idea. Maybe they were kidnapped — have you considered that?"

"And where is your son?" His face was a granite mask.

"Why, Alex took off to tour some sights! It's his first vacation in a very long time, Inspector, and I certainly did not want him to waste any more of it than he has already, because of all this upset."

"Where was he going?" Grey was not giving an inch.

"He had no set plans, although I think he was making for the Lake District. He did mention that he might look up an old school chum in Edinburgh — he went to school here, you know," she said, strewing as many red herrings in the path as she thought feasible.

"The name of this friend?" Grey queried, pencil poised.

She gave it. "But I've no idea of his address," she added hastily, "I believe he's a civil engineer. Now, Inspector, suppose we cut out any more of this nonsense and get back to the case? I think I've made some progress, but there's one very important question I have to clear up with you. While we were staying in Fulham, did you have the house under surveillance by a team of plainclothes detectives on motorbikes?"

Grey looked at her in silence for a moment. "That's the second time you have mentioned this. I thought the first time you were just talking, but why is this so important?"

"I'll tell you when you answer me! Please do so."

"Then, no, I did not. London is a high-crime city, as you well know, and there is a limit to the number of officers to be spared for round-the-clock surveillance. As it was we were stretched very thin keeping an eye on all the principals of the ballet company, and we thought two people of responsible reputation like Sir Tobias and yourself could be trusted. In that it appears we were gravely mistaken."

She ignored this, for, with her fears confirmed, she was thinking furiously. "Just one other question, talking of surveillance, is there *any* possibility that Gregorvich could have eluded your men that night, just as poor Mala did?"

He shook his head. "No. The man on duty outside his room heard Gregorvich's phone go around midnight and him answer it. He did not leave his station at all until seven-thirty the next morning when he was relieved. His relief reported that Gregorvich appeared, evidently fresh from the shower for his hair was all wet, to go down to breakfast at eight-thirty. So he definitely is out of it."

"That brings us right back to Long and Spence, and I think I can now point the finger definitely at Long," she said triumphantly, and went on to lay out her case.

Grey heard her out in silence, but at the end of it shook his head and sighed heavily. "You may well be right, but you have not got an atom of proof or anything that would stand up for a minute in a court of law. It's all circumstantial and, on the negative side, Long has no apparent motive and *two* very strong alibis. He was down at Alfriston when Mala was killed."

"Both alibis provided by Spence, who may be a very interested party," she protested. "You said yourself that their alibis in the Pavilion did not jibe all the way! And, although I cannot put my finger on a very strong motive as yet, there *has* to be one. Think about it! We have established a link between Long and Carstairs. We know Litvov was *waiting* for Carstairs that night with some important information. What that was, we don't know, but Litvov was obviously going to put the screws on Carstairs for a large sum of money in order to finance his own defection. He was confident he was going to get it, too, because he had already booked those passages to South America. Neither he nor his murderer knew that Carstairs had changed his plans, and the murderer had to silence him before he got to Carstairs. Long is the *only* one to fill this bill. Surely, with all the resources at your disposal, you can dig out the motive or — better still — break Spence down? He *has* to be lying."

"Now you're beginning to sound like a gangster movie," Grey said in a dull voice. "This is England and we simply don't do things that way, as you well know. How far do you think we'd get hounding an employee of MI5 and a respected Foreign Office official?"

"But Long may be a 'mole,' have you considered that as a possible motive? In which case MI5 should be extremely interested."

"Oh, I will certainly see that they get whatever concrete information we have," he murmured, doodling on his notepad. "But so far as Spence goes, I don't think we are going to get very far. As a matter of fact, I've just been talking to him — I'm surprised you didn't run into him on the way in. A rather bizarre little scenario: a package arrived at the Yard last night addressed to him via myself. He opened it in my presence this morning. It contained the icons taken from his house the other day."

"Really!" She was genuinely surprised; what on earth was Vadik up to? "How very odd! Still, I expect he was happy to get them back."

Grey was eyeing her. "Yes, extremely odd. One of them was still missing and he was quite upset about that. Said that it was not because it was so valuable but that it was of great sentimental value to him; a present, apparently.

"From Long?" she asked quickly.

"He didn't say. Do you know something about it?"

She opened her mouth, then shut it again. She could not reveal the true facts about the icon without giving Vadik away and she wasn't about to do that unless she had to. Instead she said, "Maybe we can trick Long into betraying himself. What if you contact him and let it out that I've come to see you with some new information: that I talked with Mala before she died and am going to make a statement?"

Grey gave a derisive snort. "Oh, you really do have a penchant for the melodramatic, Dr. Spring! I know enough about your other cases to see that has been a favorite ploy of yours—a very foolhardy one too, I must say. But do you think for an instant it would *work* in this case? Long isn't stupid! He would know damn well that all you'd have would be hearsay evidence from a dead girl. Why would he even bother to rise to such bait?"

"But there must be something we can do," she cried. "He's a double murderer!"

"Yes, I think he probably is," Grey said heavily. "But if I had a thousand pounds for every murderer that's walking scot-free about England at the moment I'd be a rich man. I can name you at least a dozen. The police *know* they are guilty, but proving it is something else. I'm very much afraid that Long may well join that unholy group—particularly in view of all the rest of this hubbub."

"So you're just going to sweep it under the rug, is that it?" she said indignantly.

"Oh, I'll keep digging—you can count on that." He sounded unutterably weary as he got up and walked over to the window. He gazed unseeingly out into the courtyard, his hands in his pockets, his neat shoulders hunched in dejection. "But aren't you overlooking something, which I'm sure must be extremely important to you? Even if we do nail Long eventually, it is not going to make one scrap of difference to what happens to Sonya Glendower and her father. On that our hands are tied and our duty all too clear. Once they are caught Sonya will *have* to be handed over to the Russians. There is absolutely no way of avoiding that so far as I can see. The only thing I could do for her would be to make it clear she did not have a hand in either of the murders — for whatever good that would do." Again he sighed. "I don't blame Sir Tobias for what he has done — if I had a daughter in such dire straits I would probably have done the same myself. But I'm afraid he has put himself on the wrong side of the law for nothing — they *won't* get away."

Penny was desperately torn between her mounting fears for her nearest and dearest and her abiding faith that Toby would make good their escape. How far did she dare go? "I think in your present single-minded pursuit you are overlooking other possibilities," she said, grimly controlling herself. "Long has been ahead of us all along the way, and he may still be. Now that I know those motorcycle watchers in Fulham were his men, and what thugs they are, I am seriously worried about the safety of the Glendowers. If Long is a mole as well as a murderer, what better way to get himself in the good graces of the Russians than to bring ridicule and suspicion down on the British government by capturing the fugitives himself — or, more probably, making sure the Russians find them first? You'd all look pretty silly then, wouldn't you? He may already have them and is just waiting for the right moment to hand them over. I've already told you the names and descriptions of the gang, and that at least three of them are no longer in London — Vadik has established that. Why don't you get after them and round them up? They are hired hands and may talk."

"Ah, yes, Gregor Vadik," Grey murmured. He returned to his chair and looked across at her. "Since he seems to be taking such an active interest in all this, I did some checking on him. Very strange company you keep, Dr. Spring. What exactly is *he* after?"

It was something she fervently wished she knew; she took refuge in indignation. "He owes Sir Tobias a favor from way back and he is merely trying to repay this debt. He has very valuable sources of information not available to me—nor to you, apparently—and he has been *extremely* supportive. I am thankful for his help."

"Sure of that, are you?" he appeared grimly amused. "His reputation doesn't exactly paint him as such a creature of sweetness and light. But to get back to your suggestion—I will indeed look into this so-called 'gang' you mention, but for now I really must get back to following up my latest lead."

"Lead?" A chill ran up her spine. "What lead is that?"

"Oh, I had an interesting chat on the phone with Dr. Jessup in Oxford last night. You know him, of course? I asked him if he knew Sir Tobias' favorite spots in the British Isles—somewhere remote and where he could go to ground. Jessup was a bit vague but said he did have the impression that sometimes Sir Tobias went back to his native Wales—which of course would make a lot of sense. I assume you know of this?"

Damn Jessup, damn him to bloody hell! Penny raged inwardly. That pettifogging little bureaucrat who bore no love for either Toby or herself because their reputations so overshadowed his own! "I know nothing of the sort," she said stoutly. "Sir Tobias' father, Arthur Glendower, as you may know, was a noted Celtic enthusiast, one might almost say a fanatic about all things Celtic, but since Toby never got along with him it was my impression that he *shunned* all things Celtic. If that's the sort of lead you're following, you'd be better off looking in Greece or Ionian Turkey—that's where his heart lies."

"They are still in this country." Grey was implacable. "And Wales—though a wide enough area—is a lot smaller than the whole of the British Isles, so we'll be focusing our search there."

Was he trying to bait her, trying to panic her into contacting Toby? If so, she was now definitely on her guard. She got up. "Well, I think you'll be wasting your time, but I'll let you get on with it. I'll check back with you, if I may, about your progress in locating the motorcycle gang."

"By all means," Grey was back to his imperturbable self as he got up and gravely shook hands with her.

She simply flew back to another rendezvous with Vadik in the British Museum, where she recounted the details of her interview, carefully suppressing any mention of Toby. To needle him into further action she told him of Grey's researches on himself and of his doubts that Long would ever be called to account for his crimes. Neither appeared to faze Vadik in the slightest.

He ruminated for a while, then said, "Obviously it is time to attack the weak link in the enemy's armor — I shall make an official call on Herbert Spence."

"No rough stuff! — that would just make things worse." Penny was alarmed.

He clucked his tongue in reproof. "How you underestimate me! Have some faith!"

"But what are you going to do? You have no *official* clout!"

"Oh, but I have," he purred. "At least enough to satisfy the insecure Mr. Spence." He flipped open a small leather folder that showed an Interpol ID card. She could scarcely believe her eyes. "You're working for *Interpol*?" she gasped.

He grinned savagely at her. "No, not really. But, if asked, they would not deny this ID — they could not afford to."

"Well, I give up. I don't know what you're up to. I

only hope you know what you're doing," she said help-lessly.

Vadik got out another small folder—this contained the photos of Long and his cronies taken in The Purple Pigeon. "Notice anything about these?"

She peered at them. "They're a lot lighter than the first prints I saw—a lot more details." In one Long had his arm around Geoff, in two others he was holding the hands of Anders and the black man.

"Anything else?" he pressed.

She shrugged and shook her head. Vadik again clicked his tongue. "I see anthropologists are not as keenly observant of details as archaeologists. I would wager Toby would pick it up in an instant." With a stubby finger he indicated a spot behind the heads: it showed a single-day wall calendar, the dates clearly visible. They were all during the past two weeks; one actually on the date of Mala's death.

For a second she was bewildered, then light dawned. "You've faked them! They're all fake—the originals weren't a bit like this!"

"Ah, the marvels of modern technology," he said in high good humor. "But by the time I show him these, Mr. Spence will be in no mood to harbor such doubts."

"But I still don't see what you expect to gain?"

"Don't you?" Vadik got up and chuckled. "Everyone knows that 'Hell hath no fury like a woman scorned.' That's what I'm banking on. . . ."

Chapter 18

"You can tell 'is Nibs from me, Cannon, to get off 'is 'igh 'orse! If he's so bloody upset, let 'im come 'imself and give it a try. Cor! — you should just see this place — talk about the end of nowhere! Nothing but sheep and 'ills and people that gibber at yer in some strange lingo. You never fink you was in England at all." The bullet-headed man leaned close to the phone in the wayside call box, as he listened intently to the disembodied voice at the other end, an aggrieved expression on his battered face. "Well, I *told* you what happened already — didn't you tell 'is Nibs? It was that silly sod Anders wot mucked it up. We was on the tail of the Rolls right up the M5 and on to the A5 right the way through Shrewsbury. Going great we wos. Then Geoff had to stop for some petrol and Anders and I went on. Then *I* had to stop and take a leak in a lay-by and Anders kept after them. Next thing I knew the silly sod was back with his mouth hanging open, saying he'd lost them. Playing silly devils he was, roaring on ahead of them making for Bangor — dark by then o'course — taking a look back every now and then. Then 'e realized it was some other perishin' car's lights 'e was seeing. By the time he got back to where he passed them, they were gorn, and ain't been seen since. That bloody Rolls has vanished. They've got to be *somewheres* on this fucking peninsula, but it'll take us a while to case all these bloody little villages. . . ." He listened some more, then took up his plaint again. "We've done all that. Sent the ones who don't really know wot it's all about to cover the main roads into Liverpool — that's my bet where they're 'eaded — and all the likely spots in the city. Sent a couple off to Holyhead, just in case they're after the ferry there. To be on the safe side, I even sent a couple off to Manchester, tho' I don't think they'll make for an airport. Me and Geoff and Anders are 'andling this end. Camping out we are, and perishing awful it is too, but we got such a frozen mitt in the pubs we hit that we thought it better to stay out of sight — talk about 'ostile! These perishers treat us like *we're* the bloody Commies."

The phone crackled again and he listened, eyeing his companion, who was lolling against the outside of the booth smoking a reefer, his Mohawk crest tousled by the brisk breeze. Geoff lifted his eyebrows enquiringly and the ex-pug grimaced at him. "Where are we? On the A487 just outside a place called Penygroes. Anders is doing the villages to the south and we're 'eading north. We ain't got a base, so I'll have to call you — be at the Pigeon? Oh, I see. Don't like the sound of that much. All right then, you stay put where you are and I'll call back tonight about six — sooner if we've got anything." He slammed the phone down and shouldered out of the call box, his low forehead wrinkled in thought. "Cannon thinks there may be some trouble brewing," he informed Geoff, who yawned and stretched gracefully. "Couple of odd ones in the Pigeon last night with photos of us. We'd better get crackin', mate. I don't like the sound of it."

Geoff nodded his crest at the small road that made a T junction with the main one at the call box. "Why don't we try this road first, Bob? I've been having a dekko at the map. Now, according to Anders, 'e lost them on the A5 just abaht 'ere, see? Place called Capel Curing? So they probably turned off on this A4086 and that splits — see? — around Snowdon. Now this little road just 'ere runs between the A487 to the A4085, and I'd think we'd 'ave better hunting there than here."

"Talk abaht needles in 'aystacks!" Bob grumbled. "Still, we got to start somewheres, I suppose." They revved up their bikes in unison and roared down the secondary road. As they came to the first signs of habitation on it they throttled back and proceeded at a more sedate pace, looking anxiously around them. Geoff suddenly braked hard and put his foot down, " 'Ere, look at that!" They gazed at a small village hall; above its modest oaken double doors hung an equally modest sign: "Glendower Memorial Hall."

"Well, the name's the same," Bob muttered. "Worth a try. There's a post office in that shop over there — hope the perishers speak English. Better let me do the talking, they don't seem to take to your 'air-do. Wot's the name of this place anyway?"

"The sign outside the village said Pen y Nai," Geoff muttered. "I'll go and take a dekko in the garage along there. I need some oil and I can ask abaht the Rolls."

"Righto — meet you back 'ere then." Bob carefully parked his bike in front of the hall and went over to the post office. He made a show of studying the small rack of postcards outside of the door, while ascertaining there was only an elderly woman inside. He shouldered in. "You speak English?" he demanded.

"I do indeed," she said with dignity, her mild hazel eyes wary. "What can I do for you?"

His eyes flicked over the motley conglomeration in the crowded shop. "Three packets o' crisps, three bottles o' Fanta, and three of them sausage rolls—oh, and a bit o' information, please, if you don't mind." He smiled ingratiatingly, revealing uneven nicotine-stained teeth. "Noticed that sign over your 'all out there. Same name as a bloke I worked for once. Nice chap 'e was, name of Tobias Glendower. 'E came from around here, I fink. Do you know if he's still got a place here? Drives a lovely car, he does—a Rolls?"

Her hazel eyes widened innocently. "After the great Owen Glendower our hall is named," she murmured. "So I'm afraid I can't help you there. Have you looked in the phone book? Visiting around here, are you?"

His face fell. "Nah, just passing through." He dug in his leather jacket and paid for his purchases, then mooched gloomily back to his bike just as Geoff came roaring up behind him. "Wash out!" he said grumpily.

"I'm not so sure about that." Geoff was excited. "I asked about the Rolls and got nowhere, but while I was putting the oil in my bike I noticed the man at the garage muttering away at some kid who came by, and the kid took off like a bat out o' hell. See, there he goes up the hillside now! Think we should follow him?"

Bob was looking uneasily over Geoff's shoulder towards the post office, where the old lady had come to the door and was now staring at them both. And worse, a policeman on a bicycle had just pedaled into sight. "Nah, I think we'd better get out of here—almost time to meet up at Penygroes with Anders anyway to see if 'e's turned up anything. Just keep an eye on where the kid's heading, we can check on it later if need be." They roared back the way they had come.

At the rendezvous, the tall Swede was pacing excitedly up and down as they screamed up to him. "I fink

I'm on to something," he burst out. Despite his Scandinavian name and appearance, his Cockney accent was just as thick as his companions', both of whom had been born within the sound of Bow bells and hence were true Cockneys.

"Found the Rolls?" Bob demanded eagerly.

Anders' face fell, "Well, no. But there's a car parked in the pub lot in Nebo wot's got a London registration — only one I've seen in this God-forsaken place — and it's an 'ired car too,"

Bob looked at him in disgust. "Must be 'undreds of them around — still a lot of tourists about this time of year!"

"Yeah, but wait, that's not all!" The Swede was aggrieved. "I nobbled a simple-minded bloke wot cleans up in the pub. Slipped 'im a quid, I did. Made aht I was waiting for a friend to turn up from London, see? Bloke said that the only one had turned up from those parts was a Yank doctor — a Doctor Spring. And ain't that the same name as that funny old geezer who was in the papers with our lot?"

"I think you're right," Bob said. "We're on to something. Wot d' you think, Geoff?"

Geoff was again studying the map. "Makes some sense that does — see, there's Pen y Nai and here's Nebo. I suppose we'd better check aht all these other little places, but my bet is that they're somewhere up there. . . ." He looked, squint-eyed, at the grey crest of Pwhelli Tor. "But first let's go 'ave a look at that car and the Yank doctor. One of us better keep tabs on 'im, 'e might lead us right to 'em!"

In a state of high excitement they roared southwards to Nebo. But as they came into the parking lot of the pub Anders' face fell and he let out a string of curses. "It's gorn!" he said forlornly. They looked at each other in dismay. "Ere then, you try and get hold of that dimwit. Slip 'im another quid if you have to, but see if the Yank's checked out," Bob sounded a little desperate. "We'll go on with the checking and meet you back at Penygroes in two hours — right?"

"Yes, let's check this first." Geoff was back at the map and he indicated a little byway that appeared to run uphill between Moel Herog and Pwhelli Tor. "We might spot something from up there — a farmhouse or something. Got your glasses, Bob?"

Bob nodded slowly, for quickness of thought was not one of his strong points. He handed over the binoculars. "You go on then, I fink I'll stay with Anders. Don't want 'im mucking things up again. I'll call Cannon and tell 'im to tell the others to keep a sharp eye out for that car in the towns along the coast. Got the description 'ave yer?" He glared savagely at Anders.

The sullen Swede towered above him, "Better than that. I took the fucking number," he mumbled and handed over a crumpled bit of paper.

"Well, that's a bit of all right then." Bob was mollified. He grinned crookedly at his companions and curled a hamlike fist. "We might 'ave quite a surprise in store for this Doctor — fucking — Spring."

"Glendower-bach — there's trouble I think." Williams' anxious voice followed upon a furious rapping on the door, dispelling the peace of the cabin, where father and daughter were browsing through another late lunch after a peaceful morning's dig in the cave. Toby's state of euphoria vanished in a flash, as he leapt up and opened the door upon Williams' worried face. "What is it? Come on in."

The farmer had his three black and white Welsh

collies with him, and bidding two of them stay, he came in with the third and smallest and slumped into a chair. The dog immediately took up guard by his side. He mopped his forehead and muttered. "Not good, not good at all is the news I bring." He drew a deep breath and looked up at Toby, "My grandson came up from the village. First the constable from Penygroes came with a flier about you. Put it up in the post office he did and made a big noise about it, but he's not a local man so there's not too much to worry about there, I would say. But then Myfanway Evans at the post office and Hugh Griffiths at the garage say that two men from that motorcycle gang that's been around were in the village at the same time. Asking questions they were — about the Rolls and about you, *by name*. They went off again, but Griffiths didn't like the looks of it, so he sent Tammy right up and I went down. Seems they've been in all the villages 'round here, but in the others they only asked about the Rolls."

"Are they of the police?" Sonya broke in nervously.

"Not like any I've ever seen," the old man said. "Sound more like city ruffians up to no good. It's why I brought the dogs along. I'll leave my Jess here with you." He fondled the dog's black and white head. "She's the oldest and smartest of the three, and best sheep dog in Gwynedd. She won't bark, but she'll let you know for sure if there is anyone around. She's the mother of the pair outside. The dog is fair daft and a real barker, so I'll keep him with me in the farmhouse, but the bitch is almost as smart as her mother. I'll leave her roam free and she'll come tell me if there are strangers on the hillside, and I'll chase them off. Just you don't show yourselves for any reason whatever."

"If we can only keep away from them tonight, we'll

be gone by tomorrow," Toby said tightly. "But I won't have you putting yourself in danger on my account, Williams, particularly if there is a gang of them."

"What about Alex?" Sonya said, her eyes anxious. "He's coming back here tonight. He must be warned to stay away!"

Toby looked at her helplessly. "Easier said than done, my dear. We've no idea where, how or when to contact him, except in Nebo. And short of sending someone from Pen y Nai over to wait for him at the pub with a message, there is no means of alerting him. Maybe, if the gang have been there also, he'll hear of it soon enough and be on the alert." He eyed Williams. "Is there anyone from the village who'd be willing to go, do you think?"

Williams did not answer him directly but got up and made for the door, "There's that fool dog barking his head off again! Probably just after a rabbit, but I'll have to quiet him. Care to come out with me for a word, Glendower-bach? You stay here with Miss Sonya, Jess-girl, and look you after her." Again he fondled the head of the collie, who looked at him and grinned.

As soon as the door was closed and he had quieted the dog, Williams turned to Toby, his face grave. "I did not want to tell you the worst of it in there to upset the young lady, but it's worse than I let on. The constable from Penygroes was full of himself and free with his talk. Went on about how the search for you is concentrating now in Wales and that they're on the lookout for you in all the ports around here. It's as if someone's tipped them off. That they know where you are. Why not change your plans? We can hide you in these hills well enough until they tire of it — and sooner or later they will, I'll be bound."

"No, the longer we delay, the worse it may get. Let us

hope it is not already too late. If Alex Spring has been successful today, we'll make for Liverpool at dawn tomorrow and take our chances there. The only snag is that I can't use the Rolls, and if the police *have* tumbled to the fact that Alex is assisting us, they may have got his rental car number also." Toby looked inquiringly at Williams.

"Well, if you're set on it, Sir Tobias." The use of his formal title indicated the depth of the old farmer's disapproval. "On the transport we can help. I can drive you down to the village in my old lorry. It's too open for the rest of it, but Hugh Griffiths has a panel truck. He can drive you in that and you'll be safely out of sight until the time of the ferry. And I'll see someone from the village gets to Nebo — tho' fair strange they'll think that. Our chaps don't go over there much, their soccer team and ours being dead rivals."

"Thanks, that would be splendid," Toby said with a great deal more confidence than he felt. "Tell Griffiths he'll not be the loser for this."

The old man grunted. "Then it's on my way I'll be to see what can be done. I'll be back tonight to see how the young man has fared. And if Jess starts acting up, take heed and douse your lights. I'm thinking you might be better off in the cave once the young doctor is back here." He stomped off with the two dogs following on his heels.

Toby did not immediately return to the cabin. He badly needed time to think away from Sonya's anxious eyes. He lit up his pipe, squatted on the lee side of the cabin away from the brisk breeze, and gave himself up to gloomy thought. How they had been tracked down so quickly he had no idea. There had been no mention in the papers of any kind of reward for their capture, so the provenance and motivation of this motorcycle gang were a complete mystery to him, unless. . . . It was this "unless" that made his blood run cold. Maybe the Russian, Korkov, had had Sonya under surveillance all the time. In which case they knew in general, if not in particular, where their quarry was and for reasons of their own were waiting to pounce at a moment of their own choosing—for motives he did not care to think about. The remoteness of the Folly had seemed such a good idea initially; now he wondered if he had not led them all into a trap. But, if it came to confrontation, it was a defensible trap. His round jaw set grimly. Rather than have Sonya fall directly into the hands of the Russians and their hirelings, he'd raise enough of a rumpus on this quiet hillside to bring in the police. Then he would take his chances with the Law of England, which is probably what he should have done all along. If he could draw the Russians out to attack him, there would be public outcry, grounds for appeal, grounds for delay . . . and time was what he needed. He smiled faintly—he was sure this was a plan that would appeal to Penny no end, for it was something far more along her lines of thought than his own.

He got up, stretched, and went back into the cabin. "We've got to get busy," he informed Sonya, who was curled up in a despondent heap on the cot with Jess curled beside her. "To be on the safe side I think we'll beat a retreat into the cavern. We can set up camp in the great chamber, where lights and a fire can't be seen on the hillside; we would not dare show any lights here. So let's clear everything out—the bags, the stove, the groceries, the bottled water—all except the table, chairs and cot. Then, if they do stumble upon the cabin, they'll think we are already gone."

She jumped up. "What about Alex," she demanded instantly.

"I can wait for him here after dark and then bring him to the cave."

"We wait together," she said in a voice that brooked no argument, and set methodically about packing up. The sheep dog watched the proceedings with interest, and as they made trip after trip to the cavern she trotted to and fro with them. At last, the cabin stripped to its bare essentials, Toby switched off the small gas-driven refrigerator — his sole luxury in the cabin — and took out the ice trays to melt along with a bottle of Mumm's Cordon Rouge. "May as well use this up," he said dryly. "We've done everything else — and we've enough stuff in the cave to withstand a week's siege at least."

They toasted each other silently. "It is very bad, isn't it?" Sonya murmured. "This spot we are in."

"Bad, yes, but not impossible," Toby said stoutly. "I've been in worse spots. Come to think of it, a lot of them were connected with caves or variations thereof. Want me to tell you about them?" She smiled and nodded. And so, as the shadows lengthened on the hillside, he related some of his more bizarre adventures. He was coming to the end of his lengthy narrative, when Jess suddenly got up from where she was curled at Sonya's feet and went over to the door, her ears pricked. She let out a faint whine and looked back at them. They strained their ears but could hear nothing. She came back to Toby and looked up at him, then returned to the door, her hackles slowly rising. Toby fingered the revolver in his pocket, his nerves tightening. Then suddenly there was the sound of stumbling footsteps and a pounding on the door. "Anyone there? For God's sake, if you are, open up! They're after me." It was Alex.

"Call the dog!" Toby yelled at Sonya, and sprang for the door. He opened it and a shadowy figure stumbled and fell across the threshold panting heavily. Toby shone his flashlight down to reveal Alex covered with mud and grass stains and with a cut, streaming blood, above his left eye. "Men on the hill" Alex gasped. "Jumped me—but I managed to get away from them. I think we should get fast and far away from here—right *now. . . .*"

Chapter 19

"Didn't you get my warning message at the Nebo pub?" Toby demanded testily, watching Sonya fussing over Alex's cut and generally cleaning him up by the harsh light of the Coleman lamp. They had beaten a hasty and silent retreat into the cave shelter and were now cozily ensconced on the sleeping bags in the great cavern, arranged around the camp stove on which a coffee pot was perking busily.

"I was so late getting back from Liverpool that I decided to forego dinner at the pub and come right on. So I just parked the car and started my hike," Alex replied. "Never went inside the pub."

"*Liverpool*?" Toby queried.

"Yes, well, before hearing *your* bad news, you'd better hear mine." Alex grimaced as Sonya dabbed Mercurochrome on the cut and covered it with a bandage. "The booking is definite now from Dublin, day after tomorrow. I was a little concerned when I saw so much police activity around in Caernarfon and Bangor, so I thought I'd go on into Liverpool and scout out the docks there, both for the quickest route to them and to see if there were any police in evidence. And, boy, were there ever! They are searching all the cars on the car ferries, and even have two cops on each gangplank checking foot passengers. It is going to be hellishly difficult to get you on unnoticed. I suggest you just take a small carry-on bag each; I'll fly direct to Dublin with the rest of the stuff and check it in ahead of you. Luckily, there seems an almighty crush as sailing time approaches so the police can't check as carefully then. You'll just have to disguise yourselves as much as possible and try to slip through the crush. Alternatively, we could scrap this whole plan and I could hire or steal a boat from one of the smaller ports around to take you direct to Dublin. Or I could put up a false trail a couple of hours before sailing time with an anonymous phone call to the cops telling them I've spotted you and you're planning to board the Holyhead ferry. That might make them let their guard down in Liverpool long enough for you to get on and away." He paused for breath and looked enquiringly at Toby.

Toby shook his head in dazed disbelief. "You most certainly are your mother's son!" he said with fervor. "But before considering all this proposed derring-do, you'd better hear what we now seem to be up against . . ." and rapidly filled Alex in on the events of the day. "I'm waiting for Williams now to see exactly how things stand," he concluded. "In fact I ought to get back to the cabin in a few minutes."

Alex favored Sonya with a long speculative stare. "So someone has already blown the whistle, and both the police and, more importantly, this gang are hot on our heels. Well, that does alter things a bit, and it explains a lot." He got up and helped himself to a mug of coffee, his handsome face set and stern. "At least we've had one small bit of luck. If it hadn't been for a goof-up on their part, I might have led them right to you in the cabin. As it was, I was quite low on the hillside, using my flashlight of course to light my way, when I heard the noise of somebody falling not too far behind me and then some choice swear words in a very Cockney voice. Naturally I put the light out at once and got off the path. Damn, but there must have been at least two of them — the next thing I knew this shape came hurtling out of the dark at me, knocked me down and started lashing out with some kind of chain. That's what caught me here. . . ." He touched his brow and winced. "He yelled as he went down — a name, I think it was 'Bob' — but I was too busy fighting him off to pay much mind. Anyway, I managed to land a good one on his jaw; he went down again and I raced off. The first rock I ran into — quite literally — I stayed put behind for a while. I could hear them stumbling around and cursing — they didn't have lights — and after a bit they moved away and then I ran on up to the cabin. Somehow they must have spotted me at the pub, because I swear no motorcycles have been following me around the past two days. The problem now is, how to get rid of them long enough to get away from here?"

Toby also got up. "Well, we will talk of this later on, when I've seen Williams. You stay here with Sonya, I'll take the dog with me."

Alex grinned down at her. "Gladly. I've always wanted to play cave man. Besides, we've a lot of catching up to do. I have been deprived of the pleasure of her company for the best part of two days and am positively pining. Don't hurry back!"

Toby snorted and stamped away, the sheep dog at his heels, as Alex turned to Sonya, his face solemn. "You and I *do* have a lot to talk about, my sweet. There's no sense in ignoring the plain fact that things are about as bad as they can be, however . . ." he sat down beside her and took her hand. "I have a proposition that I want you to listen to very, very carefully, and it is something I *don't* want your father to know about. . . ."

In the darkened cabin the minutes dripped by like hours as Toby gloomily puffed away on his pipe and contemplated the moonlight that now slanted across the cabin floor, while Jess sat motionless beside him. Eventually she got up and went noiselessly to the door, her head cocked, her feathery tail slowly wagging—Williams was on his way. At the first audible footfall, Toby went to the door and opened it, as the farmer, armed with a shotgun, came into view. "It is good that you show no light," the old man muttered as he came across the threshold. "For it is no good news that I bring—there are men on the hillside."

"I know," Toby rumbled back. "We have moved into the cave. Shall we talk here or there?"

"There would be safer." They closed and locked the cabin and went silently through the grille before the cavern. As they entered the big chamber, Sonya and Alex started up, looking a little disconcerted. After Williams had been formally introduced to Alex, the latter said easily, "Well, I expect you two want to confer, and I'm dying to see what Sonya has been up to in that deep pit, so why don't you show me around?" He looked keenly at her and she nodded, her face impassive. They took a lantern and descended the chain ladder into the pit, Williams watching them in mild-eyed astonishment.

He turned to Toby after the couple had reached the depths and said quietly, "I'm afraid the plans will have to be changed. When I drove down to the village there were two men on bikes blocking the track. Stopped me they did and tried to question me as they looked the lorry over. I pretended I had no English, and I had the dogs with me, so they did not dare pull me out, and let me go on. Then, after I had spoken with Hugh in the village, I drove around a bit and there're a pair of them on each of the main junctions around here. I came back the back way—the Moel Herog path, you know?—and two more there who stopped me also. Livid they were when I only talked Welsh to them, and followed me they did until I took the turnoff to the farm. Then I stopped the lorry, got out with the dogs and my shotgun and pointed to the PRIVATE PROPERTY—NO TRESPASSING sign. Stood there until they took off, I did, but if they're watching they could be back at the farm by now snooping around. I can't lock the barn, so best I could do was to leave the dog on a long chain to the door, and hope his barking keeps them off. If it doesn't, they'll find the car for sure. Then David Evans—My fanwy's youngest—came back from Nebo by way of the farm. Didn't find the young man but said the whole area is up in arms—these bikers seem to be everywhere, and more pouring in. Two of them got run in in Penygroes for raising a rumpus at the pub there, but the constable has his hands more than full, I can tell you! He sent to Caernarfon for some help, but Heaven knows how and when they'll go about that." He paused for a moment and looked at Toby. "The only thing I can think to do is for you to get yourselves down the mountain before dawn, and I'll tell Griffiths to meet you at some point along the road. How about that junction in the Pen y Nai road where that lane goes off to Llanlyfyn? He could go a little way down the Llanlyfyn road and wait for you there at dawn — say for thirty minutes? Then, if you don't show, we'll raise the village and come to the cave."

Toby was thinking furiously. "We could try that. But how will you let Griffiths know?"

"I'll walk down again." The old man drew his shepherd's cloak around him as if suddenly cold. "And then I'll rest on the mountain for the night, as I have done many a time. If there are men searching here I will see them, but they won't see me."

"There is one other thing," Toby said. "This gang must be getting their orders from someone and, if I'm correct in my thinking, that someone should be coming on the scene very shortly to direct our capture. If you are going to see Griffiths, ask him to alert the village for any car with strangers in it — probably from London. These strangers may be foreign. If they do arrive, have the police called *immediately*, and do you think the village could arrange some interference until the police get here?"

"*You* would call in the police?" Williams looked at him under beetling brows.

"If it comes to that, yes." Toby was firm. "I have my reasons."

"Good enough." The old farmer got up stiffly. "Then I'll be on my way, and we'll see what can be done. Then it is six for the rendezvous?"

Toby nodded. "And, for Heaven's sake, take no chances Williams-bach! This is not your problem, it is mine."

"I am making it mine," the old man said gruffly and walked back out into the night.

Before locking the grille after him Toby stepped through it and looked out and down to where the few scattered lights of Pen y Nai could be seen far below.

The moon was surrounded by a misty halo and he could feel the light damp fingers that were part mist, part drizzle, trailing across his face. It was, he thought, a slight plus for their side: if the gang were all city-bred they would have little stomach for a sustained search of a wet Welsh mountainside during the hours of darkness. With morning light it would be a different matter. . . .
He closed and locked the grille and retreated to the comparative warmth and welcome of the big chamber. There he helped himself to a swig of brandy, settled on his sleeping bag and studied the large-scale ordinance map for the best route down to the rendezvous point. He could hear voices in the pit, and by the pitch of them he diagnosed a spirited argument going on. He smiled faintly to himself and went on with his study. The voices dropped to a murmur again and then silence. He got up and went over to the top of the ladder. "Hey down there! Are you on your way up?" he demanded. "There's been some developments and a change in plans, so we'll have to get an early start."

"Be right with you." Alex sounded a little breathless. There was quiet muttering, the creak of the ladder, and they emerged from the pit, both looking somewhat dazed. "So now what?" Alex asked, as they joined him around the spread-out map.

"The gang are covering all the roads, so we'll have to walk down the mountain just before dawn to rendezvous with the Pen y Nai garage man in his panel van, here . . ." Toby indicated the spot. "This will be our best route. We'll have to circle around those two small ponds that give birth to the brook that flows through Pen y Nai, otherwise there's no bridge or ford across it. After that, it should be plain sailing down to the Llanlyfyn road. Griffiths will drive us into Liverpool, and once free of this lot, we'll have to decide whether to go

209

on with the original plan or not. We don't want to be encumbered by baggage, so just take whatever you can get into one small holdall." He looked at Sonya. "We can restock later in Ireland." She nodded mutely, her eyes blank and unrevealing. He felt a curious sense of unease, as if an invisible wall had suddenly descended between them. He cleared his throat uncomfortably. "Now we'd better try and get a few hours sleep. We should be up by four-thirty at the latest."

"But I couldn't sleep a wink!" Sonya protested. "Not here, not with all this!"

"I agree. In fact I'm all for going *now* and waiting down there," Alex joined in.

"No, there's no sense in doing that. By morning we'd be wet through and in no shape for what lies ahead. We must *try* to rest," Toby said firmly. "Tomorrow is going to be a very nerve-wracking day and we'll need all our wits about us."

Muttering to herself in Russian, Sonya took off her shoes and slid into her sleeping bag, as he turned down the lamp to its lowest setting and extinguished the camp stove. The two men got into their sleeping bags and the cave settled into its primeval silence. But long after the even breathing of the two young people signaled that, despite their protestations, they were firmly asleep, Toby found himself gazing up at the unseen roof and grappling with a mounting premonition of danger.

He could have sworn that his eyes had not even closed, and yet the next thing he knew was Alex's urgent hand on his shoulder. "We've got to get a move on, it's almost five. Sonya's making coffee." Toby struggled up to see the cavern fully lighted and Sonya, her face still flushed with sleep and heavy-eyed, bent over the camp stove. "Damnation!" he exploded.

While Alex gulped the scalding coffee and Sonya

stuffed her holdall, Toby took his mug and walked along the long passage to the grille, unlocked it and stepped out into the starless darkness preceding the dawn. He could feel rather than see a mist swirling about him, scurried along by a brisk wind from the northeast. Jess came out and stood scenting the wind and looking up at him. When he went back in she hesitated, and only came reluctantly to his call.

"Leave everything just as it is," he ordered, as he got back to find Sonya automatically tidying up and rinsing out the mugs. "We'll need all the time we have to get down the mountain; we dare not show our lights too often, and it'll be slow going in the dark. Got your flashlights? The important thing is to stay together. . . ." He picked up his own small holdall containing the money, tickets and a few toiletries, and shooed them out before him, extinguishing the lanterns and locking the gate behind him. "First we'll be heading to the left, then down," he instructed. "You take the rear, Alex and we'll keep Sonya between us at all times."

They had negotiated the first stretch and were just starting their downward plunge when, from somewhere below them on the hillside, came the unmistakable crackle of gunfire. Toby froze in his tracks, his mind in ferment, as behind him the sheep dog let out an indescribable strangled howl. "Oh God! Williams! Here, Jess!" he grabbed at the dog's collar. In a flash his mind was made up. He wheeled about. "Alex, come here!" The tall figure appeared beside him. Toby pressed the holdall into his hands. "You go on with Sonya to the rendezvous. The tickets and money are in here. The important thing is to get her away. But I *have* to see that Williams is all right or if I can help him. I'll join you at the rendezvous if I can, but don't wait beyond the appointed time, just go — all the way if you have to!"

"Are you sure about this, Toby?" There was a strange note in Alex's voice. "How the devil will you ever find him?"

"Certain—just go on, as fast as you can. I have the dog, she'll find him."

Suddenly Sonya's arms were around him, her wet cheek pressed to his. "Oh father," she sobbed, "I love you. Whatever happens now remember that. Please remember that and forgive me!" She was tugged away from him by Alex's impatient hand and they disappeared into the darkness.

The dog was tugging frantically at Toby's restraining hold and uttering pathetic little whimpers. He tried to soothe her as he dragged her back up to the cabin, hastily found a short length of rope and tied it to her collar. Then he whispered in Welsh, "All right, Jess, go find him, go find Williams. . . ." His arm was almost wrenched from its socket as she lunged urgently forward. They hurtled downhill at a breakneck pace and he lost all sense of time and direction. There came the sound of two more shots, this time much closer at hand. The dog made a frantic leap, unbalancing him and he went sprawling, the rope slipping from his hand. By the time he scrambled up she had disappeared.

He stood like a statue, filled with helpless desolation: to continue to look for Williams now would be futile until he could see, and once it was light enough for this he himself would be a sitting target for the men on the hill. He looked out at the unseen horizon that was already greying into the first flush of dawn. So be it then, he thought, but I'll damn well give them a run for their money first. Then he started to climb back up the mountain.

Toby climbed rapidly, his ears straining as the light behind him strengthened into a pearly grey. Now he could see the crest and the black maw of the cavern's mouth. Increasing his pace, he climbed to within a hundred yards of his goal, then turned and looked behind him. Lower down, he could make out at least six black specks advancing towards him. With a final spurt he reached the grille, unlocked and reversed the padlock so that it hung inside and locked himself in. Then he strode down to the big chamber, collected his sleeping bag, binoculars, and a bottle of brandy, and returned to the grille. There he cleared out the digging equipment from the nook just inside the entrance, spread out the bag and settled full length on it so that he was out of sight. He pulled the gun and a box of ammunition from his pocket and placed them beside him, then trained his glasses downhill. The figures had taken on clearer definition and he could hear faint shouts. He sat up, took a long swig of brandy, gave a satisfied sigh, and lay down again to resume his scanning.

Nothing short of a bulldozer would penetrate that grille; they could not smoke him out or burn him out, because he could always retreat into the inner fastnesses of the cave. All they could do would be to starve him out, and that would take time, a lot of time, and time was what he needed more than anything else. A new sound came upon straining ears, the unmistakable throb of a helicopter. Could it be the unknown organizer of all this, appearing from the skies for the last act? His spirits began to rise — if so, they were playing the game his way at last. The siege of the Folly had begun, and he was ready for them.

Chapter 20

Penny sat clutching the phone in a state of dumb-founded bewilderment, as Mrs. Walker's anxious voice crackled with excitement at the other end. "Ever so insistent he was that you get in touch with him right away! Said it was a matter of life and death to you. Of course I pretended I didn't know where you were or what he was talking about, but he just went on and on. Wouldn't take no for an answer. Said I was to have you contact him at that number I gave at the earliest possible moment; that he wouldn't wait beyond four this afternoon and that the blood of you-know-who would be on your head! So I said I'd do my best, but he just repeated what I just said — very threatening-like — and rang off."

"Are you sure it was Selwyn Long?" Penny was still trying to grapple with the implications of this bomb-shell.

"Well, that's who he *said* he was." Mrs. Walker's voice soared. "Oh, Dr. Spring, whatever are you going to do? That poor girl! Fair gave me the shivers, he did!"

"I don't know," Penny said flatly. "But don't you worry about it, I'll take care of it. If he calls you back, just say you've passed the message and not to bother you again. And if he does, call Inspector Grey at the Yard." She hung up and sat gazing vacantly at the phone. A very large orange cat, a member of Miss Penrose's growing horde, who had taken an unaccountable and violent fancy to her, sprang heavily into her lap. It proceeded to gaze adoringly up into her face, amber eyes slitted in bliss, as it kneaded her lap vigorously with needle-sharp claws. She absentmindedly stroked it, eliciting a purr like a diesel engine, as she tried to decide what to do.

When the phone rang she had pounced on it, hoping for an update from Gregor Vadik, but to hear from Long was the very last thing she had expected. She glanced in agonized indecision at the clock: two-thirty, an hour and a half until Long's set deadline, although the significance of that hour totally escaped her. Dare she wait for Vadik? Her mind reasoned one way while her edgy nerves shrieked for immediate action—the nerves won. She picked up the phone and dialed the given number. A Cockney voice answered and she asked for Long. " 'Ang on," the voice said, and she sat trying to analyze the background noises. There was music and a faint clatter—dishes, glasses? It must be a restaurant or a pub.

"Selwyn Long here. Who is this?"

"Dr. Spring returning your call. And to say that I'm surprised at its reported content is a vast understatement. I have not the faintest idea what you intend to convey with all this melodrama."

"So the old biddy did know where you were." There was an edge of satisfaction on his voice. "And come off it! You knew damn well what I was talking about. I suppose you think you've been bloody clever about all this, but let me tell you something. I've one or two trumps of my own yet to play. So I suggest you listen

215

and listen carefully. I know *exactly* where Toby Glendower, the girl, and your son are, and have the means *and* the motivation to throw them to the wolves at any moment I damn well please. Whether I do so is entirely up to you. I'm proposing a deal—you play along with me and I'll forego the pleasure of seeing that smug rich bastard get his comeuppance."

"Deal?" she echoed stupidly. "And if you do know where Sir Tobias and Alex are, you are way ahead of me. I haven't the faintest idea where they can be or what you are talking about."

"In a pig's eye you don't!" His voice was shrill with mounting anger. "Does Pen y Nai mean anything to you? Or a handy little hideaway nearby? So cut the bloody nonsense and listen. The deal is this. I know you've been playing footsie with Gregor Vadik and that you must have something big on him for him to fool with the likes of you. So get hold of him and tell him he's to get me out of the country by tonight. I'll tell him what I want and the ongoing details when you put me in direct touch. He can do it—he's the original Invisible Man when it comes to borders. It's not that the police can get me for anything—they can't, in spite of what has just happened. But I'm not going to stick around for all the fuss and furor—I have more important fish to fry. What's more it is up to you to lean on Vadik and make it very clear that if he crosses me then you'll cross him. And if *you* cross me I'll make damn sure you never see any of that trio again, and that's a promise." His tone was vicious. "So get at it, *now!*"

"I think you must be mad," she said quietly. "Quite mad. In the first place, I think you're bluffing, and with a very weak hand, too. In the second, I have no means of getting in touch with Vadik at a moment's notice, even if I had a mind to. It is he who contacts me and I have no idea if he will do so before this deadline of yours — whatever that's supposed to mean. And lastly, I have no hold on him — Vadik is in this for his own purposes, and you probably know what they are better than I do."

There was a moment's silence at the other end and then Selwyn said in a much more controlled voice, "So that's the way of it, is it? But I am not bluffing, and *if* things are as you say, it makes no odds, I can handle Vadik. The important thing is for you to act as go-between." His voice dropped and became cajoling. "After all, what's Litvov's death to you? He was a miserable self-serving traitor and no loss to anyone. Aren't you more concerned about the welfare of your loved ones? Just do as I ask and I swear they'll come to no harm."

She was overwhelmed by a furious wave of anger that sent the cat with a startled yowl from her lap. "Aren't *you* forgetting something?" she hissed. "The death of a very gifted young woman whose only fault was that she was too naive and trusting? It's just too bad that England no longer has capital punishment, because I'd like to see you hanged higher than Haman for that. As it is, I hope they put you in prison and throw away the key for the rest of your miserable life!"

"You stupid old cow!" he shrilled. "Why should I kill Mala? You don't understand a bloody thing, do you? Your time is running out fast — *will* you get me Vadik?"

"Go to hell, you murdering bastard!" she cried and slammed down the phone, trembling with rage.

There was an outraged snort behind her and she swung around to see the convulsed face of Miss Penrose staring at her. "If it's not bad enough to be driven out of my own sitting room for these unending calls of yours!" the old woman quavered. "But to hear such terrible profanity in my house! — no, that's too much, just too much. I am a God-fearing woman, so I'm afraid I must ask you to leave immediately. I should never have agreed to let such a horrible person under my roof!"

Penny controlled herself with a vast effort. "I'm sorry to have upset you, Miss Penrose, and I'll go soon enough, but, there's just one more phone call I have to make, then I'll be gone." And she dialed the accommodation number Vadik had given her.

"I want you out *now!*" Miss Penrose shrilled.

Penny held up a commanding hand, as a foreign voice answered the phone and she made her urgent demand. "He's at Scotland Yard," came the surprising answer. "You might catch him there if you hurry. Otherwise where can he reach you?" All she could think of on the spur of the moment was Mrs. Walker's. "Ah, I know that one," came the satisfied reply. "And I'll see he gets the message."

"It's *extremely* urgent," she pressed. Hanging up, she immediately redialed and called a cab. "I'll be out of here as soon as the taxi comes," she informed her outraged hostess, and hustled upstairs to throw her things in her bags.

In the taxi, zipping through the relatively light traffic of a London afternoon toward Scotland Yard, a measure of calm returned. She began to wonder what had spooked Long into making such a daring and rash move. He had as good as confessed to Litvov's murder, although she realized this damning verbal admission, so easily denied, would not stand up as evidence in an English court. She also realized, belatedly, that by letting her own temper get the better of her, she had done the worst possible thing. She ought to have played along with him, set up a meeting and then left it up to Vadik or the police to corner him. Worst of all, she had needlessly added to the hazards of the fugitives in their escape.

By the time the taxi screamed into the Yard her spirits had plummeted. She crawled out, bag and baggage, deposited them at the feet of the startled, familiar sergeant, and inquired anxiously after the whereabouts of Inspector Grey and Gregor Vadik. "A very burly and hairy man, with a big beard?" she gulped. "I've been told he's here and it is vital I see him immediately."

The sergeant had conceived quite a fondness for this strange little woman who kept popping unexpectedly into his otherwise routine life, so he looked down at her indulgently. "Yes, I think I know the one you mean. Came in earlier with another man. I believe they're still with the Inspector, but let's find out." He hefted the cases. "What shall I do with these?"

"Oh, could you just stow them somewhere and I'll pick them up later?" she said mournfully. "I got kicked out of my lodgings, but I couldn't take the time to drop them off. Please! — every moment is vital."

They trudged through the maze of corridors, abandoning the cases at a reception desk on the way, and elicited the fact that Vadik was no longer with Grey but still in the building. They tracked him to a small waiting room, where he was sitting like a hairy Buddha, his eyes closed and a smug smirk on his full lips. "Oh thank you, thank you so much!" Penny almost hugged the benevolent sergeant in her vast relief. "I'll be fine now." And the minute he was gone she wheeled on Vadik, who had opened his eyes and was regarding her with quizzical surprise. "What in the name of Heaven has happened? I've just had Long on the phone and he as good as confessed to Litvov's murder!"

His dark eyes opened a shade wider and the smirk

became a grin. "Oh, yes? Spooked is he? Good! Spence must have sneaked off and warned him about me. My visit to Herbert worked like the proverbial charm. The stolen icon was my foot in the door but it was the photos that did the trick. Not a very strong character is Herbert, and very spiteful to boot. He's in there now making a statement to Grey that effectively shoots down *both* of Long's alibis, although he won't put himself on the hook by saying Long admitted anything to him. Anyway, it's enough for the police to go after Long, and with some solid digging they should be able to get enough evidence — at least for Mala's murder. The police will be glad to get their hands on him — where is he?"

Penny looked at him with a troubled expression. "I don't know, and oh, it's not as simple as that! You'd best listen . . ." and related the substance of the phone call. Vadik's face transformed as she spoke into a glowering, threatening mask.

"Damnation! Why the devil didn't you play along with him? It would have been so much simpler that way. My way," he growled. "It would have solved everything."

She felt an icy chill at the implication. "I lost my temper," she faltered. "All I could see was Mala's face. I didn't think." She looked at her watch which showed twenty minutes to four. "But what about this deadline of his — four o'clock? What do you make of that?"

He shrugged. "Nothing. And before you say another word, let me make something very clear. I don't want to know anything about Sir Tobias, his daughter or your son, their present whereabouts or ongoing plans. You'll notice that in our last meetings I carefully avoided the subject. There is nothing I can or will do about that. I came in on this to help Toby clear his daughter of a murder charge and that I have done. The rest I *cannot* get involved in."

Her temper, egged on by her own guilt feelings, flared again. "Damn you, Vadik! You were in on this from the start for purposes of your own, so don't try to snow me! I think the least you can do now is to tell me *why*, and who the hell you're working for. I'm in no position to go shouting it from the rooftops and it may help."

He softened as he looked at her outraged little face and held up a placating hand. "All right, I'll tell you what I can. I'm an independent operator, as you know, and a good many countries find me very useful. In this instance I was wearing two hats—helping the Russians about the icon business, and helping your own CIA on another matter." His expression became grim again. "A series of coincidences between the two led me onto Long's trail. I discovered that for some time he had been a double agent and, as such, was the direct cause of the death of an American agent. He sold him out to the Russians for cash. I owed that agent, just as I owed Toby—he saved my life once—so I agreed to help the CIA get the man who did it and stop the leak in MI5. As I see it, that was Long's motive in Litvov's murder. Litvov was ready to bolt; he needed more money but had already bled Long dry. He planned to blackmail Carstairs using evidence of a prior sexual relationship with Long. And, more importantly, he was going to reveal Long's activities as a double agent. Long knew that would be the kiss of death. Even if Carstairs hushed it up for the sake of his own career, a powerful man like him would certainly have seen to it that Long was quietly kicked out, and he could not afford for that to happen. I imagine Long had one last desperate go at

Litvov before Carstair's anticipated appearance, and when that failed he lost his temper and in a blind rage did that spur-of-the-moment killing. I think Mala, in all the hide-and-seek the Russians were playing that night, must have spotted him either going to or coming from the kitchen. For that she had to be silenced." He stopped abruptly.

"Yes, that all makes sense," she said edgily. "But it's of small help to me now. What am I going to *do*? Toby's in danger and I've no idea how to help him. I can't even warn him"

Vadik eyed her. "Well, as I've said, I can't help you with that, except to try and get on Long's trail myself, which I will do. But if you want some advice, I'd say better the devil you know than the devil you don't." He smiled grimly. "Maybe you should ring Grey in on this before it's too late. I have considerable faith in the British police."

"But if I do that it might ruin their escape plans!" she cried. "And if they're caught, Sonya will have to be given up to the Russians."

"I think you should have more faith in your eminent partner," he chided. "Toby is a very resourceful man. They may already be gone and Long's statement an empty bluff. Is it that motorcycle gang that worries you?"

She looked at him in sudden suspicion. "Why are you still here at the Yard?" she demanded.

"Oh, that. Well, our Herbert is a very nervous sort, so I promised I'd keep a personal eye on him until Long is safely in custody. Grey was all for it—he obviously thought it would also be an excellent way of keeping an unobtrusive eye on *me*." He grinned sardonically at her.

Their confrontation was interrupted by a uniformed constable. "Mr. Spence is ready to leave now, Mr.

Vadik. Inspector Grey wishes to know if there is anything else you need?"

Vadik eyed Penny significantly. "Just that this lady be shown into him immediately. She has some important information concerning the case."

"Certainly, sir." They were ushered along the passage and before Grey's door stood Herbert Spence. He was sweating profusely, his large face a pale green, his eyes haunted and flickering wildly. He positively grabbed at Vadik like a drowning man as the latter came up to him. He was in such a state of panic that he did not so much as recognize Penny as she was shepherded past him into the office. The constable went over to Grey, who was on the phone, murmured in his ear and took a discreet departure. Grey hung up and looked up at her. "Well, what now, Dr. Spring? Come to make a clean breast of it and to tell me where they are?"

"I've heard from Long," she said, and launched again into a carefully edited recital of the phone call.

"It's an interesting confirmation of what has just happened," he said heavily. "But a verbal confession would not stand up without witnesses, as you well know. It might add a little to the accumulating weight of evidence however."

"I realize that," she cried. "But that's not what's important. What is the significance of that four o'clock deadline which . . ." she glanced in agony at his wall clock, " . . . has already passed? Whatever he was going to do, he'll have done it by now. It somehow concerns the Glendowers."

"I've no . . ." Grey began, then paused and rifled madly through the papers before him. "Wait! Maybe this is it. Korkov just made a swift trip to East Germany. According to our information, he was booked to return to Heathrow at two forty-five. Four o'clock would be about the time he'd get back to the Russian Embassy. That imaginative scenario you hurled at me the other day may not have been so wild after all. It looks as if Long may be about to sell the Glendowers out to the Russians in a last desperate attempt to save his own hide. In which case there's nothing to worry about."

"What do you mean there's nothing to worry about?" she shouted. "They're in danger!"

Grey was unruffled. "It must be quite evident to you that we've been keeping an eye on Korkov. If *he* moves on this, we move. It is just what I wanted. We trail him, he leads us to the Glendowers and we'll have two birds with one stone. Not to mention a very nice screw to turn on the Russians."

She pounced on that. "Would that mean you could get Sonya off the hook? That she could stay?"

"I'm afraid not. As I have repeatedly explained, there is nothing we can do about that. If she had asked for political asylum *before* all this started there may have been some hope, but now . . ." he shrugged resignedly.

Almost beside herself with frustration, Penny yelled, "So is that all you're going to do? Sit there while Toby and the girl might be in God knows what peril from Long's thugs?"

"And I advise you to calm down," he snapped. "Beyond confirming what Vadik had already discovered — that three of them were no longer in London, we have no indication that this so-called motorcycle gang are involved at all with the chase after the Glendowers. If we *do* get any indication then we may move on it, but, as I've said, our best bet is to wait and see what Korkov does, if anything. And to send out a dragnet for Long. It is really up to you, Dr. Spring: if you want your mind at rest, tell me where they are and we'll pick them up. If not, my best advice is to go home, calm down, and I will let you know if anything develops—that I promise." He got up. "Now I really have a lot to do, so you must excuse me. Where can I reach you?"

"Oh, the Fulham number, I suppose," she said grudgingly. Still desperately torn between her desire for immediate action and her duty to Toby, she stamped angrily out. The baggage was collected, another cab summoned, and she was deposited before the little shop just as Mrs. Walker was closing for the night.

Having already received an irate phone call from her sanctimonious cousin, Mrs. Walker was both unsurprised at her reappearance and flatteringly solicitous to Penny's careworn spirit. "I'm ever so sorry Clara went on like that; crazy, she is, just like I told you. But you just come right in and sit by the fire and I'll get you a nice cup of tea and you can get settled in again at your leisure. You can stay here as long as you like, my dear," she clucked. And tea, hot buttered crumpets and honey having been provided, she wisely made herself scarce, leaving Penny to gloomy contemplation.

Fortified by her tea, she dragged herself upstairs and, foregoing yet another unpacking, sank exhaustedly onto the bed for a nap. When she again opened her eyes the room was dark and Mrs. Walker was shaking her urgently. "The phone, Dr. Spring. The man from the Yard."

She scrambled down to it, still groggy with sleep. "Yes? What is it?"

"There have been developments." Underlying Grey's even tones there was suppressed excitement. "Korkov has just taken off in an official Embassy car with their intelligence officer and two of their armed Embassy guards. He's heading west. Further, reports are in from the Caernarfon police of complaints from several small villages south of there, about the activities of a large motorcycle gang roaming the area. Naturally we are keeping an eye on Korkov's progress, but I put it to you that now is the time for you to speak up. If Korkov meets up with that gang they will undoubtedly converge on wherever the Glendowers are hiding out. It would be advisable if the police were there ahead of them to head off possible violence. The jig's up. One way or another the Glendowers will be trapped. So I suggest you tell me where they are and save a lot of unpleasantness."

She realized it was put up or shut up time. "On one condition," she said, " . . . that I go with you." And to forestall his protest hurried on. "Sir Tobias is an extremely stubborn man, but if I go with you he'll listen to me. I guarantee it."

"It's irregular, but then this whole affair has been irregular. All right. Agreed. I'll pick you up in a police car in about half an hour. Where are they."

"As I've said,. I don't know exactly." She was still cautious. "But I know approximately where he *might* be in Wales. He has some property near a village called Pen y Nai. I believe it is somewhere in the area of Snowdon." She could hear the shuffling of paper. "Got it!" Grey was triumphant. "Now where exactly is this property?"

"That I really don't know," she confessed. "But if we go to Pen y Nai we could probably locate his tenant farmer, a man named Williams. The rest would be up to you."

"Good enough. Then in half an hour?" He hung up.

But things were still not to be as straightforward as she and the police anticipated. Reports on the progress of the Korkov car, which was an hour and a half ahead of them, came in at regular intervals over the two-way radio as they headed for Wales. Then, to their consternation, the Korkov car stopped in Shrewsbury and the Russian party booked into a hotel for the night. Grey cursed softly, "What the hell now? Well, keep an eye on them. We'll be there ourselves in about an hour." He cheered up somewhat when the next report came in of a large black man on a motorcycle who had held a brief conference with Korkov in the hotel's parking lot and then had roared off into the night. "They must be waiting for daylight. Good! That gives me an idea." He looked searchingly at Penny. "Nothing else you'd like to add to what you've said? It would help with the positioning of my men."

"I believe Sir Tobias has been excavating a cave shelter somewhere near Pen y Nai," she admitted. "It is probably high up on one of those mountains — but I don't know which." She fully expected that they would stop in Shrewsbury, but after a brief consultation at the main police station, Grey rejoined her in the car. "Liverpool," he ordered the driver.

"Liverpool?" she exclaimed, her fears returning in full flood. "Why are we going there?"

"We're going to the airport. I'll arrange for two police helicopters to be ready at first light, if Korkov starts to move. By helicopter we'll be over Pen y Nai in twenty minutes at most. It should give them one hell of a surprise."

It was well after midnight by the time they arrived. "Would you like to check into a hotel and get some rest?" Grey asked, "We won't be taking off until six o'clock."

"No, I'm far too worried to sleep," she said tightly. "I'd rather stick with you, if you don't mind."

"Then we'll park by the helicopters and maybe we both can get some rest," he comforted. "Don't feel too badly about this, Dr. Spring. I'm sorry for the Glendowers, but it is best this way, I assure you."

"I hope you are right," she retorted grimly. And after

he had completed the arrangements for their dawn
flight a somnolent silence descended on the darkened
car. In spite of everything she did drowse, and by Grey's
even breathing he too had drifted off. They were roused
by an insistent rapping on the window. A uniformed
constable stuck his head in and muttered at Grey, who
stretched, groaned and nodded. "Get the pilots and the
squad ready," he ordered and turned to her in the back
seat. "Korkov's just left Shrewsbury — it should take him
less than an hour, but we'll be there in thirty minutes.
He's right on schedule and should be there by dawn."

With a quickening sense of excitement Penny boarded
the helicopter, and as it lifted off the pad and circled
over the grey, flat waters of the Mersey she could see the
misty beginnings of dawn to the east. By the time they
reached Pwhelli Tor and were circling the village of Pen
y Nai, they could make out the dark shapes of men
advancing up the hillside, as well as a black car thread-
ing its way up a little mountain road and flanked by two
motorcyclists. "Right!" Grey said into the radio. "Move
your men in now and begin rounding those blighters up.
Anywhere you can see to put down?" he demanded of
the pilot.

The pilot grunted and took another circle around, as
Penny's anxious eyes made out the telltale dark opening
of a cave just beneath the crest. "Seems to be a bit of flat
pasture by that farmhouse," he shouted above the throb
of the engine. "I could put down there."

Penny clutched at Grey's arm. "Look, there's a cave
and some of those men are almost up to it. Can't you do
something? They may be armed!"

"Circle around the crest again as low as you can,"
Grey ordered. "Make sure those men see the police
markings on the copter. Then put down." The pilot
swooped obediently and Penny had a vision of upturned

startled faces. Several of the men started to scramble back down the hill. The few who remained milled around for a minute in confusion before the steel fence and then started helter-skelter after their more faintly hearted brethren. "That takes care of that," Grey said smugly, as they settled down in the pasture.

He set a brisk pace up the hill, flanked by the two policemen who had accompanied them, while the second helicopter settled by the first and discharged its squad of police, who started to chase and collar as many of the fleeing bikers as their numbers permitted. Penny puffed along beside Grey, gazing anxiously upwards, but there was no sign of life at the cave mouth. As they got to within earshot, Grey used the bullhorn. "Sir Tobias!" he roared. "This is the police. I must ask you to give yourself up quietly and to surrender your daughter. We have the area blanketed. There is no hope of you getting away." He waited expectantly but there was no response or sign of life. With a snort of disgust he handed the horn to Penny. "You try!"

"Toby!" she called anxiously. "If you're in there, please come out! Right now."

Again for a few moments nothing happened, then his tall spindly figure appeared from the blackness and peered myopically through the grille's bars. "Somebody call me? Good heavens, Inspector Grey! And Penny too! What on earth are you doing here?"

Grey went up to the grille and rattled it impatiently. "Open up, Sir Tobias, you're wasting time. It's all over. I'm sorry but I must take you both into custody."

"Both?' Toby echoed blankly, unlocking it. "Whatever do you mean? I'm here alone. Digging. Very interesting site this."

"Oh, come off it! If she's hiding here we'll find her. Tell us where Sonya is."

"In Moscow, I presume—how should I know?" Toby's round blue eyes were widely innocent. "I dropped her off at Heathrow airport, just as I promised. Then I came on here. I often do that when I'm upset, and I was—very." Grey had pushed past him and was snapping orders at the policemen who in somewhat bewildered fashion started to search the passages. "There's no one here but me," Toby reiterated. "Come, let me show you around." He led them back into the big chamber where a lone sleeping bag lay beside the lantern and the cook-stove on which a single mug sat. "I've been camping out," he explained blandly, while Penny hugged herself in secret glee. "Would you like to see my excavation?" He waved the lantern over the deep pit.

Grey was quietly swelling with rage. "Do you mean to try to tell me that you were unaware there has been a general hue and cry out after you and your daughter for the past few days? I'm telling you it is no use! Give it up right now."

Toby looked at him in blank astonishment, "*Has* there? Good Heavens, no! You see that up here I am quite out of touch—quite. . . ." He waved his hand vaguely around. "No radio, no papers, not even the telly . . ." he giggled fatuously. "Dear me! Do tell me what's happened. I have no idea what this is all about."

"Perhaps you'd like to explain why you were locked in here and why this place was being besieged by a gang of thugs—apparently hired by Selwyn Long—when we arrived?" the inspector grated. "And why a contingent from the Russian Embassy, headed by Korkov, are now being questioned down in Pen y Nai?"

"How extraordinary! Yes, I *did* see some people tres-passing on my property, come to think of it. So many of these vandals around these days even here, it's really too shocking! Nothing is safe, nothing!" Toby was at his pompous best. "So I just locked myself in and got on with my work. Nothing really for them to steal around here, so I knew they'd go away sooner or later."

Grey glared helplessly at him. "You'll have to come with me, Sir Tobias. You are under provisory arrest for impeding the police in the pursuit of their duties."

"Well, of course, if you insist, Inspector," Toby said mildly. "Although I don't quite see what I've done wrong—digging on my own property and minding my own business? Doubtless I shall be allowed to call my lawyer?" He held out his bony wrists. "Are you going to handcuff me?"

"Oh, for God's sake!" Grey growled disgustedly. "Just come along!" and stamped out of the chamber. Behind his back, Toby favored Penny with a sly wink and a mischievous grin. She could have kissed him.

Chapter   21

Their secret elation grew in proportion to Grey's mounting frustration. The villagers steadfastly maintained that they were aware of Toby's presence but were unaware of anyone else up at the shelter. The rounded-up, unhappy bikers, though questioned and cross-questioned singly by a battery of police, were of equally small help. Many of them were only vaguely aware of their purpose in being there. "Kind of like a treasure hunt, it wos," one bleary eyed biker explained. "Ten quid a day expenses and an 'undred' for the one who spotted the Rolls and got the old geezer wot owns it. Girl? Nah, I never 'eard of no girl."

The police had their hands full in keeping the irate villagers and the bikers apart, and frequent shouting matches erupted between the two groups. The ringleader among the complainants was Williams, who, to Toby's vast relief, appeared to be all in one piece. "Trespassers they were!" he roared. "Scattered my sheep, killed one of my dogs — had him chained to the barn and they bashed his head in and broke in — thieving they were! I want the law on them." He identified five of the group, whom the police, thankful for something concrete to do, promptly arrested.

Several of these hurled counter accusations, claiming they'd been shot at. "Crazy old perisher was going to kill us! Set his dogs on us too—I got bit," one shrilled.

"Within my rights, I was. Defending my home," the old man countered. "Trespassing, they were. Killed my dog and done destruction to my property. I warned them, and shot over their heads. Gun all licensed too."

All this while Penny was sitting quietly by Toby in the back of the police car, unable to communicate because a uniformed driver was also on watch over them. Deprived of the chance to vent the questions that were seething within her, she concentrated on what was going on outside. Of the group from The Purple Pigeon, only the stocky ex-boxer was in evidence. He had apparently sprained an ankle for he was hobbling painfully. He was, she noted, also being very uncooperative, answering the police with curt monosyllables or shrugging disdainfully. No one seemed to know the source of the money offered. "Ask Cannon," said one biker, and was rewarded by dark looks from his fellows. But of Cannon, the big black man, there was no sign. Another complained piteously that his bike had been stolen ". . . while I was having a bit of a kip," but in all the rest of the hurly-burly no one paid any attention to him.

At one point, one of the villagers, a dark, thin-faced man, managed to edge up to the car and mutter something in Welsh to Toby. The driver immediately sprang out and waved him away. Penny could feel Toby tense and his mouth clamped in a grim line. "What did that man say to you?" the driver demanded.

"Just asked if there was anything he could do for me in this ridiculous situation," Toby said tightly. Suddenly he was restive. "Where *is* Inspector Grey? I really must insist, if I am under arrest, that we get on our way. I have not yet been allowed to contact my solicitor and I demand my rights."

The driver looked unhappy. "The Inspector has gone to deal with those Russians. I'm afraid you'll have to wait, sir."

Toby consulted his watch pointedly. "I have already been waiting over two hours—held incommunicado on a ridiculous charge for which you have had no substantiation. This will not look well for the police in a court of law."

"I'll see what I can do." The driver beckoned another policeman over, muttered at him and watched him disappear into the crowd. When he reappeared some twenty minutes later it was to announce Toby could make his phone call from the post office under his escort. Toby got out, and to Penny's amusement, some of the villagers immediately struck up a full-throated rendering of "All Through the Night," the Welsh national anthem. The circus-like atmosphere grew as they followed him, singing and clapping to the post office.

Before Toby reappeared, Grey returned to the car, his face flushed and mirroring his inner frustration. "The Russians claim they were on a sightseeing trip, but were rather hard put to explain keeping company with one of the bikers—the mohawk-haired one; the other was gone before our men could get to them. I could not hold them on any charge, but fortunately their intelligence officer seems as upset by this ridiculous situation as I am, so they are heading back to London. We're holding the biker on general principles." He looked helplessly at the singing, cheering crowd that was now escorting Toby back from the post office. "This is the most absurd position I have ever been in, and I hope for everyone's sake Sir Tobias has some satisfactory explanation for all this and is now prepared to help rather than hinder us." He looked searchingly at Penny. "The hunt for Sonya Glendower is not going to be called off, you know. So tell me, Dr. Spring—where is your son?"

"I haven't the least idea!" she cried. "And that is the plain, honest truth, Inspector. I only wish I *did* know!"

Toby got back into the car. "My lawyer will be at the Yard to meet us. I told him we would be there by four o'clock, for I trust we will be starting very shortly." Again he looked pointedly at his watch. "He has advised me to say nothing until I arrive and I shall follow his advice."

Grey snorted angrily. "Very well, if that's your attitude. I had hoped for more consideration. I have to give some ongoing orders, but we'll be on our way in about twenty minutes. Sooner, if you can get rid of those followers of yours."

Toby smiled faintly, got out of the car and held up his arms for calm. He let forth a string of mellifluous Welsh; there were smiles and nods, and the crowd immediately began to disperse. Williams came towards the car. "I hope you don't mind, Inspector, but Williams is also my caretaker and he'll have to secure and tidy up the cavern and the cabin. Since you have searched both, I assume you have no further objection?" Toby said smoothly.

"Go ahead," Grey snapped. "But I must insist you converse in English."

Toby reached into his inner pocket, extracted several ten-pound notes and handed them to Williams. "If you would be good enough to tidy up and move my camping stuff back into the cabin—all of it—I'd appreciate it." He looked squarely at Williams. "This should cover it for your time and trouble. Perhaps you could use some of it to join your wife for a holiday, I'm sure you could use a rest after all this turmoil."

Grey pounced on that. "Your wife isn't here?"

"No. Went to see my daughter in Caernarfon, oh, two or three days past."

"And what would her address and telephone number be?"

The old man gave them and slid an amused look at Toby, a twinkle in his eye, as Grey scribbled it down. "Took a sudden longing to be with our Gwenny she did."

"Er—I think, considering the complaints you've lodged against these bikers, it would be best if one of my men went over your house and outbuildings to check if anything is missing," Grey said casually.

"Most welcome to, I'm sure—any time." The twinkle intensified.

"I'll be in touch as soon as this nonsense is settled," Toby broke in. "Oh, yes, one other thing. Would you have Evans drive the Rolls to London and leave it at my solicitors? You have the address." He handed over the keys. "I'll send a message through Mrs. Evans as soon as possible and we can talk on her phone. Many thanks for everything, my friend."

"It was a pleasure, Glendower-bach—a real pleasure. And if there is anything else, just let me know." The old man grinned, and was ushered away by a policeman.

When the police car finally did get underway and they distanced themselves from the village, the Tor shrinking to an insignificant speck behind them, Penny could feel some of the tension go out of Toby. To while away the tedium of the trip, she recounted, in stream-lined form suitable for Grey's keen ears, the outcome of her own adventures and Vadik's investigations. It did not seem to cheer Toby as much as she had hoped, although he made appropriate comments at suitable intervals to show he was listening.

At the Yard they were met by a stony-faced Pontifex, who insisted on a preliminary private interview with his client. Penny was left to cool her heels in a waiting room for what seemed to her an inordinate amount of time. To calm her jumping nerves she made up various scenarios of what had happened on Toby's mountain, and comforted herself with the fact that Sonya—and presumably Alex along with her—had got clean away. When Toby did finally reappear, accompanied by a now-smug Pontifex, she almost sprang at them. "Well?"

"I'm free to go." Toby was still very preoccupied. "But I have to hold myself available, so I am going back to the Athenaeum. We'll have dinner there. Pontifex will drive us."

As soon as they were in the car and away from the Yard, she said eagerly, "Well, did they get away? Is everything all right?"

"I hope so," he said heavily, and related the bare bones of what had happened. "The thing that worries me is that Evans—the man who came to the car— managed to tell me that they did *not* make the rendezvous with him. I don't understand it and I don't like it."

"But they *couldn't* have still been there, the police and the bikers were all over that mountain!" she cried. "They *must* have got away somehow."

"I hope so," he repeated. "But how?"

"That biker—the one whom no one paid any attention to—who claimed his bike had been stolen. Maybe they pinched that!" she exclaimed.

He brightened. "Yes, that is a possibility. Well, all we can do is wait and see."

And so the waiting began. A fillip to their hopes came

when they learned the stolen bike had been found in Liverpool. Penny was quietly jubilant. "They must have made it to Ireland. If they make the flight from Dublin, we should be hearing from them tomorrow." But on the morrow no such message came, or on the day after. She made some discreet inquiries from the airline as to the presence of the Doctors Spring on the Dublin to Brazil flight and was informed that, yes, the seats had been booked and paid for, but that the parties in question had been "no-show": it was then the fear had started.

"Where can they be?" Penny demanded, trying to mask her inner agony. A stone-faced Toby quietly instituted a search by the people of Pen y Nai of the whole mountain and the adjacent villages, but not the least sign of the fugitives was found. A summons to the Yard they answered with poker-faced alacrity, but it was only to parry some searching questions from Grey, who had been alerted to the presence of the abandoned rental car at the Nebo inn and had traced it back to Alex. Both of them disclaimed knowledge of how it had got there or what it signified, and, surprisingly, the inspector did not press them on it. Since his return he had regained his temper and was back to his urbane, elegant and amiable self. He unbent enough to inform them that Korkov had been recalled to Moscow and that the Russian Embassy had become a lot less intransigent than it had been. The knowledge that Long was now being sought in connection with both the murders of the Russians had apparently led to this sudden change of attitude. But of Long himself there was still no sign.

Another horrible idea had come to Penny. "What if Long went to Wales himself? What if he has got them? He has killed twice, so he'd not stop there. He may be vindictive enough or desperate enough to use them as hostages. Maybe that's why the Russians have turned amiable. They may be bargaining with him."

Toby had scoffed at that idea. "I can't see a man of Long's physique and temperament taking on a man almost twice his size and a very strong active girl on a mountain in the dark! Besides, if he had been there, one of the bikers would have split on him by now. You heard what Grey had to say about that: they've nearly all been let go, but are a very disgruntled lot because they never got paid, so they've spilled all they know. Granted that isn't much, but it does tie Long firmly into the original idea."

Nonetheless, she was not entirely convinced and so tried to contact Vadik to see if he could throw additional light on the matter, or help them with a covert search. To her further frustration the mystery man had disappeared from view, his own work apparently accomplished. A week passed thus, during which Toby aged a year for every day before her eyes. The only thing that kept her going was the conviction that her son was still alive: if Alex were dead she felt sure she would *know*, and she had no such feeling.

Then her theory of Long's involvement in the disappearance was given a sudden and dramatic quietus. Grey called the Athenaeum, where she was having another dismal lunch with the despondent Toby, and they both answered the call. "We've found Long," Grey said tersely. "Not that it did us much good. He was dead — an apparent suicide, although he left neither note nor confession. Has been dead at least five days according to the post-mortem. Took pills and booze and then stuck his head in a gas oven in this little *pied-à-terre* he had in Shoreditch. Luckily the oven was on a pay-meter or the whole place might have gone up. It was just around the corner from The Purple Pigeon, as a matter of fact. We picked up Cannon yesterday and sweated the address out of him." He paused. "Probably just as well. Now we can mark the two cases closed, but if Long had ever come to trial, I don't think we'd have had enough solid evidence to convict him."

A terrible thought came to her—had Vadik got there first and done it his way after all? "I suppose it *was* suicide?" she managed to get out.

There was a slight hesitation before Grey said, "That is how the death will be listed. Why?"

"Oh, nothing. I just wondered," she said hurriedly.

"Well, I thought I'd let you know. In our files Long will be named as the murderer of both Litvov and Mala, and that, of course, exonerates your daughter completely of any complicity in either murder, Sir Tobias. Otherwise it does not alter the present situation, although her continued absence at least gives you more time to regularize her situation."

"I am doing just that," Toby growled.

"Good luck to you then," Grey said surprisingly, and rang off.

"I wonder if Vadik did get to him after all," she muttered as they returned to the dining room.

"Offing murderers is one of his specialties, as we know from past experience," Toby said gloomily. "And in this case I, for one, don't give a damn." And they resumed their cooling luncheon.

Three more days dragged by with no further word, and Penny felt she was quietly going out of her mind. Then the long-awaited bombshell burst. She was giving Mrs. Walker a hand in restocking the shelves of her little shop, when the phone went and she answered it. "Ma, it's Alex. . . ." She almost fainted at the sound of his voice. "Sorry we couldn't call before, but this is urgent.

Get Toby and come over to the American Embassy in Grosvenor Square right away—Room 221."

"Where have you been all this time? Are you all right? Where's Sonya?" she yelled.

"Later, ma, later. We're both fine. Just get Toby as quickly as you can. I have to call Grey now."

"You're not giving yourselves up?" she cried in horror.

"No, I'll explain everything, but I can't talk now. Just get here."

She was in such a daze that later she could never remember how she and Toby got there. In what seemed a small eternity they were being ushered into an office in the Embassy, where a widely grinning Alex and a radiant Sonya flanked a very unhappy-looking bald-headed man at the desk. As her son rushed at her with arms outstretched, she didn't know whether to hug him or hit him, and could feel the tears of relief starting to pour down her face. "It's all right now, Ma. Don't get upset," Alex whispered as he kissed her. "Trust me. It's going to be all right." Sonya was in her father's arms, equally bathed in tears and gabbling at a great rate in Russian.

On this tender scene of reunion erupted a grim-faced Inspector Grey. He marched up to Sonya, "I'm afraid your abortive flight is over, Sonya Danarova Glendower. I'm sorry but you'll have to come with me and remain in protective custody until such time as the British government confirms your being handed over to your own government. I'm glad you've at last had the good sense to give yourself up."

In a flash Alex was by her side and, detaching her from Toby's possessive grip, took her hand. "No, Inspector, that is what you cannot do, and that is not why I called you here. I may remind you that here in the Embassy you are on American soil and you have no authority here, and that this is no longer a matter for the British government, it is a matter for the *American* government. Sonya is no longer Miss Glendower, she is *Missus* Alexander Spring—the wife of an American citizen. We were married on the US Nato base in Iceland yesterday morning, and I have already claimed political asylum for her. . . ." The bald-headed man at the desk looked as if he might burst into tears at any moment.

Penny felt her knees give and she sank hastily into a chair. Toby, equally astounded, tottered and collapsed into another one. They gazed open-mouthed as Alex produced several official-looking bits of paper which he handed to Grey and continued, "Why I needed you here is to verify that Sonya is not wanted by the British police for any *criminal* act. Mr. Hayes here . . ." he nodded at the miserable Foreign Service officer, "needs that verification before he can issue her a visa for the United States. Since I see by the papers that the Litvov case is over, I hope you can do so."

For a breathless moment Grey just looked at the young couple, then to everyone's surprise he threw back his head and laughed. "You Springs certainly have a lot of nerve! But . . ." he grinned wolfishly at the despondent Mr. Hayes, "I am sure the British government will be only too happy to toss this hot potato into American hands. So yes, Mr. Hayes, bring on your forms—I will duly certify that Sonya is not a wanted criminal. However, I would like to know what your ongoing plans are for getting these young escape artists out of the country. They cannot remain here, as I am sure you understand."

Hayes cleared his throat and blinked nervously. "Quite so," he muttered. "I am far from happy about this myself, Inspector, but. . . ." He glared menacingly at Penny. "Certain branches of the Embassy have indicated their strong support for this step, so I must perforce obey. In short, Dr. and Mrs. Spring will remain in the Embassy until the paperwork is completed and then will be taken by embassy car to Heathrow where they will be placed aboard the first available American plane to New York by an embassy escort. Is that satisfactory?" He sounded as if he wished fervently it would not be.

"Eminently," Grey said affably. "So what and where do I sign?"

"Er, since this may take some time, is it all right if we go elsewhere while you get on with it?" Alex broke in. "We'd like a private word with our parents before saying our goodbyes."

"The man in two-twenty-six is on vacation. You can use that," Hayes glowered. "But you are not to leave this floor."

"Understood," and Alex led the minor stampede down the corridor. Once behind closed doors, he swung around, still holding tightly to Sonya's hand, and addressed Toby. "You are probably very upset about this, but please listen. On my part this was not some madcap quixotic gesture. I've known almost from the first that Sonya was the one for me. I love her, and so for me this is for keeps. However . . ." for the first time he seemed uncertain of himself, and glanced at Sonya then at Penny. "I've told Sonya that once the situation is regularized and she has her American citizenship, if she doesn't like America — or me — I'll give her a divorce, whenever she asks and with no strings. I'll put that in writing if you like." Again he looked at Sonya, whose fine-boned face was impassive, the blue eyes slitted. There was moment's heavy silence, then a devilish smile curled her lips. "Oh no you won't, Alexander Spring," she purred and cuddled up to him. "Me too. I marry not for convenience but for keeps — you crazy, rich American doctor, you are not going to get rid of me." She

243

looked over at Penny. "It has happened at last, you see, just like I said. He is the one for me too."

Toby was making strange little growling noises, so Penny said hastily, "Then I'm very happy for you both, but since we have so little time we must know — how did all this come about. Where have you been all this time and what happened? We've both been frantic with worry."

"Yes, we're very sorry about that." Alex looked contrite. "But we simply did not dare to contact you before we were married and we only managed to do that yesterday, there was so much red tape to go through."

"But *Iceland*?"

"Sit down and I'll tell you as quickly as I can." They sat, and Alex continued. "I had this in the back of my mind all along. Before I left London even, I made inquiries from the embassy here about how and where an American could get married in a hurry to a foreign national. To me it seemed a far better solution than Toby deep-sixing his career and reputation by whisking Sonya off to South America."

"Damn cheek!" Toby muttered.

"However, I went along with the original plan since that is what they both seemed to want. But when things started to go awry I put this other plan to Sonya and she was all for it." They grinned delightedly at each other. "So when Toby left us, we wandered about that damned mountain and missed the rendezvous. But we did come across this biker who was asleep and, more importantly, his bike. We helped ourselves and made for Liverpool, but rather than risk the original direction, which was solid with cops, I decided to head in the other direction. We made for Aberdeen. No one was on the alert there, so we got an airlift with a bunch of American oil riggers to one of the North Sea oil platforms, and another lift from there to Iceland—one of their R and R spots. The US base there was one of the places on my list, and so we stayed until the deed was done. We flew from Iceland to Gatwick—no one was looking for us coming *in*, you see—and came up by train this morning. Oh, and that reminds me . . ." he reached into an Icelandic airlines totebag, pulled out a large manila envelope, and handed it to Toby. "Here's the money and papers you gave me. It's all there." He looked over at Sonya. "She has the rest and has been our treasurer. I think we spent about five thousand—being a fugitive is expensive." Sonya dipped into her totebag and came up with another enevelope which she profferred to her father.

"I don't want it," Toby growled. "Keep it!"

"Certainly not! We can't accept that. There's almost fifty thousand pounds there," Alex exclaimed.

"Am I not even allowed to give my own daughter a wedding present?" Toby bellowed. "It is nothing to do with you!"

Here we go again! Penny thought resignedly, but Sonya asserted herself. "Stop it! Both of you!" she commanded, her eyes flashing. "This is not what I am going to put up with—all this fighting, fighting . . . is nonsense! You are my father, you my husband and I love you both. If you love me you will be friends and nice to each other. Thank you, Father," she kissed Toby and put the envelope firmly back in her bag. "That is a very, very generous present and I will use it wisely, I promise. You are a good and generous man and *I* appreciate it." She glared at Alex. "We *both* appreciate it, don't we?"

"Er, yes. Very good of you, Toby. Thank you," Alex muttered. Penny suppressed a grin and looked at her new daughter-in-law with an approving eye.

The door opened and Grey popped his head in. "My side is all taken care of, and Hayes says that you should say your goodbyes now, because there's other paperwork to be done and the car for the airport will be here in half an hour. He seems to be in quite a hurry to get you off his hands—I can't imagine why!" The head withdrew.

Alex broke the sudden painful silence. "Well, this is only a temporary goodbye. As soon as Sonya gets her papers and we can safely leave America, we'll be back over here on our delayed honeymoon." He grinned ruefully at his bride. "My vacation is all used up so I'll have to get back to work. Maybe you can both get over to America before that?" He looked at Penny enquiringly. "First thing we'll do is find a bigger apartment that we can all fit in. Have you ever spent much time in New York, Toby?"

Toby groaned faintly. "Yes. Terrible place!—but some very fine museums there," he added hastily, seeing the frosty glint in Sonya's eyes.

Hayes appeared at the door. "You'll have to come now," he snapped. And under his forbidding eye they embraced and muttered embarrassed farewells, before the young couple followed him out.

Feeling drained, Penny and Toby found their way out of the labyrinthine embassy. Grey was leaning against the Rolls as they came up to it. "I just wanted to congratulate you on the fortunate outcome of all this, before getting back to business," he said dryly. He looked keenly at Penny. "You are certainly a woman of many parts, Dr. Spring. You should have told me about your CIA connections. It might have helped and I certainly would not have given you such a hard time. I got out of Hayes that it was they who insisted the way be cleared. Quite amazing!" He raised his hat and went on his way.

They looked at each other in stupefaction. "CIA connections? Me?" Penny gasped. "What the hell was he talking about . . . ?"

Epilogue

The phone call from New York arrived: all was well with the newlyweds and there was nothing left to do or worry about. A celebration of sorts was in progress at the Athenaeum, although by the funereal expressions of the celebrants it appeared more a drowning-of-sorrows than a festive orgy. "Well, I had a daughter, but I didn't have her for very long, did I? Just when I was getting used to the idea and was enjoying having her around too," Toby complained.

"Oh, what nonsense, Toby! You'll have her now for as long as you live. Recall the old saying 'but a daughter's a daughter for all of her life'?" Penny said. Remembering the rest of the saying so depressed her that she hastily helped herself to another glass of the vintage Veuve Cliquot they were drinking and downed it in a couple of gulps.

"Go easy on that stuff! We've already got through one bottle, and at this rate you'll be potted to the gills," Toby reproved. He also helped himself to another glass and reverted to his theme. "Anyway, it's probably just as well—I don't think I'm cut out to be a family man. Too set in my ways, I suppose." He sighed heavily.

"Oh I don't know about that! I'd say you showed amazing flexibility — not to mention considerable imagination — over the past few weeks. I think you acquitted yourself in this a lot better than I did," she said. He refilled her glass and after a reflective sip she went on. "Never have we been involved with a case where I've felt more on the outside. I don't feel I ever came to grips with it at all. I mean, I was so busy chasing around after the Russians that I scarcely paid any mind to the real murderer. And I never even spoke to Herbert Spence, who turned out to be the key to all this. Maddening!"

"But you *did* solve it by process of elimination, and with no help at all from me," Toby pointed out magnanimously.

"Even there I would never have done it without a lot of *outside* help," she complained.

"Ah, yes, *that*," Toby muttered, and they fell silent.

"I was always running *behind* the action." She took up her plaint again. "I've never felt so. . . ." She was interrupted by a discreet cough and looked up to see a waiter hovering at Toby's elbow. "Excuse me, Sir Tobias, there's a foreign gentleman asking to see you. He's in the lobby. Says his name is Gregor Vadik. Should I show him in here?"

They looked at each other in sudden alarm. "By all means — and bring us another bottle," Toby boomed.

Although he was soberly and conservatively attired, Vadik still looked exotically foreign in this august English milieu. He advanced towards them, his gold tooth much in evidence as he grinned widely. They eyed him warily as he bowed over Penny's hand. "Won't you sit down and join us for a drink?" Toby said. "This is quite a surprise."

"Thank you, but I can only stay a few minutes," Vadik said, settling next to Penny. "Ah, you celebrate —

and with reason! That is nice. Now you are one big family, eh?" He took a sip of his champagne, examined the label on the bottle and clucked with appreciation. "Very good, very good indeed!"

Toby cleared his throat. "So what can we do for you?"

"Oh, nothing, nothing at all! I go home now — back to Vashti and my Stefan. I merely come to make my good-byes." Vadik's dark eyes gleamed with amusement over the rim of his glass. "And to say we are now quits, Toby Glendower: you did me a favor and I have done you one. Not that I expect our paths will cross again — but then, one never knows. . . ."

"You know about Long?" Penny said, eying him suspiciously.

"Yes, of course. The best solution in the circumstances wouldn't you say?" His face was blandly uncommunicative.

"Meaning?"

"Meaning that the subject is closed; all parties are satisfied, and that no more questions have to be asked — or should be."

She felt a little chill. "Grey had some extraordinary idea that I was in cahoots with our CIA. Would you know anything about that?"

He shrugged. "I may have mentioned how valuable your help had been to me in this affair to certain people. I thought it might help with . . ." he hesitated, " . . . the other matter." He laughed suddenly. "You have very resourceful children, but then who would have doubted that, with such parents? You must be looking forward to the next step."

"Next step?" Toby queried.

"Why, your grandchildren, of course, your mutual grandchildren! With such a genetic heritage they should be truly remarkable," Vadik said genially.

They looked at him open-mouthed. "*Grandchildren*," Toby muttered. "I had not even thought of that. Good Lord! I had better put the boy down for Winchester right away."

"*Boy*? They come in two kinds, you know," Penny said sharply. "Anyway the idea of putting him down for Winchester is ridiculous. He'll be an American, with American parents. It's absurd to think of him being educated here! You know how Alex hated his English schools. They have excellent prep schools in America."

"But not to compare with *Winchester*!" Toby said testily. "I'd pay for it, naturally."

"Alex would *never* stand for that!" she cried, as they eyed each other with mounting antagonism. "Besides, aren't you forgetting something, Toby. . . ."

Vadik eased himself out of his chair. "Well, I really must be going," he murmured, suppressing a smile.

They looked at him blankly. "Oh, yes, er — goodbye and bon voyage. Our best to your family. . . ." And turned back eagerly to their mounting argument.

As he made his way out, Vadik chuckled to himself. They were off and running again and true to form, all sorrows and questions banished. The case was closed. Well-satisfied with his handiwork, he went out into his own shadowy world.

Available from Foul Play Press

Margot Arnold

The complete adventures in paperback of Margot Arnold's beloved pair of peripatetic sleuths, Penny Spring and Sir Toby Glendower:

The Cape Cod Caper	192 pages	$ 5.95
Death of a Voodoo Doll	220 pages	$ 5.95
Death on the Dragon's Tongue	224 pages	$ 4.95
Exit Actors, Dying	176 pages	$ 5.95
Lament for a Lady Laird	221 pages	$ 5.95
The Menehune Murders	272 pages	$ 5.95
Toby's Folly	256 pages	$ 5.95
Zadock's Treasure	192 pages	$ 5.95

Joyce Porter

American readers, having faced several lean years deprived of the company of Chief Inspector Wilfred Dover, will rejoice (so to speak) in the reappearance of "the most idle and avaricious policeman in the United Kingdom (and, possibly, the world)." Here is the series (in paperback) that introduced the bane of Scotland Yard and his hapless assistant, Sgt. MacGregor, to international acclaim.

Dover One	192 pages	$ 5.95
Dover Two	222 pages	$ 5.95
Dover Three	192 pages	$ 4.95
Dead Easy for Dover	176 pages	$ 5.95
Dover and the Unkindest Cut of All	188 pages	$ 5.95
Dover Goes to Pott	192 pages	$ 5.95
Dover Strikes Again	202 pages	$ 5.95
It's Murder With Dover	192 pages	$ 5.95

Our mysteries are available through bookstores. For a free catalog, write: The Countryman Press, Inc., Dept. APF, PO Box 175, Woodstock, VT 05091-0175.

Other books from Foul Play Press

Phoebe Atwood Taylor

The perennially popular Phoebe Atwood Taylor whose droll
"Codfish Sherlock," Asey Mayo, and "Shakespeare lookalike,"
Leonidas Witherall, have been eliciting guffaws from proper
Bostonian Brahmins for over half a century.

Asey Mayo Cape Cod Mysteries

The Annulet of Gilt	288 pages	$5.95
The Asey Mayo Trio	256 pages	$5.95
Banbury Bog	176 pages	$5.95
The Cape Cod Mystery	192 pages	$5.95
The Criminal C.O.D.	288 pages	$5.95
The Crimson Patch	240 pages	$5.95
The Deadly Sunshade	297 pages	$5.95
Death Lights a Candle	304 pages	$6.95
Diplomatic Corpse	256 pages	$5.95
Figure Away	288 pages	$5.95
Going, Going, Gone	218 pages	$5.95
The Mystery of the Cape Cod Players	272 pages	$5.95
The Mystery of the Cape Cod Tavern	283 pages	$5.95
Octagon House	304 pages	$5.95
Out of Order	280 pages	$5.95
The Perennial Boarder	288 pages	$5.95
Proof of the Pudding	192 pages	$5.95
Punch With Care	224 pages	$5.95
Sandbar Sinister	296 pages	$5.95
Six Iron Spiders	288 pages	$5.95
Spring Harrowing	288 pages	$5.95
Three Plots for Asey Mayo	320 pages	$6.95

"Surely, under whichever pseudonym, Mrs. Taylor is the
mystery equivalent of Buster Keaton."   —Dilys Winn

Leonidas Witherall Mysteries (by "Alice Tilton")

Beginning with a Bash	284 pages	$5.95
File for Record	287 pages	$5.95
Hollow Chest	284 pages	$5.95
The Left Leg	275 pages	$5.95